What People Are S

Begotten

Begotten is a work of rich and impassioned gothic splendour, from a writer deeply versed in the history and intricacies of the occult. This immersive, atmospheric novel speaks powerfully to the dark forces of a lost era. Readers will get utterly lost in it.
Guy Mankowski

Begotten is a richly detailed, chilling debut steeped in gothic tradition. Kate Cherrell brings her intimate knowledge of the murky past of Spiritualism to haunt her narrator on a tormentous descent into madness.
Sophie Cleverly

Kate Cherrell's debut novel is drenched in the very dark energy of Gothic. It is a stormy sea of human emotion, wild nature and tempestuous relationships and melancholic mystery played out in the damp and dusty old mansions of a forgotten time. Full of power, intrigue and magic, this is a captivating debut that will leave you spellbound.
John Robb

Begotten

A Gothic Novel

Begotten

A Gothic Novel

Kate Cherrell

ROUNDFIRE
BOOKS

London, UK
Washington, DC, USA

CollectiveInk

First published by Roundfire Books, 2025
Roundfire Books is an imprint of Collective Ink Ltd.,
Unit 11, Shepperton House, 89 Shepperton Road, London, N1 3DF
office@collectiveinkbooks.com
www.collectiveinkbooks.com
www.roundfire-books.com

For distributor details and how to order please visit the 'Ordering' section on our website.

Text copyright: Kate Cherrell 2024

ISBN: 978 1 80341 804 9
978 1 80341 814 8 (ebook)
Library of Congress Control Number: 2024933764

A CIP catalogue record for this book is available from the British Library.

Design: Lapiz Digital Services

UK: Printed and bound by CPI Group (UK) Ltd, Croydon, CR0 4YY
Printed in North America by CPI GPS partners

We operate a distinctive and ethical publishing philosophy in all areas of our business, from our global network of authors to production and worldwide distribution.

For my parents

Prologue

County Duncain, Northern Ireland

It was generally understood that ours was the age of success, of development, and discoveries, that God was bestowing blessings on this generation above all others. The roar of machinery brought about new triumphs and wealth while elevating man's role in creation. These new societies thrived in wide city streets, where glass dress beads would clatter across pavements, inviting the young and beautiful to sing and chatter in the smog of progress.

Alice Crofton had waited to thrive for longer than most. She had basked in the warmth of the city and all its glittering indulgences, finally spread before her eager hands. But her time in the sun had been brief, and grief had brought her home where affairs had to be settled. But in Duncain, the old ways remained and the dead refused to stay silent.

When the body of Sir Kenneth Crofton was discovered one crisp Sunday morning, it was met with the same dulled inconvenience as a farmer finding a few smothered chicks in a henhouse. The elderly Lord lay rigid across the threadbare corridor carpet of the servants' quarters, an area of the house he had rarely frequented. He would have been horrified to know that his final moments were played out closer to the twisted iron beds of the scullery maids than the silk plumes of his own untouched bedstead.

In life, Sir Kenneth had been a stout man. He was short and stocky, a man whose chin was too keen to meet his shoulders, leaving his neck as a mere hopeful memory. Many of his associates, who would no doubt mourn his passing — for the additional administrative efforts, if nothing else — were fond of likening Sir Kenneth to a standing stone. A Pagan remnant from an uncivilized age long past; hardy, grey, and immovable.

As he lay on the floor, his limbs twisted in some arcane knot, his stature was more of an imp than a man. His once-rounded shoulders were hunched, angular, with wasted muscles stretched like sinew over thin bone. His once globular nose that hung like a pendulum had wasted to all but naught. What sat in its place was a shard that jutted from his face like a flint. A crueller friend might have likened his lifeless frame to the picked carcass of a Christmas goose.

The magnificence of the house's decor lay long in the past; its ragged tapestries and slick marble steps offered a certain faded charm that its inhabitants were not always so keen to mimic. In death, Sir Kenneth maintained his legacy of inconvenience. Sprawled across the floor, his spine compressed against the fibres of the carpet, the twisted manner of his corpse seeming incongruous with the cultivated order of the house. His mouth was most troubling of all, fixed in a foetal scream that never uttered a sound. His greying skin, as thin and waxy as butcher's paper, was pulled so taut in horror as to nearly tear his jaw from his face. From this gaping maw sprang sparse ivory pegs, pushing through the black mulch that filled his mouth, like weeds from compost.

It was not a friend, cruel or otherwise, who discovered the tragic sight of the former Sir Kenneth. Within the shade of the servants' chambers, the woman who rustled with starched petticoats could have been forgiven for walking through the body; she was accustomed to such obstacles. The cats had made frequent deposits to the carpet in the past, spreading carcasses far and wide like scattered children's toys. The frame of Sir Kenneth seemed little more than a crumpled robe, disproven only when indelicately kicked with the pointed toe of a house slipper.

In any other household, for a servant of thirty years to stumble upon the corpse of her master and utter less than a whisper would invite question. Yet Duncain House had always operated efficiently, coldly, and without comment. In life, Sir Kenneth was vigilant in his inspection of the homestead, taking some strange delight in berating the younger maids who dallied in their duties. His vicious, verbal bouts of religious fervour would frequently echo through the corridors, seeping through the walls like rising damp. The younger boys within the household soon learned to make themselves scarce when Sir Kenneth took to one of his fits. It was known throughout the county that the peal of Sir Kenneth's proverbs rang through the house like a call to the workhouse. Of course, that was many months ago. The old man's voice had withered on the third day of his insomnia and no one could recall its return.

Despite dying in indignity, Crofton's legacy of cruel efficiency was upheld to the last. Before the sun traced its fingers through the window frames, the familiar ebonized cart of McAfferty & Son carved its way across the house's great drive, leaving tell-tale trenches in the crushed stone.

Lady Crofton had already retired to her chamber and, after a period of persistent wailing, had taken to her bed, where she'd be sure to remain for the rest of the day. The Lady hadn't been able to comprehend the death of a flowerbed in frost, so the presentation of a fresh corpse was understandably outside her remit.

The housekeeper went about her duties with little comment or deviation from routine. After hearing the two tell-tale knocks on the reception doorway, she unlatched the lock with deft familiarity and gestured towards the curved staircase that wound, serpentine, across the upper floors. It had been some years since McAfferty's last visit; with dwindling staff and the nursery untouched for years, the necessity for such services had been eliminated. Into the house stepped two gentlemen; the older of the two, McAfferty himself, had spent his youth in the confined chimneys of houses such as Duncain. A childhood of such feats had left his spine warped and curving to the left, like a tree growing towards water. The older man removed his hat and bowed, revealing to the housekeeper a fairy circle of straw-covered tufts sprouting unevenly from his scalp. The old woman pursed her lips and began to ascend the staircase.

The men remained unmoving, standing in their sagging suits, hats in hand, like schoolboys waiting for discipline. As the woman made her way up the crudely patched stair runners, the younger man watched her swollen ankles with peculiar interest. Upon reaching the first landing, she swivelled to look down at the waiting men. The faint scratching of her skirts against the floor sent an uncomfortable ripple up the young man's spine. The woman's stare was unyielding and fixed like a bird of prey. The young man was left with no further concern for swollen ankles and busied himself with needlessly correcting his shirt buttons.

The elder, still holding his dented hat and staring at the floor, made no movement.

'The master is reclining in bed, where he has lain for several hours...'

The younger shifted his weight between his feet, waiting for some nod or familiar command from the old man beside him.

'The mistress has no desire for him to remain here. As you may well comprehend, a wake, public or otherwise, will not be necessary —'

'Are you sure, Madam?' croaked the old man, brow furrowed in practised concern. The housekeeper's gaze fixed on the old man's face, slowly moving to the curve in his spine and coming to rest on the hat between his hands.

'How long have you lived in Duncain, Mr McAfferty?'

'Why, all my life, Madam. Man and boy —'

The housekeeper cut in with all the precision of a mistress clipping her needlework thread. 'Then you will know,

Mr McAfferty, that few men or boys have concern with the master and his family. It would be better for his tenants and their... progeny... to keep their noses —'

A slow creak rolled from the floor above. The young man's eyes moved to meet it.

'— out.'

The older man returned the hat to his balding head, while the younger busied himself with wiping some imagined dust from the top of his own.

'There will be no ceremony other than the necessity. We will have no priests, no Lords, no publicans, no children encroaching on my mistress's mourning. As such, with my mistress being currently indisposed, I trust you will have no objections to following my instruction.' She began to make her way up the second flight of stairs, suddenly stopping halfway. 'Sirs. The master is deceased and cooling in his sheets. The groundkeeper may have carried his body to the bed, and the Lord has carried his soul to the heavens, but I will not be bringing his carcass downstairs.'

The air prickled from her words; the young man's already ruddy complexion flushed red-hot. 'Follow me, if you'd be so kind.'

As the men carried the unfortunate Lord down the stairwell, both kept their eyes fixed on the linen-wrapped bundle between them. While the housekeeper's eyes warmed their backs, they busied themselves with their business, working in double time. Whether it was through diligence or fear of the matronly woman standing at the balustrade above them, no one could be sure. She was contented to see them leave, whatever their motivations. The Lord was carried through the great doors and, after a short walk to the carriage, the young man turned to watch the iron latch of the lock swing into place.

'How queer —'

'Don't dwell on old Mrs Curry. You'll be accustomed to the ways of that lot in no time at all. Rattling around in a big empty place like that for years; it's enough to send anyone batty.'

The old man fixed the hearse doors in place and waddled unsteadily to his seat. He was soon joined by the younger, who grasped the reins and began the slow, arduous journey along the stony path.

'No wonder the children ran away. I would've thought they'd have been with their mother, or nanny, in a place like that.'

'Children? You're seeing things, lad. The youngest must have been locked away, and you know full well that the young Lady Crofton scarpered as soon as a man would look at her.'

'As God is my witness, Father, there were at least two by the Lord's room. I saw them peeking through the doorway, as clear as day.' The force of the horses' hooves scattered gravel in noisy parabolas as they reached the garden wall.

'Well, William,' old McAfferty whispered with a glint in his eye, 'you must have seen a ghost.'

Chapter 1

The border of Duncain was unmarked, but a rising sickness in my stomach made sure I didn't miss its boundaries. Ballymena and Cookstown had millstones and elaborately painted boards with crests and swirling script, welcoming visitors with pride. But there was no great fanfare when I entered Duncain; there were few signs signalling its existence to travellers at all.

Between the last town of Dungannon and the county of Duncain was over an hour's worth of fields, empty of crops, only occasionally punctuated by a lone sheep that had strayed too far from its flock. The county sat in a valley, although its depth was unclear to unfortunate interlopers until they had travelled too far to attempt a return journey with tired horses.

The southern roads into Duncain had always lain in perpetual shadow, assisted by the dense bracken that grew taller, like a barricade, with each long winter. I disliked the wetlands the most. At times, the sitting water across the county lasted for so long that sheep's legs would rot where they stood.

The fields were foul in the warmth of the summer, with peat bogs barely worth the toil of the old men who laboured past sunset. The peat was never plentiful enough to sell and was back-breaking work for those who tried. When the lodgers in Father's crofts burned peat for fuel, it smouldered in burners that filled the huts with an acrid stench that burned their throats, coating the inside of their noses and ears in a brown sludge that stuck fast and flaked like tree bark. Nothing escaped the dirt of Duncain, I was sure of that.

The surrounding counties had found lucrative work in the bog-oak trade, bringing buried wood to the surface and passing it to nimble-fingered tradesmen to carve. There proved to be quite a cottage industry in carving fanciful brooches. Likenesses of harps and abbey ruins sold well to eager tourists, with split beads circling the necks of their wives, darkening from sweat and oils, noose-like in the summer warmth. I often fumbled my neck chains when thinking of these wooden trinkets, counting each bead like a rosary, thankful that I'd never had to wear such cheap wooden novelties. Besides, the bogs of Duncain were barren, revealing only the occasional carcass, the curve of a ribcage or jutting splinter of a shattered skull, coughed up to rest beside the road.

I would never have expected a polite greeting from Duncain, let alone an elaborate one with steps flanked with expectant staff. Between the trees, long stripped of their leaves, the full frontage of my father's house was visible from some fields away. It sat like an enormous ink blot on the landscape, stained from years of untouched filth, blown in from neighbouring farms. Yet the sight of a lifeless yard, free from footmen, troubled me. With each turn of the carriage wheels, the muddied gravel increased in its crunching ferocity, as though it were goading me with an apathetic arrival. The house and its many dulled windows obstinately maintained their stillness in the face of my frustration. Each cruel turn of the carriage wheels was taking me further away from London, and Algernon.

The carriage took its time navigating the rough tracks leading to Duncain, for which I was thankful. As it crept closer, the reduced speed permitted me a panoramic view of the house's façade and, in turn, a protracted opportunity to study the crumbling gables of the rented houses I was sure to inherit. Once the relevant paperwork had been completed, of course.

To be wealthy in property was no great boast; most people I happened upon in Chelsea had several properties to their family's name. If my family's houses had been in London, I would surely have skipped down the streets myself. Instead, they were workers' cottages in Duncain. They spoiled the views from the house's upper floors, afflicting the hills like some mottled pox. However, the punishments for submitting to such a common form of transportation were soon upon me. At each turn, hunched women with faces like rotted apples squinted through the windows. Heather was in bloom and pockets of weather-worn women gathered at the edges of the road and at the foot of rising hills, filling their baskets with bundles of purple spray. The women were older than I, indistinguishable from one another. I had watched them from the house as a child, and watched them with the same absent-minded interest from the cab. I knew that the house was still some time away.

Soon, the groups of women dispersed. First reducing in number, until only occasional pockets of one or two women emerged. As the carriage rumbled further into Duncain, the last few women seemed older than the rest, wrinkled, with frail arms emerging from layers of shawls like withered pea shoots. All of them looked like widows, yet whether their husbands had died, or if it was simply wishful thinking, was a secret known to them alone.

Although I could list the cab's failings for the remainder of my journey, its black lacquered cocoon offered some welcome privacy. My bag, a little more mud-flecked than before, still held a cluster of unopened letters from dear little Elsie. Wiping the bottom of the bag with my cuff, I twisted to look behind myself. There was no window for prying eyes, simply heavily pleated black bombazine, fraying faintly at the edges like baby hair. To pass the time, and sate my lingering curiosity, I flicked open the lip of the envelope with my thumbnail.

Sissy,

I hope you are healthy and happy. I miss you so much, and I miss our little talks through the latch in the mornings. The house is so cold and quiet now you've gone. I hope London is just tremendous, and you are wearing the prettiest dresses and jewels in your new big house.

Please come and visit soon. I'm so lonely, all I have are the crows. They're going to help me leave like you, Sissy. They're going to tear out their wings and help me fly away. They tell me to wait, but they keep me awake with their screams, so I don't know what I'm waiting for.

I know I'm a terror for asking so much, and I know England must be so exciting, but I don't like being without you any more. Father has been ill again. I didn't see his sickness like last time. I didn't see it happen, but he's been in bed. Mother has been crying again, but I cannot tell if Father is the cause. I think the visitors have moved. The ones I told you about before? Not the crows, but the others. I think Mrs Curry was talking to them in the night as she was giving them a real telling off for disturbing the kitchen after we had all turned in for bed. I tried not to giggle at her cruel little hisses, but it was so funny, hearing her silly voice shout at the children. They went quiet when they heard me, so I ran back to bed.

When everyone's asleep or poorly and Mrs Curry won't let me go outside, there's nothing to do but read, practise my penmanship, and wait for you. Visit soon. You promised you would. Please.

Yours, Elsie X

Elsie was a child of rich and wild imagination. I had always loved her for it, even when our parents questioned the sanctity of its source. But she was always more of me than of them. They never tended to her long enough to fall under her impish spell. When looking at the tight little loops of Elsie's letter, I was reminded just how delicate she was. She would have grown a little since I left to marry, but I knew she would always remain as gossamer-fine as spider's silk. As soon as Elsie was able to stand, our mother remarked that she would have men fighting for her hand, and for once I was inclined to agree. While the Crofton name had waned a little in recent years, her sweetness and beauty was sure to override any talk of familial foolishness.

Leaving her behind felt like the cruellest betrayal. But I had to. I had to before the misery of Duncain consumed me like it did my mother. I refused to become a twitching wreck of a woman spending weeks in bed for maladies that God himself couldn't comprehend. I got out and I would get Elsie out too. I just needed the paperwork, the deeds, then we would all be free. Algernon had helped me enough already, and this brief trip would be unpleasant, but necessary. I needed Duncain signed over to me. Then Elsie and I could leave, never to return.

The view from the cab's window was as grey as the day I left, when I had dashed into a carriage with not so much as a second glance, let alone a prolonged farewell. Duncain had continued to exist inside a bubble, but now a bubble left to the whims of my mother. The smallest inconvenience had always been a disaster of biblical proportions; from a poor crop of apples to a woodlouse in Mother's washstand, the Lord was punishing our family for our wrongdoings and we were sure to all know it. The bubble had not popped when I left for London, but rather re-formed, leaving a residue impossible to remove. With each word of Elsie's letters, it was clear that little had changed, or would ever change. Now she was alone, curiosities had become enormous fantastical stories, and squirrels in the attic became young friends for a lonely child. I sat with the remainder of Elsie's neatly sealed letters on my lap, hearing her voice beside me as I read the scrawl. I hadn't meant to leave them unopened. As a child, I had lived for Elsie, treating her like a doll of my own. But in London, my excitement had carried my mind away, and it was only when cracking the dried gum of long-sealed envelopes that guilt began to bubble within me.

Sissy,

I don't like the house at all. I know you promised you'd get me out when you could, but your silence feels so cruel. I often feel like the house has become this monstrous mouth, ready to chew me up. It waited for you to leave so it could have me, and now I'm waiting for you again. You promised you wouldn't leave me here, sissy. You promised.

My nightmares are getting worse. I wake with such a start thinking that some voice has shouted my name, but I'm always alone. Mrs Curry comes to comfort me at night if she hears me, or I go to her if she leaves the doors unlocked, although she seems to do so less and less these days. The night before last, I let myself out of my bedroom to find Mrs Curry. I thought I would find her in the kitchen, and she would comfort me with some hot milk, but she wasn't there. It was too cold to be outside as the winds have picked up again, so I don't know where she could have been. Perhaps she was hiding from me. She's been so kind, far more than Mother ever has, but perhaps she has her own children to tend to. But when I went towards the kitchen that night, I saw Father and his friends in the parlour. They had left the door ajar, so I simply cannot be blamed for peeking. Father was being very silly, which was very funny to watch. It made me sad that he can't be silly with us, only his dull friends. He never wants to joke with me. I peered into the parlour and I promise to you, Sissy, he had a little cloud of sick coming out of his ear. It was frothy like Mother's best soap, but looked stringy between his fingers when he tried to pull it out. I couldn't help but laugh when he tried to wipe it away with his handkerchief, but it kept getting stuck.

He seemed very angry that I'd been peeking, and one of his tall friends slammed the door in my face without so much as a good night!

I haven't heard from our visitors. I think they must have gone home.

E X

Such letters had a strange disorientating effect on my travel-worn mind. The pile of envelopes seemed unshrinking, no matter how many times I moved on to the next. I had been in London less than a year, but Elsie must have written every week, if not occasionally every day. The guilt I had evaded for so long ambushed me with a cold, unfamiliar rush. While I was fretting about drapery and the newest silks, Elsie was where I'd left her. Waiting. I was expecting little tales of seeing fairies at the bottom of the garden, something warm and homely to return to, but as the letters progressed, the tales lost their warmth. Each note was of Father's illness and Mrs Curry's kindness, of the cutting winter when the outer rooms grew icicles in the corners, and how Mother took to her bed for her latest malady. As the stamps ticked over, I grew sickly as I read through the notepaper — from the travel or the fear of Elsie's happiness, I couldn't be sure, but I wafted a canister of salts beneath my nose to steady myself as I tackled the pile.

Sissy,

Father has been sick again. It wasn't as funny this time.

Mother was out of her bed arguing with Father in his study. They weren't laughing, and Mother didn't help Father when he was sick again. She didn't seem sad about it. The white came out of his mouth this time, and sounded wet when it hit the floor, like when Mrs Curry prepares fish on her big slab. I couldn't see much through the crack in the door, but there was someone else by the far window. I heard his voice, but I didn't recognize it. It sounded a little like the old gardener, but Mrs Curry said we won't be needing staff again.

I don't think it was the children as it was definitely a man's voice. I think it must have been one of Father's business partners. He had such a thick accent, I think he was from the lowlands. It would have been funny if he wasn't so angry. Why aren't you writing back to me? Have you forgotten the address? The envelopes are a little old, but the address is printed on the back.

E x

For all this talk of white froth, it was the repeated mention of children that flummoxed me the most. There had never been any children allowed into the house outside of Elsie and me, and we often felt that we existed within its walls by the grace of God. There had been no children in Duncain but us for years. The old schoolhouse in town had been disused for decades, requisitioned by cows and farmers seeking shelter from the rain. Unless there had been a great influx of workers, Duncain had no children. It didn't nurture youth.

Sissy,

Mother came out of her bedroom today. I thought she might like to sit with me for a while, or share tea with Mrs Curry and me, but she had more important things to do. I think it was something with Father as he hasn't left his room in days. Instead, Mother made me read scripture aloud in my room, loud enough that she could hear it through the door! I don't know how long she listened, but I read until my tongue was dead in my mouth. I may be young, but I am no fool and know how Mother favours the belt.

It rained all day, but Mrs Curry went to town to send lots of money orders to the post office. I watched her write them in Mother's pocketbook myself. They must be important for Mother to send them so secretly, especially in such rotten weather. With my birthday so close, I think Mother must have arranged them for me. Please visit me before my birthday! I would so love a London dress.

E x

Ah. Elsie's birthday. I couldn't help but empty my breath from my body. Drat. I know I had been foolish and I know I should have remembered, but shouldn't Mother have reminded me too? Or Father? Or Mrs Curry? She in her sainthood was supposed to be the soul keeping the Croftons afloat. Especially since my 'insensitive' absence. How I was supposed to remember that alongside all my new London commitments escapes me. I crumpled the letter into my handbag and took time to examine the views from the windows. I would subject myself to one more. I loved Elsie, I really did, but I deserved a life beyond Duncain, and the whole family had to come to terms with that. All of them. The windows were far too steamed and mottled to see the views anyway, despite the efforts of the rain.

Dear Alice,

Mother's orders arrived in great big boxes. I stole away the catalogue on top, but it was so terribly dull. There were no pictures of hats or dresses, just drawings of bits of wood and men in cupboards. When Mrs Curry saw, she snatched it right out of my hands and tore my glove as she moved.

She slapped my wrist and said I shouldn't go looking through other people's things. I think this to be most rude of her when they're Mother's deliveries anyway, and not hers either. I couldn't help myself, I'm so very frustrated and lonely here, and I kicked a box with my foot, putting a dent right in the corner. When I kicked it, the box made the most curious sound and jingled like a jester. Mrs Curry was in one of her moods and told me not to pry, saying it was for Mother and Father, but it's a surprise. She makes little sense sometimes. I know adult matters are not for my ears, but I wish I knew what was happening with Mother and Father. Whatever it is, I think it is stupid.

Elsie x

When my initial frustrations subsided, something about the letters niggled at me. Elsie may have only been thirteen, but she had always spoken beyond her years. We Crofton girls stick together. All we had was books and each other, and childishness was never entertained, not even by ourselves. Elsie had always spoken soundly, and written as such, but these letters were becoming those of a child, not *my* Elsie.

In truth, I missed Elsie far more than I allowed myself to admit. When summer season came to London, thoughts of her excitability sparked into my mind during laps of city ballrooms; how Elsie's elegance would fall away and how she would squeal and clap to see so many extravagant dresses. After a short time apart, it seemed that Elsie's imagined squeals and the warmth of unspoken sisterhood between us had grown colder, with the chatter of society fast becoming all I could hear.

Elsie would be taller now, and older. I had never been one for milestones; that was one of the few privileges afforded to the poor, growing in close quarters. We sisters knew one another through dividing walls, locks, and visiting times; a tight segregation, for learning, and for safety.

Elsie wouldn't stay in Duncain forever. I had promised her as much, and I would stand by my word.

A cold unease grew in my stomach as the coach drove deeper into Duncain, the house appearing like a thimble on some distant hill. I felt drunk, my limbs heavy and unwieldy, my posture too rigid, as though I had forgotten how to sit. The weather was too cold to allow for clammy hands, but my skin pulsed nonetheless, tight and unpleasant against my bones. I was a woman now, and Duncain held no power over me. Should I recite the sentiment enough times, it would become a mantra, and close to truth. Or so I hoped.

I attempted to centre myself, opening a compact and blotting my face. My skin was dry, too cold for beauty's hand to reach. I was free, however, and I always would be. Duncain was just a county; the house was just a house. Brick and mortar, nothing more. Every assurance was a moment idly wasted. The churning travel-sickness of my stomach agreed, and I lay back, closing my eyes, sweeping my sister's letters from my mind.

The gritty mustard-wash coating the carriage windows had become darker and thicker with the splashing of wheels against silage. Familiarising myself with my environment proved difficult at first, as though time engaged in societal pursuits had somehow 'pushed' any domestic thoughts from my head. With a new season of balls and theatre creeping ever closer, I had furiously tried to remove such ingrained images of Duncain from my mind, arguably with some success. Yet the threads remained, and with each turn of the wheel, they knitted together, as though thought alone trained a link between us.

I was sure I had outgrown Duncain, served my time, and was free to spend my time thinking of little else but brocade and dress trimmings in a simplistic, indulgent, and quiet life of well-dressed respite. The journey itself was a compromise, and travelling unchaperoned even more so. I was sure that I would have strength, should Algernon have been at my side, but as ever, business had called my husband away.

Duncain House rose between the hills like a canker. The town itself had been dispersed over years of inactivity, scattering into smaller groups of houses, leaving a high street of repurposed post offices and greengrocers, too poor and unwilling to reopen. The remaining buildings were mottled and unremarkable, the walls, bricks, and people all streaked with the same muddied grey wash.

The roads past the high street and old market square were perilous should you meet another coming the other way. The ditches were deep and severe, the troughs cut in deep 'V's by unseen, enormous blades. They seemed to serve little purpose other than to trap those unfortunate enough to fall from the road above. Should a coach creep too far to the edge, the carriage — horses and all — would meet their end in a knot of flesh and split wood.

Horses would drown in inches of water, their upturned hooves cutting through air in a breathless frenzy. The fortunate ones would break their necks on impact. As a child, the metallic clatter of reins and splitting wood would drive me into the yard, where I would peek over the walls, watching strong men gasp and die, my little toes wedged between bare trellis slats.

Deeper into County Duncain, there were signs of life continuing: a wisp of smoke from a distant chimney, the distant murmur and swing of farm workers, hacking at sheafs in a tuneless dirge. The arching oaks of the country roads soon gave way to snaking lines of yew trees. Once meticulously sculpted harbingers of my family's grounds, they grew crudely, long-neglected by human touch. There were no wildflowers, no joyful butterflies, only the occasional fly-ridden carcass of some unfortunate hare.

Chapter 2

The Croftons had never been a family of excessive staff, rather in possession of what my father would call 'a practical amount'. Yet, regardless of time, our employees had never previously failed to line the steps leading to the door. The cab pulled into the carriageway without due ceremony, and the great doors remained obnoxiously still. My hands, rigid from cold, became clammy, while my ears began to ring from straining in silence. I readjusted my gloves repeatedly until the seams puckered and the stitching sagged.

The driver, grown weary on his perch, began to huff with such force that his breathing began to match that of the horses. I had been sure to send ahead the date of my arrival to avoid any confusion. The visit was streamlined to within a hair's breadth. From the steamers to the carriages, nothing was left to chance; such was Algernon's way. This was all aside from the weather, and that wretched and unexpected overnight stay at the coaching inn by Portadown. After briefly dwelling on the latter, my body retracted with such unexpected violence that staring at the house's brickwork briefly offered some lucid comfort. After a little while, the empty minutes were pierced by the caws of disinterested crows, searching for mischief beyond the garden's walls.

The coach juddered forwards a little, the gravel surrounding the wheels giving way and spitting malicious shards across the path. The horses were restless. I made sure not to move, but slowly emptied my lungs and once again smoothed out invisible creases in my skirts. The coach driver forced a cough, phlegm rattling against his throat in a crude animalistic bark.

I remained sure that soon enough, the doors would clatter open, footmen would spill out like marbles and I would be wrapped in a haze of apologies. The driver forced another raking cough, his rattling breath drawing up a thick viscous globule that he spat, with an overloud 'pfft', onto the gravel below.

In a moment, the wheels juddered once more, the horses' bridles ratting against their buckles, the cab rising several inches. The driver, whose face had turned a burning scarlet, stood beside the carriage window, staring and rapping at the glass. 'You'll have to leave, Madam. It'll be a long journey back home and I don't want to be up here when darkness falls.'

He quickly cast his eyes back at the house, his eyes scanning the windows at lightning speed. 'And of course,' he added as an afterthought, 'I have other fares to collect.'

I relented and dismounted with no offer of his hand. Turning to glance at the back of the carriage, I found my bags to have been roughly toppled from their lashings. The trunks had not fared well. The brass corners had wedged into the soil beneath the gravel; the leather was torn and curled on impact.

The driver loosened his collar with a single fat finger and kicked at the waves of gravel, eyes still scanning the estate.

'Well —' he began, nodding upwards at the fast-gathering storm. 'My poor back does not permit me to aid you with your bags, Miss. I'm afraid that is a job for your own good self.' The driver wrung his hands together and forced a small tight-lipped smile back at me.

'I'm sorry, Miss. Please take care of yourself.' He paused. 'This is no place for the young.'

I stared at my luggage, stacked awkwardly like children's building blocks. While help would have been welcome, it was some meagre relief that nobody, neither staff, society, nor family, was nearby to see the shameful sight, save for Duncain's crows. I could hear Mrs Curry's pseudo-jovial remarks already ringing in my ears. Oh, how the mighty have fallen, Alice.

The driver shuffled and secured the door of his carriage. 'I —' He stopped a few beats short of his next word, the blood draining from his face. His eyes were fixed on an upper window, unblinking, his body rigid with terror.

I stood, inspecting his face with concealed alarm. If the man were to die on the gravel, the removal of his body, let alone the horses, would be too much for my strained heart to take.

'Sir?' I began. 'Sir, are you quite alright?' I gently tapped his shoulder, uneasy with the silence of the once-jovial driver.

The man was shivering, his throat dry and rigid. When he managed to finally tear his eyes away, his movements were pained and stilted. He hobbled back towards his seat with urgency, his eyes reddening with each second that passed. Before mounting the small steps to his seat, he cast his eyes back at me as I stood expectantly, awaiting a change of heart with my pitiful luggage situation.

'I'll be taking my fare now, Miss.'

Chapter 3

I took a few tentative steps to peer around the far side of the house. Peeking through the flowerbeds was the glint of dark water and the not-too-distant snarl of the lake against an unwilling shore. Not everything had changed. The drapes parted only to reveal the vague outline of my father's old wicker-strung chairs. Stained from years of use, they kept a certain ghost of him, an expectation of impossible movement. The trees in front of Father's window had grown into the adjoining thicket and had become so dense with thorns that any bird caught in their coils would tear itself to shreds in any attempt to leave.

In truth, I struggled to recall any situation in which I had been called upon to announce my arrival alone. The whole motion seemed cruelly alien to me. The bell pull was long gone from the frontage; Father had refused to replace the mechanism after its demise, arguing that it would only encourage visitors. The bell's empty bracket still peaked out through a blanket of ivy, like a gold tooth in a rotting maw. I readied myself, clenched my knuckles and rapped three times on the splintered wood.

I waited. Above, the skies were gathering darkness, the house dragging it closer like a magnet. I readjusted my bodice, to the left, then back again. I paused, rolling my wedding ring around my finger with my thumb, twisting the finger of my glove slightly in the process. No one was coming. The household staff were either occupied with arrival preparations or some horrid accident. Either that or my mother had wittered herself into yet another state and was requiring a bank of servants to reassure her.

Tensing myself, I pushed against the door, one hand flat against the panel, the other twisting the brass knob with difficulty. With a heavy click the door opened, scratching against the stone flooring with a toe-curling screech.

Ten feet in front of me was the rotund figure of the housekeeper hunched over a sideboard with a feather duster. She finished dusting an oil lamp, but only after removing the glass shade, polishing, wiping and returning it to its base with no haste. She draped her cloth over her shoulder and turned towards me with little more than a raised eyebrow of interest.

'Hullo, Mrs Curry.'

'Oh,' said the old woman, little above a whisper. 'Welcome home, Miss Alice. I trust your journey was pleasant.'

'Pleasant enough, Mrs Curry. I hope you are well?'

'I am always quite well, Miss,' she thinly smiled. 'Why wouldn't I be?'

London society never prepared me for the conundrums of Duncain niceties. We stared at one another. Small smiles fixed unnaturally on each of our faces.

'No hat?' began Mrs Curry, smile firmly in place. 'How very modern.'

She turned her back and carried a basket of cleaning supplies into the dining room, disappearing from view.

I was once again left alone, the house void of willing help.

'Can someone help me with my luggage, please?' I shouted into the house. Waiting a beat, I received no response.

Mrs Curry reappeared from the corridor, visibly perturbed, and thinly veiling her grievance.

'It really would be best if you quietened down. The mistress is sleeping.'

'My cases,' I coughed, throwing my arm towards the open door in a sudden, overblown sweep. I had always been keen to uphold my standards of etiquette, whether I was talking to a tinker or a Lord, but something in Mrs Curry's obstinate face always managed to kick the legs out from beneath my best intentions. She meant well — she always did. It was my own intolerance sabotaging myself; I had to remember that.

The silence of the house rang heavy as church bells.

'Has Mother not risen to meet me? It is nearly dusk. I thought —' My voice petered out, my eyes pulled towards the new cracks in the once-familiar greying walls.

I dropped my smile and exhaled in frustration at Mother's unenviable nature. She could have prepared for my arrival; a basic string of niceties at the very least. A little movement before she joined Curry in their nightly curious dance of hot tea and bedside comfort, but such politeness continued to elude my remaining family. No wonder Father died so keenly.

I quickly ascended the stairs, roughly hitching my skirts, taking two steps at a time. As I reached the top, a wall of bombazine stepped out from behind an empty planter, sending me wobbling on my heels.

My mother, a bell of sunken silk, seemed shorter than before; compressed. As our eyes locked, she shrieked in overblown shock. Before a sentence left my mouth, my mother grasped at an approximation of her heart, stretching the already-taut fabric to its limit.

'Oh I cannot possibly deal with you!' Mother yelped, arching her back with an audible crack.

Whether it was corset boning or joints that snapped so uncomfortably was unclear. Welcome home, Alice. Welcome home, indeed.

Holding her hand to her brow, Mother quickly disappeared into the back rooms of the house like a spider scuttling back to the safety of its web. Whereas I, travel worn as I was, lacked the energy or inclination for confrontation, lest the old woman return with a senseless rage that would only hinder proceedings. My mother was a petulant child at heart and I knew full well that the legal issues within Father's will were undoubtedly already known. My journey was fine, Mother, thank you. Although I do believe my birthday cards were lost in the post this past year. I changed by name to Algernon's, so why must I still entertain the Croftons? Have I not suffered enough?

Chapter 4

Mrs Curry and I stood by the entranceway, unmoving as statues, as the clatter of widow's feet hurried above us.

Any ordinary child would have been moved to curiosity by the commotion, but such allowances were not permitted in Duncain. Elsie was invariably back in her room, locked in with books and such, as was our father's familiar insistence. Children being seen and not heard was never of particular concern, but the propensity for childish hands and feet to wander to the jetty and rose garden was of curious perpetual concern to my parents, not least when my mother acquired a new fleeting ailment with which to force the house into bolted stillness.

Staring in stalemate, Mrs Curry smiled.

'Miss Alice, she is in mourning,' she said, nodding in a strained approximation of empathy.

Women in mourning do not spend all day in their bedclothes, hiding themselves away, I thought. When they rise and dress, they function. But Mother was no 'regular woman', as every visitor for decades was made perpetually aware. Raking against the floorboards, before coming to rest on the crunch of a bedstead, were enough beads to sound like a hailstorm above our heads. It hardly seemed appropriate considering how recently Father passed, but there would be no breath wasted over trimmings.

'Hmm,' agreed Mrs Curry, answering the noises. 'The mistress finds comfort where she can. I'm sure you understand,' she crooned, rolling her words with unsettling warmth.

'Well, yes —' I began.

'— and will respect those methods,' added Mrs Curry, a little too loudly, smile still fixed. 'It's the grief you see, Miss Alice. It hurts me to see her in such a state. I care deeply for her. For all of you.'

The housekeeper's tone was strange, but the crack of thunder drew my eyes back to the open doorway where my cases languished on the gravel. As we watched, a trunk slowly slid from its awkward perch atop another, the metal corners scoring the leather beneath in an uncomfortable parabola. In overstretched seconds, the henge of caged dresses and books disassembled itself in an inelegant crunch.

The old servant tilted her body to see behind me.

'Were all of those necessary?' she gently laughed.

'Yes. Well, I didn't know what engagements —'

'So, you call me out to brag?' chipped Mrs Curry, baring blackened, sparse teeth through a thin-lipped smile.

I sighed. 'I'm not calling you at all, Mrs Curry.'

'I'm just jesting, Miss, you know me,' chuckled the housekeeper, before turning on her heels and disappearing into the bowels of the house. 'You girls keep me young.'

As her voice drifted through the hall, all that remained was the cold company of the outside world, an empty foyer, a jumble of cases and heavy, blackened, creeping clouds.

In all of Mrs Curry's years of servitude, I had never seen any glimpse of a husband, but regularly pitied the man who became entangled with such an obtuse woman. With the housekeeper back in her burrow, her marital affairs, or lack thereof, would be a discussion for another day.

Returning to the threshold, a spear of pain shot behind my eyes. I crumpled, slamming my hand into the door in a sudden, violent reflex. My nails dug between the fibres of the wood, my other hand grappling at my head. The curious alignment of my bones was the only support keeping me upright. Bile rose in my throat, the few scraps of breakfast from the coaching inn threatening to leave my body as the last vestiges of the world beyond Duncain.

My vision was wiped rapier-fast with a screaming agony that forced my eyes shut and threatened to cleave my head in two.

Tearing my nails into my head to relieve the pressure, there was laughter. The muffled chatter of unfamiliar voices punctuated the throbbing of my own pulse in my ears. The sounds were too quiet and low to decipher, but rolled like marbles behind my thoughts as the pain grew stronger and louder, deafening in its fury.

Relinquishing the last of my strength, my knees fell from beneath me, meeting the marble floor with a wet thud. My skirts did little to soften the blow, but took a little of the blood that seeped from my torn fingernails, whose tips still hung a little above the lock. As soon as it arrived, the pain was gone. My vision, blurred at first, returned slowly, but remained feathered around the edges. I examined my bloodied hand through a slow vignette as the other traced my scalp, skimming for cuts of my own making. I was fine. I was anxious and stressed from the journey. The food disagreed with me and I was concerned for my family. I would unpack, rest and give it no further thought. No one saw, and no one would have to know.

My luggage remained on the driveway. Wincing as I pushed myself from the stone floor, I turned back towards the cases, my head and fingers throbbing, tongue thick with sour spit. Taking tentative steps, I moved into the cold air just in time to see the first heavy droplets of rain bouncing on the lids of my trunks.

Chapter 5

Climbing across two small landings and countless gradually shortening steps, I made my way to the summit of the house's first staircase. The last of my trunks made full contact with the rug with a damp, fibrous thud. I didn't have to turn around to know they'd be fit for the incinerator. Another cost to justify to Algernon. Behind me, two repeated scuffs, like rodent bites, marked the brass corners' inelegant and imprinted route up the staircase. My beautiful soft gloves were soaked and stained from their journey through the house, having turned from pea green to mottled brown. When they dried, they would invariably become ridged and tear with use. Pea-green suede. Of all the gloves to ruin, Alice, you chose those? I could have slapped myself for my stupidity. I had bought them for travel, but not to be treated like this.

As the leather slid between my fingers, a moderate sense of grief passed over me; I'd hoped they would at least join me on the return to Chelsea. After unpacking, I made a note to squirrel them away, lest they be another precious thing irreparably damaged by Duncain. In moving my own possessions, I had taken little notice of my surroundings, least of all, the patterning of the rugs under my feet. Beneath my shoes was an enormous black mark, soaked deeply into the rug and boards in approximation of a man's prostrate figure.

Across it all grew a dark mould that sat flush with the boards in a sticky black puddle that never dried. From the curve of its back and the imprints of its calves and head, it was clearly the form of my father. I tried to assure myself that if such a sickening mark had been made by my father's poor form, Mrs Curry would not be so cruel as to leave it untouched. I hoped so at least. It was an upsetting coincidence; it was not my father.

The estate was in a perpetual state of damp anyway, with the stain existing as just another unpleasant incarnation of rot and mould, thriving in the airless shadow of the main house. Although my stomach turned a little as I inspected the damp marks, I swallowed my rising bile and made a note not to make a fuss. The stain is not my problem; the stain is not my father. The human mind can be fooled by shapes — it can seek order and familiarity in chaos. It was an unfortunate likeness, nothing more. It was a problem with soft furnishings, and I would not be affected. When the house was mine, then I could concern myself with such matters of damp and mould. Or, at the very least, I could order the carpets removed and burned once Father's body had been committed to the earth. If I wanted, I could cry and stomp and paint the whole house vermillion, but until then, I had to wait and knit together my tattered nerves. I was still my father's daughter, and I would do my darnedest to see things through his eyes. Firm and focused.

I attempted to force such unhelpful thoughts from my mind and shuffled around the edges of the stain, pushing my trunks along the familiar route to my childhood bedroom. That blasted mark was not so easy to avoid, nor forget. I paced around it again with my luggage, but couldn't avert my eyes from its blackness, as though it might move at any moment.

Turning back to examine it, I couldn't help but notice the feathering at the edges. Darker than the centre, the curve of his bent knee opened into the carpet weave like rose petals. It was beautiful in a way. It felt soft and damp like tree bark after a shower. In patches, it was glossy and metallic, thick and undrying like oil. My thoughts floated away without me, and I found myself dropping my bag of ointments, and pressing my hands into the edges of the mark. Wide, tactile and dark, it seemed warm and inviting, like a marriage bed at daybreak or a blanket waiting for a body to cling to. It was a warmth that had become an unfamiliar sensation. It was warmer than my own flesh, pressing into my palms, soft and forgiving like a kiss. My fingers moved to my tongue, rolling across my tastebuds without my control, as I softly tasted the sour paste. Like fingers tracing my spine, I couldn't help but arch my back forwards, my skin hot and sensitive, as though prickled by a lover's touch.

A breeze wove its way through the house, whipping the bedroom door from the latch.

A creak from a distant room caught my breath as I no longer felt alone with my thoughts. The unfamiliar sweetness in my mouth turned cloying and bitter like pipe ash, and a rancid taste quickly snaked up my nostrils. Immediately, as a crass reflex, I began spitting at the floor, ferociously rubbing my tongue against my sleeve in an attempt to remove the noxious flavour.

The tell-tale thud of Mrs Curry's feet against the kitchen stairs pushed me up the remaining steps with a reawakened keenness to escape any interactions. Pushing the cases awkwardly against the splitting fibres of the exposed floorboards, I breathlessly rushed into the bedroom, relieved to enter the closest form of sanctuary the house offered.

The door to my childhood bedroom had been unlocked in some unexpected, gracious allowance. The room did not seem so much expectant and welcoming as somewhat resigned to the inevitability of my return. Draughts aside, the relief of avoiding another meeting with Mrs Curry was enormous. As generous as she could be with her time for the family, my mind still did not feel my own, and explaining the damp black smears on my silk cuff was a conversation I'd be keen to avoid altogether. As a child, I had often thought that the temperature seemed to drop in her presence, like some great tottering void. It was a thought that made me shiver as I dragged my cases into the once-familiar territory of the front-facing bedroom.

The view had changed little from the window. The bumpy leading around the glass was a little looser and there were fewer flowers in the garden below, but the grounds had never been abundant in terms of non-functional decoration. Everything within my family's gaze had required a purpose; from chairs to trees, practicality blanketed it all, with no requirement for decoration. Children were to operate under the same principles: simply raised and with clear usage when they came of age. My usefulness in marriage could not have come soon enough, I thought. God bless Algernon. I owe him more than words can convey.

Curiously, the room had remained as it was when I left: sparsely decorated and clumsy, with a heavy oak bed dominating the far wall. I had always thought they'd repurpose my room when I married, but perhaps they had not yet thought of a decent usage. Nearby was a linen closet, dresser and reading chair. I had surreptitiously and poorly reupholstered the seat in my early teenage years with muted colours of pastel floss, forming rudimentary flowers and foliage that warped and pulled as soon as the chair was used. It was sweet, in a way. But the kind of sweet that I'd have to keep in a room far away from Chelsea visitors. Sentimentality so often warms my heart, but chills most fashionable minds. Nonetheless, the female realm was evidently of no interest to my father, and thanks to Mrs Curry and my mother's disinterest, the chair remained in its modified form. Little did I know that in a matter of hours, what was first endearing would become a considerable irritant as the loose threads hooked around the curled brass handles of my writing slope after a mere second's rest.

With the bedroom door fully open, I was afforded a clear view across the landing to the far room, which was clearly bolted. There was no warmth to be found behind the door to Mother's room, just a well-worn sickbed and a selection of 'best silverware' which was somehow too appealing to be on display. Instead, it clattered together in crates, denting and warping into one amorphous mass every time Mrs Curry desired access to the linen closet. I closed the door, making sure the click of the latch was firmly heard by anyone within earshot. Although the room was familiar, when closing myself within its walls, the space offered no comfort, nor a perceived privacy. It was clear that upkeep of the room had not been a priority for the household and had been instantly struck from Mrs Curry's chore list. The surfaces were dusty, with fresh brown watermarks stretching down the walls like adders. I hadn't expected bunting and a 21-gun salute, but a wipe around the walls with a damp cloth surely wouldn't have killed them.

The bed was bare and unmade, with old blankets folded on top in what appeared to be another strange gesture of reticence by my mother, or Mrs Curry, at my return. However long the blankets had been resting was of little importance; after all, the house had never really been of interest to moths. This was a fact that only seemed curious upon my departure from Duncain, especially when I opened my beautiful armoire last summer and found my new taffeta dress ravaged by tiny greedy mouths. The old groundskeeper used to say that Duncain was too cold for little city moths to survive; they were too delicate and weak for Duncain's harsh winters. The big ones thrived. Black moths as large as teacups would throw themselves against the windows at night, banging on the glass like war drums. They came in clans when candlelight was sparingly permitted (it was a commodity perpetually deemed wasteful), or when — as an emboldened child — I palmed a handful of matches from Mrs Curry's stash. In Duncain, darkness was the natural order of things. My father professed to us all that to rest in blackness was to do God's work; to spend time in contemplative prayer with eyes unburdened. He showed very few instances of genuine Christian belief, but relished the dogma and hellish laments of the Old Testament, speaking of Belfast and London with all the ferocity of Sodom and Gomorrah.

Childish nightmares had never been permitted, and I had soon learned to endure the creaks of the house as a little girl.

But now, this hardened strength seemed to have left me. Lingering in London, no doubt. Mrs Curry closed a door in the lower floors and I twitched with every creak. I didn't dare dwell on how my mind would cope with the nocturnal whisperings of Mrs Curry and those horrid dusty thuds of thwarted moths. The windows were painted shut, so all the creatures achieved was leaving dusty triangles on glass and quickly burning into clouds of ash when they dared to venture down the chimney. I would clear my mind of such horrors and prepare my room as comfortably as I could. I would be practical. Paperwork would take a few days, nothing more. I unfolded the first blanket and felt my nails pierce through the ends of my gloves. Typical. Another bill for Algernon.

19th October 1877

Dearest Algernon,

I have arrived safely. I trust you were waiting until my arrival to send me correspondence. A very wise matter, my love! I hope you are keeping well. I have yet to speak to Mother, but Mrs Curry assures me that the solicitors will be arriving before Father's funeral.

Owing to the diversion due to this horrid weather, I have had no choice other than to put up a portion of my allowance for my board. I must tell you once more that it was upon the driver's insistence as I cannot bear the thought of you worrying about me rattling about in a coaching inn.

Although meagre, the costs have impacted on my allowance and I will require a little more from our accounts in order to comfortably return to London. I have enclosed the receipt for your records. If you could forward a few notes to the house at your earliest convenience, I would be most relieved. Also, please send a selection of furs. I feel I am a little unprepared and would be so embarrassed to return to you with a chill at my heels!

Please don't worry for me. I am strong of mind, but long for your consolation in these dark times.

Yours forever,

Alice x

Proprietor: Mrs C. Cooney
The Jubilee Coaching Inn
Dungannon

Breakfast — 3d
Lunch, Dinner — 4d
Share of Dinner Bill, Wines, Beds — 6d
Hay — 5d
Servants — 6d
Total = 2s/0d

Chapter 6

I spent a restless night above the covers, rising periodically to replace the candle in my chamberstick before returning to my position, aching from the cold. For a time I contemplated composing letters to friends, as the writing slope still rested beside the window. But to tell them of what news? Of rain and coaching inns and portly drivers whose mouths glistened black from chewing tobacco? How I could still smell the breath of the over-familiar, if attractive, barkeep on my collar? Unlikely.

Mrs Curry's thunderous feet took the stairs to her quarters, closing the door with as much consideration as a mildly perturbed bull. At last, the house was silent, save for the creak of old foundations and the occasional, frenetic tap-tap of Elsie's feet across the floorboards. Cold and prostrate, I lay in bed until the sun's muffled brightness fed its way through the window pane. With my mother's disinterest in funerary proceedings hanging heavy in my mind, I sank into my apathy — a rather luxurious feeling, considering — and remained in bed, watching imagined patterns swirl across the ceiling.

Throughout the grey morning, the house's own aches were punctuated with occasional whimpers and muffled demands from my mother. Mother's voice was weak and cracking, but loud enough to be heard throughout the house when she called for assistance. The whole performance was well considered and rehearsed; a voice loud enough to have its demands heard, but not so clear as to suggest strength. I reclined my shoulders, stiff from my restless night, and listened to the interactions in the corridor outside. Arching my back and placing my hands behind my head, I lifted my nightshirt a little too high above my ankles. I closed my eyes to focus on the imagined interactions between my mother and Mrs Curry, seeing the two rotund, hunched figures meet like overfed sheep in adjoining fields.

A needful wail from my mother became a clear signal for Mrs Curry to return to her door with more tea and food. This performance began early in earnest and cyclically repeated itself at least three times before the auditory frustrations became too great for me to remain in my room. My mother would have to be winched from her mourning bed should she become accustomed to this sweetness of grief, with all its convenient cream fillings. The recurrent story continued throughout my ritualistic dressing. First my undergarments, then my knitted stockings (I was no fool in this weather), chemise, stays, and petticoat. And another petticoat. Just in case. Lastly, my dress whose tiny buttons frustrated and pulled at my shoulders without the help of my maid. I trusted Algernon's judgement with my life, but heavens, I wished he'd allowed dear Charlotte to travel with me. A lady's maid never seems so much a privilege as a necessity on days like this. As I rolled a second pair of stockings up my calves — a paper-thin silk with little blossoms embroidered at the heel — the heavy thuds of Mrs Curry's feet on the staircase were inescapable. The creaks of the boards close to my door seemed impatient, but not loud enough to fully conceal the somewhat contrived, melancholic wails of my mother. The adjustments of my underclothes were accompanied by the jangling of empty plates against the enormous wooden handles of Mrs Curry's tray and the satiated groans of my mother whose stomach was as bloated and taut as the unburied carcass of her husband. Had I not been so cold, and so ignored by my mother, I am sure that my mind would have been far more sympathetic to her plight. Instead, I obsessed over the sweet inevitability of my departure from Duncain.

Choosing my jewellery from its travel case, the gentle satisfied crunches of sandwiches against my mother's ill-fitting teeth imagined themselves into reality. I could hear the discomforting grind of polished bone cracking through over-baked bread. Algernon had said my vivid imagination was endearing, but it often seemed to try and sabotage me.

Rattling my fingers through the case, one piece was glaring in its absence: my wedding ring. I was sure to have placed it in the centre of the case before I changed into my nightclothes the night before, but something in my travel-scrambled mind clouded my memory. I rummaged between bands set with coral, diamond, square-cut emeralds and enamel, not caring if they clattered together, and continued swirling the jewels with no luck. I scanned the floor, the window sill, and fluffed my blankets with eyes trained like a hawk for anything glinting in the meagre light. Nothing. Without the ring, my fingers were not my own. They were fingers of Duncain. They were the fingers of a girl trapped by damp walls and old ways. Most of all, without the ring, I was Alice Crofton, not Alice Marriott. I searched the room again, which skulked in shadow and still refused to give up its secrets.

The ring was my link to Algernon. It showed the world that I was his and he was mine. It proved that I had escaped. Feeling my naked finger with my thumb did nothing to ease the panic rising in my chest like floodwaters. I began searching the floorboards, first with a look, then with my hands, my face and my eyes tracing every crack and fracture in the worn-out beams. I scaled the room on my knees, keeping my breath low in my chest, in case the slightest exhalation would push the hidden ring beneath the boards. Pushing my nails under the plaster at the base of the walls, my nails split, curling back in thin sheets. Decorum became frantic, scaling the fine cracks of the rooms' perimeter, my fingertips raw and prickling from this futile exercise. My ears rang in the silence of the room, the familiar curve and clink of gold nowhere to be found. The ring was in the room somewhere. It had to be. I had been careless and would learn lessons from the incident, for that was all it would be, an incident. A blip in my day. The ring would be found.

It seemed as though hours had passed as I tore my room apart. My heart continued to beat in deafening thuds; my saliva tasted of iron, warm and wet on my tongue. My fingers had become raw and splintered, but my body seemed too anxious to bleed. I hoisted the hem of my dress, not caring about the stockings that might snag on the floorboards, and scurried animal-like across the room, squeezing beneath my bed as cobweb lace decorated my shoulders. But the ring was nowhere to be found. Algernon would not forgive me for such a loss. He often told me of my unappreciative and careless nature, and I had worked so hard to convince him otherwise. I was the perfect attentive wife. I read all the right magazines, said all the right things. I thanked him, celebrated, and treasured his every motion towards me. But the ring was gone.

I roughly hauled the top trunk from its stack. With the weight taking my wrists by surprise, the box landed with a heavy smash onto the floorboards. The lid arched open to its fullest and I pulled out dresses and blouses with boundless ferocity. Caught up in the frantic speed of my pulse, I whirled swags of fine fabrics and embroidery about myself, throwing them across the room in wild semaphore. There was nothing, no tinkle of gold against damp wood, just the swish of silk and the occasional snagging of fibres against old wood. Throwing open lids and lotions, my panic was punctuated with the crack of plaster and the sudden flight of brass corners and cream pots. Emptying my luggage, I scrambled towards the linen cupboard, my toes catching in the hem of my dress as I stumbled. Wrapping my arms around the enormous piece of furniture, I finally came to a standstill. Tears pricked at the corners of my eyes, blurring my vision.

I should never have taken the ring off. The loss was of my own making. I should have kept it tight to my finger, wearing it for every moment until a divot grew old and coarse, mottling my ageing skin beneath the band. I had been so foolish. The ring had not left the room since I worked it off my finger the night before. It would emerge. It would have fallen into some dark corner that more rested eyes could explore. As Algernon would say, 'You silly, silly girl.'

Surveying the chaos of velvet and lace surrounding me, I couldn't help but clutch at my chest. Each surface was covered in clothing, ribbons and cosmetics in a topography of frantic desperation and shame. As I sat and wept, nursing my tattered fingertips, I toyed at the cuff of a lonely glove. I would find its partner and return my things to their cases, one piece at a time. No one would know my shame, of that I was sure. And I would certainly not ruin another pair of gloves on this trip.

After Mrs Curry had completed the cycles of feeding and crockery retrieval, the upper floors sank into silence once more, with no sign of life from Elsie's chambers and only the occasional piercing caws of visiting crows from outside, fighting for rotted fish on the jetty.

The clocks in my old bedroom hadn't been wound since my departure some time ago, leaving the hands jauntily fixed at different times. Some clock hands, languishing without the protection of glass, supported thick caterpillars of dust, framing clock faces like my father's moustache. I presumed the hour to be long past breakfast, but the precise time was impossible to predict. The house was well-fed, but languished in shadow.

The sun hadn't risen as such, but rather lumbered across the sky, gently warming the thick clouds that kept Duncain in a perpetual state of timeless near-waking. As I became aware of the stiffening of my hips, I opened my remaining trunks and grappled for my warmest layers. Having little time to concern myself with mourning wear, nor keenly making haste to take an afternoon's visit to Jay's to bore myself with black crape and veils, I fixed myself into a deep violet house coat with tiny French jet buttons to the bodice. The buttons were a compromise, to Algernon's standards at least. Being black glass and not true, carved jet, each glimpse of them 'stank of budgetary constraints'. Or so he spat over dinner one evening. Indeed, they were more delicate and elaborately cast than any Whitby carver could accomplish, but the concern of having someone notice the disparity was a lingering concern for him. It was a mistake I was sure to never repeat.

'People would stare,' Algernon would say. They did already, or so I'd been told. And he did not bring me to London to have his country wife humiliate him. At first I was intelligent, 'unusual for a woman'. I was conversational, sparkling, a jewel, or a whole blasted treasure chest once his blood was warmed with brandy. I wore his 'unusual' praise like a fur stole most days. I was 'other', not elevated above women, but I often believed that my reality straddled that of a masculine world to which so few had been privy. I remember when I was beautiful, then *too* beautiful. I set down standards too high to comfortably maintain; the action of a stupid country bumpkin. I, a Crofton whose surname pierced through nightly lectures with a spittled hook, was trying to ruin him. My presence in the home became a direct attempt to distract business partners, to push their loyalties towards another firm. A child, vying for attention. Soon enough, Algernon conducted all business from his office, leaving not so much as a business card at home. With time together so fleeting, it was at times unclear what he had brought me to London for at all.

I left my clothes in piles, quickly tidying my thoughts, and left the room in silence. Nothing good would come of such things. I squirrelled my diary beneath the writing slope, ever-mindful of the wandering eyes of staff. I would be efficient, like Father, and like Algernon. My time at Duncain would be brief and assertive and I would make them proud.

Or satisfied, at least.

The upper floors were deathly quiet, save for the groan and click of distant doors. The house was still and unchanged, with the same dust that had caught in my lungs a decade before. With hunger weighing heavily in my stomach, I slowly made my way down the stairs, in search of my own underwhelming sustenance.

Without audible warning, I met Mrs Curry at the foot of the landing, narrowly avoiding a collision or violent embrace, depending on her hourly mood. Mrs Curry, suddenly unsteady on her feet, wobbled like a weathervane. In her arms, she held an enormous wooden tray, overflowing with sweet treats and hot tea. Clouded by my creeping hunger, my hands circled the tray, lifting it from Mrs Curry's arms with absent-minded familiarity. I only managed a single step before Mrs Curry's throat-clearing stopped my slippers in their tracks.

She stared at me with open hands, before a familiar tight-lipped smile snaked across her mouth. I winced a little awkwardly in the silence, the tray uncomfortably heavy in my hands.

'Some of us haven't been offered sustenance today,' I said, half-jokingly. 'I see no issue in ensuring my own health. Besides, it's unlikely the old woman will starve.'

I nodded my head towards Mother's room and forced an approximation of shared laughter. It was an invitation not picked up by the housekeeper. Mrs Curry waited a beat before silently retrieving the heavy tray from my arms. It was clearly not to be a jovial day.

'Your food is in the front parlour, Miss Alice. I prepared a table for you.'

'Ah,' I exhaled, my face burning in embarrassment.

Mrs Curry languished in the bloated silence between us. 'Beside the window.'

'Good, yes. Thank you, Mrs Curry.' I replied a little too quickly, smoothing imagined folds from my bodice.

'Could you clean this later?' I said with deliberate, ineffectual, firmness, casting my hand towards the mottled outline on the carpet. 'It's very troubling —'

My words suddenly caught in my throat with an uncomfortable globular hack. I knew I was being a little childish, stamping my feet with a little moment of authority with the staff; but navigating my role in Duncain House, especially Duncain House in mourning, was a troublesome task.

'I've tried, Miss, but it's a job beyond my abilities. He ain't moving,' smiled Mrs Curry at last, her pocked face hidden behind the veiled steam of boiling tea.

Ending our interaction, Mrs Curry turned to ascend the last few stairs with her unchanging, rolling gait.

'Oh, Mrs Curry!' I shouted behind myself. 'When you have a moment, I have a letter on my desk that needs posting to London. Could you please take it —'

'Consider it posted, Miss,' replied Mrs Curry with strange absentminded cheer as she moved up the stairs.

'Very well, Mrs Curry. I give you leave to return to your chores,' I muttered under my breath, mimicking her gait and wobbling my head like a mocking child. How frequently I forget this is Mrs Curry's house. Silly old woman.

I saw Mrs Curry's face folded inwards in anger, wrinkled like a forgotten potato. I cannot deny taking strange satisfaction at her irritation. Somewhat empowered by the sensation of fresh Duncain-free tailoring against my skin, I moved down the staircase and through the parlour door with practised elegance, my head held obnoxiously high like a show pony.

At least with my delay with Mrs Curry, a few moments without food might rouse Mother from her chambers. When Mother emerged, at last, discussions of a suitable memorial might arise between us, although I had begun to feel that such matters might have already been executed. My stomach began grumbling a little too loudly for any semblance of elegance to be maintained, leaving me glad of my return to solitude. Solicitors would invariably visit soon, being a welcome signal of my imminent departure from Duncain.

I continued into the parlour with the heavy tray weighing in my mind, still mildly perturbed at the broken fluency of my words to Mrs Curry. The musculature of my hands felt a little strained from the unexpected heft of the tray, but such concerns quickly left my mind at the full teapot and extensive spread before me. Any thoughts of torn gloves, lost rings and absent mothers were short-lived as I tucked into rolled meats, fresh bread and a thick, daffodil-yellow wedge of butter.

Above the parlour, Mrs Curry slowly moved from her footing by Lady Crofton's bedchamber and shuffled across the boards. Slowly and surely, her impossibly heavy footsteps lumbered down the staircase, across the foyer, and down the dark stone spiral into the depths of the kitchen; all the while huffing and puffing like a slowing steam train. A little while later, she re-emerged from the staircase with her clothes thick with the smell of burning coal and pig fat. The signs of Mrs Curry's approach were not a subtle affair, sending nostrils pricking before her feet made it across the parlour threshold.

I had grown bold with the warmth and weighty satisfaction of simple foods and sweet tea. I had left little on the tray, save for a few crumbs and a string of fat that proved too tough and rubbery to swallow. Not the dining habits of a lady, but who was watching?

Tearing through the comforting bubble of the sun-warmed entrance, Mrs Curry's sweeping brush scratched its way through the entrance hall and into the quiet sanctity of the parlour. The enormous brush was too rough; the fibres were fixed like crochet hooks that clawed through the boards, removing as much of the varnish as the dirt. With the housekeeper's rude entrance, the pleasantries of my feast dissipated quickly, Mrs Curry's claws digging deeper into the flooring with each swoosh of her brush.

'Mrs Curry,' I began, my voice quiet from the inevitability of a fast-approaching headache. She did not respond, but continued brushing, mounting carpet and floorboard in one violent parabola.

'Mrs Curry!'

The housekeeper stopped, punctuating my speech with a heavy thud of her brush against the unfortunate leg of a console table. She'd have me believe her destruction wasn't deliberate, I was sure.

'I am keen to know any information about my father's funeral. I have not been told if or how his body was laid out ... if he's still in the house for that matter?' I added the latter in mock, forced humour. It was always best to keep the staff on board with humour of their class, or so I had been told. Mrs Curry's eyes that had unnerved me as a child tangled my speech as an adult.

'Is he... were there undertakers?' I questioned, no longer sure of the intent of my speech.

I needlessly wrung my hands. I had not been greatly susceptible to anxieties of late, yet the growing sensation of over-indulgence and tannin-coated sustenance incited a panicked pounding within my head.

'For a grieving daughter,' I began slowly, 'having so little information puts even more strain on my heart.' What I had intended as sincere hung rather foul once it had left my lips.

Mrs Curry leaned her brush against a table and moved towards the door, closing it with a palm flat against the panelling. The other circled the brass knob with a cloth, as though she were removing fingerprints from the well-battered surface. Her hands were clumped into fists, resting on the approximation of her hips.

'Mrs Curry, my father —' I intonated.

'Undertakers got him. I know no more, Miss, truly. That'll be your mother's realm. I've got too much to do around the house than to spend my days keening in one of them back rooms anyway. Your mother was in no rush to shove him in the ground. If you spoke to her, you'd know these things. Mind your feet.'

The housekeeper had grasped the handle of the broom once more, forcing its spines back into the boards in a heavy, unyielding rhythm.

'Have you entered my bedroom of late, Mrs Curry?'

The housekeeper continued to grate the floorboards, pausing periodically to raise an eyebrow, to which I shrank a little deeper into my seat. The stuffing in the chaise seat had begun to emerge with pressure of my weight. Horsehair irritated my skin. Pieces of protruding straw were a threat to the fabric of my dress and housecoat too, let alone my stockings. With Algernon's past comments of cost and frivolity in my mind, I kept my body still, to save racking up further bills.

'You think I'm comin' in to watch you sleepin'?' Mrs Curry chuckled.

'No —' I began, still military-rigid in my seat.

'Look, Miss, what you do up there is your business. I have no interest in anything other than the upkeep of this house and the well-being of the Lady.'

The housekeeper cleared her throat, hacking the heavy phlegm into her dust cloth.

I spoke quietly. 'My ring is missing.'

'Oh, I'm sorry about that, Miss,' crooned Mrs Curry. 'Was it an important one?'

'Yes, my gold wedding band,' I said, slowly. 'I left it on my dresser — or in my box — and this morning it was gone.'

Mrs Curry supported herself on the broom handle, as though she were a music-hall act, primed to begin her routine.

'Have you checked your table? You checked your cases too?' said the housekeeper with poorly feigned interest.

I stared back at her, taking a moment of silence as my headache slowly worsened.

'I can't help you there, Miss. It probably went the way of my golden shoes and 18-inch waist. Or maybe, just maybe —' she whispered, leaning towards me, 'the *aos sí* have spirited it away as you slept!'

I sighed, reclining in pained frustration. With my sigh came the tell-tale crunch of horse hair piercing taffeta. Great.

Mrs Curry huffed her way around the remainder of the room, her brush and spitty cloths muddying each surface they touched. As she moved the dust about the room, replacing old grime with her own, I watched her, as though I might intercept some brazen light-fingered activities in her presence. There was barely anything worth stealing nowadays.

Mrs Curry visibly enjoyed her voyeur, deliberately circling tables with her back to me, over-dusting and rearranging clusters of ornaments with poorly hidden delight. After completing her circuit, dwelling a little too long on a pair of cherub-covered, pink porcelain vases, she grabbed a lone, large vase and placed it onto the breakfast tray. Catching the lip of the saucer, it came close to toppling, before I grasped its handles in panic.

'Could one of the younger girls have taken it?' I asked, quickly.

'Girls?' questioned Mrs Curry. 'There'll be none of them here.'

'A butler perhaps? Gerald?' I offered.

'It's just us now, Miss,' stated Mrs Curry.

I looked back in silence, curiously squinting at Curry's statement. Mrs Curry used her words slowly. 'It's just me, you and the mistress now.'

'And Elsie,' I added.

Mrs Curry responded as slowly and calmly as before. 'Of course, Miss, and Elsie.'

My hand snaked towards the vase that still lingered by the tray. The entire front of the vase was painted with a likeness of Leda and the swan. Leda really wasn't as beautiful as she should be. Her curls were too tight and closed around her face like the fixed halo of a bisque piano baby. The swan beside her looked somewhat demented. With its too-long beak and red eyes, it stared at Leda's exposed breasts like a lecherous drunk. My stomach twisted at the thought.

'Can you hand me the other vase?' I asked, closing my eyes to avoid another bilious attack.

'There ain't no other vase. Must have just broken,' replied Mrs Curry as she busied herself once more with vigorous dusting.

Quality porcelain *just* broken was something to rouse me from any unpleasant episode. For all of his faults, my father taught me certain things well, namely, inventory.

'*Just* broken?'

'Well, your father did have his fits.' As the clipped words left her lips, Mrs Curry shook the duster beside her in a curious semaphore of conversational closure. She turned to me with a small smile, as though such a gesture would make up for any disparaging comments.

Turning to leave, Mrs Curry packed up her basket, grasping the broom handle like a lance.

Catching Mrs Curry's ear at the doorway, I spoke a little louder: 'What happened to old Gerald?'

I had hoped to sound absent-minded, and kept my eyes turned from Mrs Curry's. I was keen not to let her have the last word in this stilted interaction.

Though old, the butler was always a stocky and reliable figure, particularly through Sir Kenneth's relentless requests to rearrange the furniture of the upper floors.

Mrs Curry maintained her stance and stared through the window as though deep in thought.

'Died. Last winter,' she said.

'Patrick?' I quipped, remembering the ginger gardener with an unbecoming beard.

The housekeeper's response was swift. 'Drowned.'

'Artie?' I asked, my voice wavering as I scrambled through old memories.

'Left, last summer,' huffed Mrs Curry.

'Where did he —?' I began.

'Well,' interjected Mrs Curry, 'probably dead now.'

'Sean?' I asked hopefully.

'Married.'

'Oh really?' I quipped, cheerfully. He had always been such a handsome man. For a local, at least.

Mrs Curry pursed her lips. 'No. Died. A wall fell on him.'

'Well —' I began.

'Buried him up by the crofts,' continued Mrs Curry, her eyes still staring through the murky window.

'He —' I began, fruitlessly.

'His family wanted to take him back to Cranagh,' sighed the housekeeper. 'But your father was having none of that.'

I sat silently, my jaw chewing dead air.

'He was a very heavy man at the end. I had to pull him out myself. Lord, he made a terrible mess. I think his foot's still in the garden somewhere,' chuckled Mrs Curry, giving little indication of truth or humour in her reply.

I tried to swallow the bile that rose in my throat, but Mrs Curry was quick to notice and dampened a small smile that played upon the corner of her mouth.

Mrs Curry was toying with me, like a cat batting at a trapped mouse, delighting in the sport between us. Her face showed more life than I had seen in many years. She was a gun dog, relishing the disgust that talk of blood brought about.

'It's just us now, Miss. Just us,' said Mrs Curry, smiling broadly, emphasizing her words like a mantra.

Chapter 7

As Mrs Curry busied herself, I sank back into the chair, my body separating at its joints. I felt rather limp from it all, tired and heavy like a play-worn doll. The food had been blissful, and I had undoubtedly been satiated for the first time in weeks, should I be truthful. But with my stomach comfortably swollen with bread and syrup, the rest of my body felt unsettled. It was as though someone was talking about me in another room. It was a strange, unsteady feeling, where a mild sickness rose in my stomach, some unseen pins pricking at my fingertips like static. Perhaps this was God's way of teaching me not to trust the ingredients of Duncain's produce. Duncain was not good for me, nor was the house. I just needed a lawyer to attend the house; I didn't even have to see a grave. The emptiness of the house was as good as a funeral wreath. I needed a lawyer, paperwork and a coach out of the county. The steamer journey was painful enough, but I'd take it again so happily, providing it returned me home to London. Home to Algernon.

The smell of the steamer rooms filled my nostrils, and thoughts of cabins of staring children and too-talkative mothers returned to my mind. One woman seemed perfectly agreeable for a time; I even thought I could perhaps make a letter friend of her. But at the mention of Duncain, she seemed disinterested, held her child closer and made a great deal of fuss about dinner plans. Travellers can be a curious bunch.

Mrs Curry had crept closer without my noticing, inspecting my position in the chair with mild interest, before leaning over me to grab a rogue cloth. Seeming distracted, she muttered in half-growled tones, 'If it were in my powers to bring a lawman up here, I'd drag him up by his collar.'

I sat stock-still, my skin fighting a cold sweat. Gathering a little of my strength, I replied to Mrs Curry in a voice just above a murmur. 'This table needs clearing. You can take that up with you.'

'You not sleeping, Miss?'

Mrs Curry roughly wiped the table and folded the leaves back into the sides. A dull, barely functional piece, it had never been removed from the wall and left a strangely bright shadow against the wallpaper behind. My vase counterpart and I stared at one another as I found myself slowly inspecting the half-naked princess for damage. Leda's painted eyes remained fixed, brilliant white and unblinking as the swan flanked her breast. Perhaps the other broken vase was a blessing.

Mrs Curry remained beside me, silent, the cloth tucked into the crook of her hip. I leaned forward, avoiding her gaze, and found a little more hot water in the pot. One cup of lukewarm tea. I would stay a little longer. The air seemed muggier somehow, as if someone had closed all the windows at once. My heart began to race uncomfortably and I knew that my legs would fail me should I try to stand. Watching the last tepid drops pass through the strainer, Mrs Curry leaned forward to watch my shaking movements. Something was wrong.

With me, or the tea, I couldn't be sure, but something was very wrong.

My head grew too heavy for my neck, lolling back onto the slats of the chair. The carved curl of wooden grapes and bowknots dug into the base of my skull like a fist. My vision blurred in waves, as though tiredness had ambushed me with a blanket. Before me, women danced in blurs of brown paint water as small black-eyed children scuttled about the floor like dogs.

'You never did belong here,' whispered Mrs Curry, her voice airless and distant.

Mrs Curry was somewhere in the room, but with a head of lead, my searching eyes could not find her.

'I don't understand why you hate me so, Curry,' I whispered.

'You've tested us all —' began the housekeeper, her voice melting into the whines and swooshes of the mottled strangers. 'Your illness—' she continued, her voice pulsing in and out of audibility, before coming to rest, 'we care.'

Jolted forwards from the chair with a sudden breathless force, I gasped with the guttural wheeze of a boulder slamming into my chest. Aching and painfully winded, my vision swirled before settling on the dimly lit parlour door. It was later, and far colder. My feet were rigid and frozen inside my slippers. The time of day was unclear, but from the tightening of my joints, I had slept for some time. With no time to warm myself or settle my thoughts, Mrs Curry crept into view, her bell skirts moving like a heavy lampshade.

'Oh look, Miss Elsie has come to join us!' cheered Mrs Curry, walking into the room with a freshness that she wore like a stranger's coat; uncomfortable and ill-fitting.

Peering through the doorway was the gentle, bright smile of young Elsie. She moved with the gentle grace of a woman far beyond her thirteen childish years and sprang, barefooted, into the room. Pinned to Elsie's pinafore was a single brilliant violet, the likes of which I had never seen in Duncain before. Her head was topped with tight ringlets that were barely contained by a wealth of pins and clips that dotted her scalp like polished thorns. Her skin unsettled me. She looked like a doll. She was such a brilliant white that she surely couldn't have seen daylight in months, if not longer.

'Elsie!' I croaked, my tongue sandpaper dry. 'Oh, how you've grown —'

I pushed myself up from the chair with all the strength I could muster. I tried to smooth my movements, but my cracking joints put an end to any such illusion.

'How I have missed you! I wanted to see you, but — you were locked in your room, you see,' I said, suddenly nervous in

Elsie's unblinking silence. She seemed so very young, but stood with such strange authority.

She smiled back blankly, twisting at the delicate cutwork of her cuffs. I watched her pushing her little fingers between the embroidered petals, stretching them wider like buttonholes. The work on her blouse and apron was remarkable, with tiny white flowers stitched with thread so fine and close that it could have been done by mice. That was not the work of a Duncain seamstress.

'You haven't written to me in a while, Elsie —'

Silently, Elsie staggered my speech by suddenly smiling widely, as though offered some sweet treat. Her breath whistled between the gaps of her teeth that were lined up unevenly like pegs.

'Did you bring me presents?'

'Ah,' I sighed. 'Not this time, but — but I will get Algernon to send some treats as soon as he can.'

She smiled and pressed her hands together in a childish clap of encouragement. This was not the same Elsie who wrote letters of concern about Father. This was Elsie five years ago, a little child, not the young woman she was. I weakly responded to her glee with a nod in agreement. We faced one another in silence, my head too dizzy to speak openly. Elsie's smile faded with the creeping window's breeze and she shuffled backwards, navigating into the crook of Mrs Curry's arm.

'Go on, give your big sister a hug,' crooned Mrs Curry, the tone ill-fitting and cold in her mouth.

Elsie, unsure of herself, looked up to the old woman for permission. Visibly inflating with satisfaction, Mrs Curry gently pushed Elsie's shoulders, her eyes folding into an approximation of kindness. To me, her eyes looked like that of a fox: cold and focused, claws poised to enter the henhouse.

'It's fine, go on.'

Like a gundog with great purpose, Elsie quickly wrapped her arms around my waist. With a momentary squeeze, she powerfully gripped the outline of my hips but suddenly rushed back to the side of Mrs Curry as I felt the unexpected grind of her bones against mine.

'Hasn't Elsie grown into quite the beauty, Miss?'

Mrs Curry kept her eyes fixed on Elsie, twisting a stray blonde curl around her gnarled finger like a leash.

'Elsie's very accomplished, aren't you, dear? She reads, writes and sings so beautifully.'

Elsie jumped excitedly, slipping her curls back into place. 'Mrs Curry says she's going to get the pianoforte fixed for me!' she squeaked in a voice far younger than her years. Although she shouted towards me, it was clear that she was addressing another. It seemed that my presence was of no consequence to her. Without my visitation, she would be equally as thrilled to see a blackbird or particularly shiny pebble by the dock. However, I made a mental note to order a new parlour organ upon my return to London.

'I tell you what,' loudly whispered Mrs Curry, crouching to meet the child's eye. 'If you run down to the kitchen, a little birdie might have left some bread and honey on the table.'

Elsie grinned and skipped back through the door without a second glance behind her.

I raised my hand to wave her goodbye, but Elsie's interest was piqued elsewhere. Mrs Curry continued to watch her as she skipped a path into the kitchen, disappearing into the housekeeper's domain. Turning back to me, Mrs Curry was standing straighter somehow, as though the tangible unrest had nourished her.

'Beautiful girl, isn't she? She's really grown into her teeth.'

With a nod of acknowledgement to herself, Mrs Curry flung the sweeping brush beneath her arm, clenched the handle beneath her armpit and carried a small table out the door, leaving me alone once again.

After a short period of silence, in which I slowly readjusted myself to the strange environment in which I found myself, a series of scrapes and bangs emanated from beneath the floor. From distant rooms, Elsie and Mrs Curry audibly re-emerged with the combined subtlety of a pack of hunting dogs.

I expectantly waited for them to re-enter the parlour and readjusted my skirts against the chair in anticipation. Wishing I had a vessel with which to pose for tea (as the handle of my last cup lay cracked and mournful by its saucer), I fumbled with a dry slice and grubby cake fork as Elsie was escorted back to her room.

With tiny, quick squirrel steps, Elsie ran up the stairs, slowly followed by the rustling thud-thud of Mrs Curry's boots and the inescapable bang of the latch against Elsie's door. I remained sitting and resigned myself to the fact that Mother was not to pry herself from her grief-bed, nor was Elsie returning.

I took a turn about the room, marvelling at the accumulated dust and grime, of which there was a substantial layer. Most curiously, this grew within a room that was supposedly cleaned but ten minutes earlier.

The far window, although painted shut, was letting in a dreadful breeze. Strangely, all of the clocks were stopped at similar times, an act which appeared to be deliberately committed, with keys nearby to each face, and only one with a small piece of paper affixing the hands in their place. The skeleton clock was stuck at 3, with the hammer rusted firmly to the bell from the fast-acting damp. I stared and whistled through my teeth in brazen annoyance. The skeleton clock was Father's greatest pride and achievement, more so than any child or business venture. Now, it was a wreck. Vandalized in his absence. It had been a beautiful contraption, catching the sunlight with such high polish that a step too close to its pendulums burned your skin from its brightness. The brass fixings were changed; gritty, stained, and bubbled as though they had been dredged from the lake. There was clearly nothing for my entertainment or use downstairs, simply the opportunity to perpetually wait for an invasion of privacy or derisory comment. Not too dissimilar to London, it would seem.

Instead, I decided that unpacking and sprucing up my chambers would merit a wiser, safer and less confusing investment of my day. If I were to be imprisoned, the least I could do was wallow in a little comfort.

I would give Mother one night, then I would beat down the bedroom door myself.

Chapter 8

22nd October 1877

Dear Diary,

I have still received no word from Algernon. I expected the postal arrangements in Duncain to be poor, but expectantly waiting for a rap at the door each day is so very tiring.

Nonetheless, I still send him short notes, to let him know that my heart still lies over the sea.

Winter seemed closer this morning. The house was speaking louder than I ever remembered, with sharp whistles forcing themselves between the horrid little cracks in the window frames. It could have been the wail of a groundsman, were it not for the cold chill it rode upon. Mrs Curry is much like her old self, proving that Duncain truly is an unchanging place. No, I mustn't be too cruel; she keeps the pantry somewhat stocked and navigates the postal route within the village. Both are such demeaning tasks, so I must find thanks where I can.

My sleep has been poor. For all my efforts, I am never rested. I have been religious in my application of cold cream, I comfort myself at night, I strive to keep myself warm and safe with locked cases and a closed latch, but sleep never comes. My stomach and mind are weakened from it, and my eyes are starting to play tricks on me. I am aware of this, so they rarely catch me unaware, but they are unpleasant nonetheless. To lose control of one's self, and one's environment, however briefly, is torturous. My senses seem to betray me a little more frequently of late, but such a concern is something I will keenly keep to myself. I have heard of women taken away for less.

Last night, I looked into my dresser mirror to apply my cream, when I saw a little flicker beneath my eye. Truly, if I had been of simpler mind, I would have believed some enchanted beetle had burrowed its way inside my eye. I saw it pucker and roll across the white before disappearing behind my eyelid. I would have screamed if Algernon had been to hand, but my conscious self knew better. The mind can be a cruel place, and so affected by the simplest things.

Undoubtedly, there will have been some insect taking a trip across the mirror, an image which I conflated with my own. Algernon often speaks of matters of the mind and how mesmerists in Europe are making such wondrous developments with magnets and mind-play. I confess, it is not yet all to my understanding, but my keenness grows with each of his stories. Algernon spoke very highly of a travelling Scottish man he met in passing called Mr Home. The magazines he tossed onto the drawing-room chairs were filled with little else. Mr Home has such great spiritual control that the hands of the deceased can lift him into the air, as though in celebration. He is a most fascinating man, and I so wish Algernon had bought more of the papers, or that I had the forethought to pack some for my travels.

Home had caused quite the stir in society circles, but something seemed to have gone sour during a trip to Rome and Algernon refused to mention him for some time afterwards. However, he told me over breakfast several times that these skilled, spiritual men would revolutionise the world. He surrounded himself in strange books for a short period: small-run cloth-bound affairs with fine-lined diagrams that seemed rather more like schoolbooks than things of a spiritual matter. Their contents were too complicated for my comprehension, and would 'trouble' me should I try to absorb them, and as such I took Algernon's guidance on the matter. I so wish he'd trust me more. I may only be his wife, but I believe I have potential to understand so much more.

He tried to conceal it from me, and I'm still not entirely sure why, but Algernon had visited the most exciting trance medium, a few weeks ago. She was a few years younger than me, and prettier too, as he informed me afterwards. I pressed him for details as I wish he'd let me accompany him. I know it would not be improper for me to have done so. He had worn a suit I hadn't seen before. It was pleasant enough, but an unexpected sight. Afterwards, he said she had spoken of 'spiritual matters' but that he'd attended with two of his colleagues who had pressed her on the financial market. I confess, I have little interest in earthly stocks, but the spirits imparted some tips as far as my understanding went. I'd have loved to have seen the medium, an American girl, blonde and slight, apparently. I thought about her frequently afterwards: if she curled her hair like mine, if her accent was the soft and charming type, and if Algernon had begrudged our union as he watched her.

I have tried to speak with him on such matters, but his initial enthusiasm for discussion on spiritual concerns has left him of late. At any mention, he insists that 'sufficient discussion is not for women', or women such as myself at least. He says this knowing full well that most of the finest mediums in London are women, and reputable ones at that. Not last week had I been told of séances with one Mrs Guppy by way of Bloomsbury where spirits brought her the most beautiful and enormous piles of flowers, being great blooms that filled the room with the most spectacular scents. They fell from the air, from the hands of spirits, freshly cut as though they had manifested from some great heavenly flower market. Truly I am giddy at the thought, and a little green with envy at those who have been fortunate enough to sit with such mediums, should I be so truthful. I should like to see the flower woman upon my return to London. While I know little of the practice, I know her circles are exclusive, with printed invitations coveted by all. Yet I believe luck may be on my side, if Algernon's interest continues to flourish.

X

Chapter 9

A storm had been brewing all night, amplifying each creak to a groan and each gust to a screech that pierced the house like a needle through unwilling flesh. As I lay in bed, I couldn't help but think of Elsie. She was locked away in a darkness of her own, with only the company of dolls and solitude. At her age, I was sure that such raucous nights would bring images of devils or goblins to her mind. The scratches of stray branches would transform themselves into hellish claws that dragged across her window pane. Instead, she lay in her childhood bed, hidden in an adult body that was somehow not her own.

Shaking Elsie from my mind, I traced the gentle, shallow curves of my body. I felt no difference between my own skin and the thickly woven fabric that surrounded me. Thinking hard, I tightly closed my eyes and furrowed my brow until my breaths were deep and low, but still I couldn't rekindle the smell of Algernon, nor his touch. His soft and heavy hands, shaped by business, with ink tracing the creases of his knuckles; those I could conjure with fearsome accuracy. However, the heavy weight of his body beside mine and the reassuring warm crescent of his body had cooled across the miles.

My body had been a tiresome vessel. I preened, plucked and pinched my skin and singed tight curls into a head of hair that cruelly grew straight, despite the iron clamps of my curlers. I had spent a childhood praying to the same God that made beauteous women and gave Jacob an army of sons, but in exchange for my words, I was gifted small inconsequential breasts and hip bones that jutted a little too uncomfortably from beneath my nightdress. It was the body of a woman in technicalities, not in practice.

Extending my hand across the linen, I reached out as though Algernon were lying a little further away. The plaster of the wall met my fingertips with a cold, damp familiarity, crumbling into minuscule pieces and nestling beneath my nails like vagrants far from home. I pushed the grit from my nails and rested my hands above the tight triangle of my hips. I rested for a time and enjoyed the gentle waxing gradient of my stomach. I pushed my hands together, warm in the thought of how my belly would swell in the summer months, that a child of his would grow within me, nourished and safe. I would flutter about the Chelsea house, nesting and nurturing our baby. Ours. He would be born from love and raised in the brilliant light of the city. Together, Algernon and I would bring him the best that life could offer, reflecting on our own beautiful existence at the end of each day. The taste of his lips that hung so heavily on my tongue and skin as a strong exotic perfume had left without notice. The Duncain bed was too small for the two of us.

I had hoped for a honeymoon child, conceived on a holiday of love and lust beneath an unfamiliar skyline. The wedding exhausted Algernon and he slept for twelve hours, rising when his cravings disturbed his dribbling slumber. Whether his desire was for food, drink or a game, I could only truly remember the fleeting warmth of his breath against my neck before his own betraying body woke him.

The scratches at my window were simply the work of nature. The Duncain beyond my windows was a joyless and grey expanse; it was cold and impartial, a likeness that brought its own cruel sense of familiarity. The winds of Duncain rarely whispered, but shrieked and wailed and, between breaths, rocked me to sleep.

Chapter 10

I awoke to find the house fully sealed off. The windows and gates were crudely and roughly bolted. From the window, the enormous iron hinges at the end of the drive had been pulled closer together, leaving black ditches in their wake. The gates had been abandoned before their latches met, leaving the estate only marginally more uninviting than before.

The purpose of the house's sudden fortitude was a rite whose details were clearly only privy to my mother and Mrs Curry, who scuttled about the house with her black, over-darned stockings peeking from beneath her dress like an enormous rain beetle. The old housekeeper clattered throughout the lower rooms, roughly dusting surfaces and rearranging furniture with no discernible rhyme or reason for most of the early morning. After Mrs Curry's circuits achieved a discernible regularity within my mind, it was evident that there were indeed two sets of feet scurrying about the lower floor.

I hoped that by approaching Elsie downstairs while Mrs Curry was so preoccupied, I would at last have a little unregulated time with her, which would be pleasant in theory, not least to assuage my guilt due to the small matter of the lack of presents. Rather more cruelly, I knew that Elsie also had the potential of offering a little more insight into the matter of my father's estate and, indeed, his elusive body. I rose and dressed, hooking myself into a lilac day dress with an enormous lace collar, affixed at the neck with a brilliant gold and amethyst bar brooch that gleamed a brilliant purple, despite the gloom's dulling efforts. Reaching the crossroads of the parlour rooms, I waited expectantly, anticipating finding Elsie in a childish and excitable solitary state, whereby Mrs Curry would lack the time or inclination to choreograph our every interaction.

The pat-pat of fast-moving slippers rumbled towards me and I practised my most genuine smile in anticipation of a meeting. Instead of facing Elsie, suddenly casting a flat, wide shadow in the doorway was the startled figure of my mother. She was trussed into a black taffeta bodice, several sizes too small for her figure, her corset audibly straining against her form.

I was expecting resistance against my imminent inheritance, but Father's will was watertight, tied up in clauses and signatures that a dumpy widow from Duncain could never untangle. There were no poison letters on my Chelsea doormat, and no talk of the chain at all in the household. The estate, main house and all its tattered contents would revert to the possession of the firstborn child upon his death; it was indelibly printed. My mother and I would sign the agreement that 'Lady Crofton' could live there until her own demise; then the natural order of things could resume. It was a great, if slightly cold, comfort that Mother was powerless in the face of legal inevitabilities.

I had never especially relished moments of power or superiority, although a lifetime of Mother's behaviour would have justified such a trait. Duncain House, however, was a millstone around my neck. It was one last, lingering link to confinement, a childhood spent skipping across broken glass, and a county of tenants whose hatred spread across the fields like fog. There was so little to be gained here, and in truth, I resented Algernon's insistence on my travel. He knew my fears of returning, and how uncomfortable the thought of revisiting the family pile made me. But I was to be a good wife. I travelled upon Algernon's insistence, on love, on a childish desire to make him proud, but I had still not decided for what.

Too exhausted to pursue my mother, I resigned myself to another period of quiet contemplation and correspondence in my own chambers. With quicker — and keener — steps than those of my descent, I returned to my room, removed my shoes at the door with the begrudging help of a miniature button hook and replaced them with further sets of stockings. It may have been a jumble of threads and embroidery, but what the world could not see would at least bring a little more warmth to my toes. Undeniably frustrated and wary of an oncoming migraine, I circled my bedroom and forced a letter opener into the painted ridge of the window pane. Chipping away at the thick trough of paint, the window cracked open slightly, allowing a little air to snake into the room. For all of my hunting, there was no key to be found in my room, with Mrs Curry invariably being the lone guardian. For what often had felt like a prison, the sudden removal of forced solitude did little to remove the ingrained sense of punishment. As the sun dully curved across the sky, Mrs Curry periodically delivered thick bowls of stew to my bedroom, leaving them with a two-fingered clatter at the door like sustenance to a loathed invalid.

I placed the bowls, still half-full despite my hunger, outside the door. I found a strange enjoyment in sitting and listening for the housekeeper's breathless rustling and pained exhalations as she bent to collect the remnants. Growing up, I had often believed that Mrs Curry would be well suited to the acting profession, were she not sculpted so crudely. When she sat, the old woman looked like an abandoned project on a potter's wheel; heavy and slick with all the overhanging elegance of hardening clay. I shouldn't be so cruel. But for such flavourless stew, it seemed excusable.

As the weather swirled outside my windows, threatening to develop into a storm front, I rummaged through my drawers for old abandoned pastimes to busy my hands. A sewing basket harboured a tangle of threads and needles that seemed as though a nest of mice had knotted their tails into one amorphous mass.

As the storm grew and passed over Duncain, each thunder crack jolted my arms with unwelcome twitches that tightened the tension on my needlepoint. I had never found much enjoyment in embroidery and sewing. I always thought them to be relatively dull pursuits and poor representations of true femininity. Although, like many more, this would be an opinion to wisely keep to myself in polite society. An old matron might well create a finely decorated tea tray, but I quickly learned that such minor achievements never did open the doors to marriage. My handiwork had suffered considerably since my youth, but I had never really been considered to be particularly domestically accomplished. Yet, as all women must, I was taught to thread and darn as though my future would be bleak enough to rely upon it. For all of my new appreciation of the arts, I was relieved to leave such rudimentary tasks to lacemakers and women with too many children.

I spent a short time berating myself for not further considering my choice of solitary entertainment when preparing my luggage for such a journey. It was entirely due to my extreme confinement that I reduced myself to such pursuits; my room was cruelly furnished with little else by way of entertainment. Forgetting the sparsity of Duncain was entirely my own fault. I should have packed some cards or books. Or more realistically, some magazines. Above the dresser was a series of old volumes of parables and inscribed books from long-passed 'Sunday School' attendance achievements, the bookplates inscribed with Mrs Curry's tell-tale scrawl. They would remain as they were. Blissfully abandoned.

Reticence notwithstanding, with Duncain's loose boards and fractured panels, I would soon find myself in need of darning skill, lest I become acclimatised to the sensation of old varnish against my toes.

Chapter 11

25th October 1877

Dear Diary,

I have yet to receive word from Algernon. Despite my best efforts, my mother continues to display some tiresome stubbornness in terms of completing legalities. Granted, I have been feeling particularly tired today, so I did not pursue her with the necessary intent to find, not least sign the paperwork. Nonetheless, funeral or not, I cannot imagine that I will be staying much longer. The signatures should take little time at all. I am so tired, too tired to last a day. I nap a lot, but never feel rested. Time slips through my fingers and I can't ever be sure if it's breakfast, noon or night. It's a strange feeling; not entirely unpleasant, but unsettling.

I don't mean to languish in my strange waking state, but have grown some vague sense of determination during my time here. I have a rising urge to produce some physical proof of my time here. I wasted many hours separating a skein of faded violet, twisting small French knots around a border of peach flowers. My efforts are not to be displayed, but may, at the very least, retain some dexterity in my fingers, despite the efforts of the biting cold. With each line of stitched petals, the blasted wind seemed to grow in intensity. I feel that should I stay too long, I will be driven mad by the foliage alone. The estate causes my mind to wander without me. Every creak sounds like a last breath, or the final, ominous rumble before a demolition.

Elsie would have provided some minor distraction had she not spent all of the day in her bedroom. I cannot recall any child being so willing to end a day before it has begun, yet it would seem that my sister shares the same willingness to speed through her days in this Duncain. Should I be so inclined, I might have woken her — suggesting a frivolous game of cat and mouse, judging by her recent regression — but the house's doors were thick with brass bolts as thick as fingers.

When word comes from Algernon, which it shall, at last I will have some reassurance that Duncain will not hold me in perpetuity. I left another letter with Mrs Curry this morning under the reassurance that the Duncain postal service was the finest in the north. However, such claims did come from a woman who believes tripe to have medicinal qualities.

X

Chapter 12

I began to explore the house and reacquaint myself with the rooms that I had once roamed with such familiar ambivalence as a child. Unsurprisingly, little had changed. Duncain existed in a lonely space without time, as though some gorgon's curse had petrified each threadbare rug in place, for no reason other than to create cruel mischief.

With each step into the upper rooms, floorboards creaked and cracked with every footstep. Wooden panels sat uncomfortably beside one another, narrowing the walls, swollen and fractured through damp. As the innards of the house swelled with each storm, its fittings grated like old hips; bone grinding against bone. Each crack in the plaster, each loose thread, jutted uncomfortably away from its root. Even the house itself seemed tired of its foundations, with each room seeming emptier than the last.

The acrid stench of Father's tobacco pipe was noticeably absent. I had tried so hard not to be too taken with sentimentality, as it frustrated Algernon to rages, yet I couldn't shake the feeling of loss. Memories of Father's mouth, filled with tobacco and snuff, were inescapable. The old man's teeth had been as bright as buttercups, pushing up through slick black gums, piled high with thick tar residue. Death is indeed a disruptor of one's routine, and I desperately wished I could be as cold as Father, seeing bereavement as an irritant in one's diary. Yet the pain in my throat kept me suspended in this state of strange, weightless grief. Foolish emotions aside, the exhaustion Duncain brought me was proving as tiresome to my constitution as Mother's perpetually poor health.

As I made a return to my bedroom, I found the door to be wedged shut. The latch had invariably been aggravated by the wind and the sneck was stuck fast.

I glanced across the banister to the lower floors, but certainly would not call to Mrs Curry for assistance. Owing to the bowl and spoon that remained in their place outside my door, the old woman appeared to be in no great haste to fulfil her post as housekeeper. I found myself thinking of how Mrs Curry certainly 'keeps' Duncain House, yet it was never specified in what condition. While I had arrived with the anticipation of a few choice words from my mother, I had not planned for the house to voice its displeasure too. I kicked the door with my toe and winced from the pain, jumping up and down in muffled rage. I emptied my lungs and addressed the door under my breath.

'Please. Enough,' I hissed.

I punctuated my rage with another kick, this one hard enough to shake the latch and open the door, albeit at the cost of a portion of toenail. Hobbling into the bedroom with a slowly bleeding toe, I removed all hopes of probate, productivity, and a beneficial evening, vowing to do little but ease the throb of my foot and find a little kindness in magazines, for such a thing was a growing rarity. The Lady's Magazine would tell me that the best colours for my skin tone were green and yellow, that my laugh was charming, that romance grew in winter, and friends would come to me in time. Father was dead, Mother wouldn't so much as speak to me, and Elsie was locked away. I'd rather take talk of fashion and dances over the silence of Duncain.

The lower floors of the house were always too cold and verged on uninhabitable on nights when storms spread themselves across the county. Regardless of the freezing temperatures, my mother once more scuttled back and forth between the rooms, repeatedly crossing paths with Mrs Curry, circling the rooms in a merry dance. I spent another day in malign solitude, ignoring my needlework partially for fear of growing calluses on my fingertips. Instead, positioned by my bedroom window, I watched and waited. While my body rested, my eyes searched for tree branches and felled trunks, frightened wildlife, or the dappled pattern of moonlight through dead leaves. Something tangible and real. I hated the house in poor weather. The creaks of old hinges pushed all rational thought from my mind and left my thoughts wandering towards darker climes.

Branches scraped the self-same lines across the glass as they had done for decades, gradually rubbing narrow divots across the window panes. In the moonlight, they glinted like veins, and on stormy nights, I swear they pulsated. Duncain grew stronger in storms. It seemed to thrive on gusts, fallen trees and the misfortune of lost travellers. I daren't ever leave the house in a storm, let alone as a married woman. It may seem foolish, but I often thought Duncain to be malicious, and in returning without my Crofton name, the house would see me as a traitor, stop protecting me, and punish my betrayal. Fantastical, I know, but Duncain was a strange county, full of strange tales and stranger people, and it served to keep your wits about you. I had escaped and would leave again. The storm was just a storm.

As the storm raged on through the dimmed light of the oil lamp, I held an unsettling vigil of my own, watching the road but anxious to view the destruction such evenings brought. It was unlikely I'd help anyone in danger, for what use could I be? But leaving the roads unmonitored seemed to pose a greater risk than retiring to my bed. If any farmers ventured out to tend to their flocks and were dealt a swift blow by some swirling debris, at least I would be the first to see it. Maybe a little excitement would revitalize the house, give Mother purpose and reason to rise. Her misery was an anchor that dragged us all down with her, and although she had always thrived in misfortune, I worried how much longer this bout would last. I worried this grief would fit her too comfortably, and she'd finally melt into her final state of never-waking depression. She was an old, selfish fool. But she remained my mother. It was at times when she was at her most delicate that I found myself terrified as to what would rouse her from such a state. Something always would — some new obsession or interest that filled her mind for a season, before the next grievance took her away once more.

I dreaded to think what the next fixation would be.

The screaming wind worsened within the house, whistling beneath the doors like vagrants on street corners. It seemed purposeful, somehow human. For all my efforts of strength, I couldn't look. It was just wind. I didn't have to look to confirm it. I could hear the lock if it opened, and that had to be enough. Please God, let it just be wind.

The gatepost lamps blazed in defiance against the wind. They had lasted years despite the hurling of stones by misspent youth. They were arguably the only bastion on the entire estate. Looking back on childhood, it seemed little wonder that they unsettled me. The twisted lamps were unattractive things, daubed with roughly-layered black paint and blazing, tall flames like monsters' eyes. On more pleasant days, they might have been fairies guarding their keep, but such days were few and far between. But the lamps were just lamps. Twisted metal and glass, bolted through stone older than the country in which they sat. I rested for a time, trying to imagine a childhood spent exploring the lawns in summer warmth, but thoughts of grass-streaked dresses were too far-fetched to a woman whose body was shaking once more from unwelcome cold. As my feet warmed through layers of stockings and my bloodied toe adhered to the fibres, I watched the lamplight flicker and slowly fell asleep.

Chapter 13

The rain continued throughout the night. I spent the morning filling many unsatisfactory hours with equally underwhelming needlepoint. The threads, once vibrant and pliable, had become damp and browning in my absence, falling heavy and limp through the needle and producing the faintest of musty smells with each stitch. For every few inches of work, a knot too tight and slippery to be untangled with ease would rear its head. I would sit, waiting for the thread to rectify its misdeeds, until I invariably nodded off to sleep, needle still clasped tightly between my fingers.

It may have still been raining when I awoke; it was always hard to tell. Duncain was cruel, grey and damp, even on its hottest days. Little would ever change, and little had, save for the lawns, which had grown untamed in recent years. Duncain House seemed reticent to remain watertight. Despite there being neither a servant's door nor a window ajar, water snaked its way inside. I had always supposed it to be my mother's doing in some way, that her grief and misery pierced the brickwork, springing leaks in the house. Every day she was in bed was another day closer to something far worse. In grief, as in life, Mother delighted in allowing things to fester. She would find something to get up for eventually. But every day she locked herself away was another day with the house under Mrs Curry's control. I always thought myself to be a modern and kindly woman, but I could never shake the concern about staff such as Mrs Curry rising above their station. She already sustained us all, with neither myself nor Mother having any competence in a domestic kitchen. I thought this gave her an unpleasant power, especially considering our reliance on her trips into town, and the isolation of the house. Mrs Curry's status never seemed to be of any concern to my mother, but had begun to trouble Father before I left. I thought him a little too cruel and reactive at the time, but with each reverberating thud of Mrs Curry's movements about the house, I wished he were still alive. Her footsteps sounded more like his every day. Too heavy, too authoritative. If Mother could not address the issue of the housekeeper, I would have to discard my peaceful intentions and do so myself. Father's words were fresh in my mind. His last grumbles before thinning over-familiar staff one year: weeds had to be removed before they sprung roots.

After I had resigned myself to daytime napping like some tragic old maid, I awoke to the sound of crunching gravel beneath my window. The rainfall had eased and the wind with it. As such, the grounds were opened to the hastening sounds of footfall; an unfamiliar and unappreciated change. Night had fallen, and the birds, whose caws would ordinarily cut the air, sheltered in their nests, too fearful to leave before daylight.

Perpetual tiredness stalked me, and I found myself only half-awake when the sounds of the world outside woke me. The flame beside me had flickered low and dull in its glass cradle, leaving dusty black clouds against the glass. It now matched that of the filthy windowpanes before it. The dirt of Duncain was unlike anything of God's creation. It grew and bred within itself, gathering and waiting to spill out like a spider's nest. The charred smut of the chamberstick was too black and grew too fast for it to be ignored. Each fleck that clung to the surface was a grain of dirt and blackness creeping closer to my skin, ready to take root. In my daze, I swore I could see it creep closer, these black, dusty clouds, rolling under my skirts, across my chest and circling my throat before coating my gums and nose in its rot. I could taste it, and chew it like Father's tobacco. Each of my breaths felt shallower than the last, filled with a damp soot that spread decay like cancer. My eyes were painfully sore and

I barely dared blink as I grabbed at the chamberstick, offering up my hands in some last stage of defence at this waking trance. The taste of tobacco faded, but my eyes still burned from soot. I was half asleep and it wasn't real. I would clean the glass and things would be fine. The house was safe, the house was ours, I was still a Crofton. No, a Marriott. I was a Marriott. Alice Marriott.

My scattered thoughts did little for my racing pulse. I slowly lifted the glass sconce above the shrinking candle, my palms sparking with pain at its heat. I kept my fingers tight to the glass and, with a clammy finger, wiped the black dust from its surface. My fingertips burned hot and sharp, leaving their own fine layer in patches across the glass. It was sore, but no great loss. This was why gloves were the finest accessory, after all. My fingers were far from the graceful digits of the ladies at Chelsea, their hands skimming across piano keys with practised ease. Through years of scrubbing and childish twitches of picking at any skin I had thought to be unclean, my hands had grown tough. The coarseness of my skin followed me to London, where gloves did little to conceal the roughness and misjudged strength of my numbed fingers, but I enjoyed the patterns and lush fabrics nonetheless. Replacing the sconce and discarding the thread into a shadowed corner of the sill, my fingers began to gently throb. Inspecting them in the half-light, the pink, puckered raw blooms glinted back at me like babies' lips.

As I slept, the needlework had fallen onto the floor, the webbing resting flat against the boards. There it would stay. The light of the room was so weak that I could not be certain of what had changed beneath my feet, but the fading visions of snaking black clouds could not be shaken. The whole tattered affair would have to wait until sunrise. It felt tarnished now, too close to the house. To Mrs Curry. Kicking the frame to the edge of the room, I moved to stand.

I hadn't intended to sleep, especially not in my day clothes, and felt the physical repercussions immediately. There was some small mercy in my enforced solitude, in that it ensured there were no visitors at close quarters to see my dishevelled state. My lips tasted tart and held themselves together with the viscous saliva of inelegant, primal, deep sleep. My tongue stuck to the roof of my mouth, my body creating its own foul fly paper. Well, haven't you come far, Alice? And you dare to worry about the improper behaviours of servants.

The clattering of the heavy latch of the entrance doors tore me from my crude preoccupations. There were visitors. Judging by the crunches, which seemed some distance away, they were expected. While it was enormously unlikely to be a visit from Algernon, I jumped at the thought that it might be the solicitors at last. I frantically ran about the darkened room, re-pinning clothes and scrambling for a compact of rouge in a stack of identical dark-brown bags.

I searched for a collar brooch to better suit my outfit, but panicked, forgetting how the tone of my dress would appear in full light. I had to look serious, of my station. I had to look as though I understood legal matters. Nothing too frivolous. What did lawyers' wives wear? Stamped silver, amber and a ringed agate all scratched their prongs against my hand until frustration brought me to a coral and shell cameo. The crisp white inlay of Nyx and her babies was pretty enough, but the clasp was misaligned. It was a problem I had long attributed to the malice of the shopkeeper, who cruelly begrudged my two-hour browsing period in Hatton Garden. Quickly, Alice. Choose quickly. You could be home tomorrow! With Chelsea at the fore of my mind, to imagine a caller entering the house while I wrestled with my jewellery didn't bear thinking about. To have the looming prospect of Mrs Curry's judgemental gaze upon me was a great enough threat.

The crunches beneath the window became louder as I fussed. I pressed my face as near to the window as I dared, careful to keep an inch between the wet glass and my fast-flushed cheeks. Two figures moved towards the house. One was tall and slim, the other short and dumpy; together they edged ever closer in small, dragging steps. The taller of the two, wearing a top hat and carrying a case, was shortening his steps so as not to outrun the figure beside. As they walked, he leaned into the shorter, sharing a quiet conversation. Curious, how they spoke so silently, when there was no one for miles to overhear them. I presumed the fat figure to be hard of hearing and turned my interest to the man beside them. Tall, slim and well-dressed in the lamplight, for a flickering moment I foolishly believed Algernon to have come good on his promises of visitation. Yet, as they crept closer to the lights of the entrance way, it was clear that neither of the figures was my husband.

The shorter of the two was indistinguishable in gender; they were round and squat with short legs that gave them the appearance of a scurrying woodlouse. The taller was clearly a man. Curiously familiar too. The brim of his hat hid his eyes, but his chin and curled sideburns were visible. Even if his eyes had been the tiniest of pinpricks, he would still be one of the most handsome men I had set my eyes on, if I dare think so childishly. His jawline was strong and chiselled, his cheekbones glinting high in the darkness. He wore a great wool overcoat that billowed behind him. It was a little too large for his frame, as though he expected to grow into it like a child receiving hand-me-downs. As I watched, it was clear to have been a poor choice for the weather; his tails and thighs would be sodden. Such a messy appearance seemed hardly appropriate when calling on a family as established as the Croftons, but I mustered no anger, nor frustration. Curiosity brought me closer to the window glass, the cool, wet surface doing little to quell the warmth that had risen within me. The man seemed unperturbed by his ill-fitting attire and walked in longer, wider strides that caused the other to scramble for footing. The toes of his oxfords shone like polished jet beneath his coat.

Algernon had worn similar shoes at our wedding. His best 'work' shoes, the soles had been scuffed and tatty, but the leather was polished so brightly that they shone like mirrors. I remembered little of the day, save for a few details that I supposed women's minds were predisposed to retain: shoes, sunlight, the edge of a dress. There had been few guests.

As the stranger's strides slowed, his trousers blew tight against his legs in the growing wind. Watching from above, it shames me to say that my heart fluttered slightly, betraying my tailored sensibilities with a reddening of my cheeks. With Algernon conducting his business far away so frequently, my heart ran loose about my chest, beating with an embarrassing, girlish excitement. Angered with myself, I drew myself back with a hard, forced cough.

'Silly girl,' I hissed.

My heart was as true and straight as an arrow in Chelsea. I sang Algernon's praises with all the satisfaction of a boastful mother, in the right company. To glance at another man, considering all that I owed Algernon, felt undoubtedly cruel and deceitful. A few days spent from Chelsea and my eyes looked to the beauty of strangers and developed a lust for things I could never have. I shuddered against myself, as though my thoughts had become a second skin, visible to all. I chastised myself again, pressing my thumb into the sharp end of my brooch.

'Stop this, stop this,' I chanted.

A voice ran astray in my head, joined by sensations free from Duncain's walls. My skin prickled with the dull coldness of Algernon's empty bed and the warm shivers that snaked up my thighs at my morning departure from the Jubilee Coaching

Inn not a few days prior. I clenched my eyes, chanting again, my voice lower and crueller.

'Stop it, stop it, stop it,' it rolled.

I chanted to myself a thousand silent chastisements. Sinning in the mind was as bad as in the flesh, Father said. I was lucky to have received a proposal at all and owed Algernon my life; he knew this as well as I did. My new life — the one I had ached for, throughout Duncain's endless winters. But the ache I felt for a life outside of Duncain had never permeated through to marriage. Algernon had been an arrangement that bore love. His proposal, although unusual — at least compared to those in my books — had offered a blissful release so great that I would have run to Chelsea to meet him. I loved him for what he provided, and he provided well, but I failed him as a piece of ornamentation. Some inconvenient clock, inherited from a distant aunt that he had to tolerate for face's sake.

'Stop it, stop it, stop it,' I continued, rhythmically.

He was agreeable enough. His face fine, his body, although rarely shared, was masculine enough. I knew the ways of a wife and had shared a bed when he suited, but such interactions had been business-like and little more. There had never been an ache, a shiver for him. There was no fawning, nor any deeper yearning between us. I tried to form bonds between us, in conversation, or through the touch of a hand after dinner. Yet he looked at me with puzzlement, and the shame of his reaction was enough to make me withdraw. My body never ached for Algernon and my heart followed suit.

I grasped my hands into ever tighter balls. 'It's not true. Liar, liar, liar.'

These were not my thoughts. They were poisoned, corrupted. As I grasped at my collar, I felt the thin gold tip of the pin slip a little too deeply into my thumb. The sudden searing pain caused my breath to fall from my chest like apples from a barrel.

I had been foolish and childish and, above all else, ungrateful. Removing my thumb from the pin, I watched my skin stretch and release against the gold, before a little blood bubbled from the tip.

The rise and fall of the latch emanated up through the floorboards, followed by an excitable shriek. Mother was free from her sickbed.

Grabbing a beaded belt, I fumbled with the hooks behind my back, the velvet pile helping to absorb a little of the blood that threatened to stain my dress. As one of my few black items, I had packed it as a grumbling gesture of oncoming mourning; a painfully dull state I had dreaded with every year of my parents' ageing. The flash of black would, most importantly, offer a little sign to the visitors that I was not so cruel as to eschew moral conventions.

I smoothed the belt around my waist. It wasn't the finest match, but since returning to Duncain, I had familiarized myself with the sacrifices of rural womanhood. First came knitted underclothes, then came mismatched accessorizing. I moved to the wall mirror, sighed, and puffed up my hair from its dropped curls.

'It's a slippery slope, Crofton. Don't let them take you back.' I paused, my mind a little fuzzy. 'Marriott. Marriott.'

I stopped and hissed my surname into the bedroom: 'Marriott. Marriott. Wake up, you fool.'

I pinched my cheeks, jiggled my shoulders, and tried to readjust my breathing.

I was not long a bride before death dragged me back to the pile of the Croftons. Crofton had always been such a vile surname. I had always thought it to sound like a thatcher's name; the name of toothless men on rooftops in tatty shirts and flat caps; the men who would pass the estate with ale-soaked laughter, shouting cruel rhymes over the gates.

I discarded the name on my first steamer crossing, never thinking it would wash up again and lure me back. The name would have been an embarrassment in Chelsea, I was sure of it.

I wrung my hands, grown warm and tacky from fretting. The sensation was uncomfortable. My palms were too warm, and gritty against my nails. It was an assault. My skin was absorbing flecks of brickwork, rotten paint and plaster, and the decaying flakes of moths' wings, trapped inside and left to the whims of the house. The house continued in its attempts to claim me, to quietly hound me and return me to its filth. I was sure of it. Bile rose in my throat as my hands itched with the imagined legs of a thousand spiders. Running to the washstand, I thrust my arms directly into the jug. Immersed to the elbows, my breaths low and heavy, the cold snap of the stagnant water brought life back into order. Stay alert, Alice, you have visitors.

Chapter 14

Standing at the top of the stairs, I enjoyed the gentle, deep breaths that cleanliness brought. My hands were cool and clean, my neck still a little damp from my washcloth. I was still a woman of Chelsea, and of London. Duncain was temporary.

I readjusted my belt, checking the hooks twice over, and running my fingers across the velvet, hunting for the sensation of dried blood. I would greet the visitors, being sure not to descend the stairs like some childish debutante, and I would present myself appropriately. Like the cultured and mannered woman I was. I stood waiting a little longer as the visitors dallied in the driveway. I had to reconsider their appearance; if they were not solicitors, then who? There were no groups or clubs in the village for Mother to immerse herself in, not that such an invitation would ever be extended to the estate. Mother had no friends, nor family, not in Duncain or elsewhere. I often thought that Mother had simply sprung up one day in the estate's flowerbeds when Father was too disinterested or busy to force her to leave.

Nonetheless, Mother was loath to entertain company at the best of times, and even travellers had long given up frequenting the village with their bags of pegs and talk of charms. She would insist on the gardener setting the old dogs loose at children that dawdled a little too long by the gates, so word soon returned to the village, and our estate quickly returned to its unbroken silence. Save for a few incidents of nocturnal curses and masonry thrown through the windows on long autumn evenings.

The clock hands struck 9 p.m., the chimes rattling from all areas of the house, unpleasantly off-key and unsteady. The silence that followed was as heavy as the oak doors that remained open, the visitors nowhere to be seen. I stared at the empty void of the entrance way, Mrs Curry propping open the doors with all the brazen confidence of a homeowner. Her boldness, while disgruntling, appeared curious from above. Mrs Curry would have no friends outside of the house. She lived and worked within the same few walls and had no family of which to speak — not that I had ever asked. She seemed like a widow who had achieved her solemn position without the inconvenience of marriage. She was one of the many unspoken curiosities of the estate's workings. Much like Mother and the hideous rot of the alcoves, Mrs Curry was a fixture, installed long before my arrival.

Mrs Curry was gesturing through the doorway — twitches of her hands and low whispers, too quiet to be heard from the landing. I considered my options, keeping my eyes fixed on Curry's bizarre movements. They might be extortionists or salesmen, hoping to snare a share of inherited fortune, courtesy of the newly bereaved. If that were the case, they would surely be visitors from outside of County Duncain. Those more local would know the Croftons were land rich, but cash poor. The crofts were not as lucrative as they once were, and the few remaining local workers made a frequent, if inebriated, show of their enjoyment at the estate's ever-growing disrepair.

On the pathway, the interlopers certainly didn't move with the authority of solicitors, not that such professionals were making house calls at such an hour. Of my quickly-cycled options, the latter was a familiar, if tiresome likelihood. The visitors would be travelling 'doctors', hoping to palm their latest restorative snake oil to the grieving widow who never knew a day of good health in her life. Nonetheless, news of Father's death would have travelled fast, not least because of the societal status of 'Old Sir Kenneth', but also owing to the enormous poster-sized death notice, lashed to the gateposts.

Relaxing into my perch, I considered that news might have indeed travelled wide of my return. It was not too bold a thought, considering my status as a successful London lady and future guardian of Duncain. Although the county was not the grandest in the country, and did not have the pretty shops or industry of Antrim or Down, it had its own successes, not least the burgeoning bog oak trade. Such fertile business opportunities were rare treats in Duncain, and my name would have understandably arisen as the owner of such valuable soil. Indeed, I thought, straightening my posture with pride, I had become quite a celebrity in the district. I had always imagined that such interest in me would arise at some stage, but at least with a little warning and certainly not so late in the day. A daytime caller would have been preferable, but Duncain was a thoughtless county and such formalities so frequently passed its people by. As Mrs Curry nodded to the closing shadows, I made sure to pinch each cheek, proud of my new and respected status. To see such a fashionable and worldly woman would be quite the exciting experience for one in Duncain, and I would never be one to disappoint.

A lady landowner too! I thought, allowing myself to enjoy my first smile in days. If the house was razed to the ground and all the land sold, I would still have the title. And, with Algernon close by, a considerable corner of Chelsea. At last, that would be something to please him. To be truly free from Duncain; free from its walls and its blasted name. Then I would smile the widest of all. I would play my part and graciously accept the niceties of the visitors, whatever gifts they might wish to bring. After all, it was only proper.

I slowly descended the stairs, reducing my steps to a shuffle as the visitors painfully prolonged their entrance. It was always a preference of mine to meet guests while moving, allowing them to admire their host, but not presume that I had been anticipating their arrival. Reaching the foot of the stairs, with not so much as a turned head of recognition from Mrs Curry, the door was still wide open. The hallway was so cold that the transition between the floors took my breath away. The wind was growing within the courtyard, sending dried leaves clattering across the tiles. Mrs Curry's housekeeping skills really were something special.

My mother, who had been expertly camouflaged until that moment, suddenly ran towards the door, stopping beside the open latch, inadvertently slamming her shoulder into the wall, coming to rest like a skimmed stone.

Mother had the same round face and watery eyes, her eyebrows as light as baby's hair, leaving her expressions as little more than an enigmatic possibility of mood.

Nevertheless, I was shocked to see her, and to see her move so keenly.

For a fleeting moment, I thought that I should jump on my mother, thrust out my arm like a rapier and demand a conversation, a discussion of our duties, or an acknowledgement of her dismissive behaviour. Instead, I stood in her own disappointment, slack-jawed, as I watched my mother strike out in excitement. Embarrassingly, Mother stood quivering, blinkered to all around her, sturdy and focused like a workhorse.

As in life, in grief Mother had little by way of self-control. I was sure that we could be separated for decades and my mother would continue to favour the movements of a passing moth more than the achievements or welfare of her children. And yet, some small part of me was hurt.

I couldn't help but nurture a childish warmth for her, lost in the hope of what she could have been as a mother. This was invariably made worse through my enjoyment of ladies' magazines. With their tales of beautiful summer nurseries and curly-haired infants, they nourished an unwelcome optimism inside my chest.

A thought lingered that Mother would soon relent in kindness, embracing her daughters with the same excitement she showed to others, confirming that I had passed the last of her great moral tests. I imagined the two of us taking tea together, parting tiny scones, and talking of dresses and future children who would cheer and play in sweet sing-song voices. I wished far stronger that such hopes would extinguish themselves, particularly as I watched my mother shake with excitement by the doorway. I had never seen her show so much as a genuine smile for any return I had made to the house. Yet I supposed such foolish jealousy would fade with time. When I became a mother myself, I would right my own parent's wrongs, but the thought still lingered, hooked through a part of my brain I could not yet put in order.

Until her keen unveiling, Mother had stood stock still, a few feet from the door like some unremarkable statue, waiting. I suddenly felt somewhat deflated, foolish, and a little more alone. Of course the strange callers would be for Mother.

Mother hunched closer to the doorframe, peering shrewishly around the latch. She turned excitably to Mrs Curry, whispering in an excited tone, so bizarrely nuanced that in my brief attempts at listening from a few feet away, I couldn't make out a word. I was soon resigning myself to the visitors simply pitching a tent on the front lawns, with Mrs Curry looking on for encouragement. Yet suddenly, after an age of waiting, the two figures crossed the threshold and moved into the light.

Mrs Curry had opened the door to its fullest extent, the howling wind amplified to uncomfortable levels. The two figures stepped through, the taller man pausing to wipe his feet roughly across the doormat. The squat figure stepped over it, more concerned with observing the contents of the hall than preserving its cleanliness.

The short visitor seemed different in the lamplight. They existed somewhere between feline and almost-feminine, but too thickset to comfortably exist as either. Two old eyes jumped and glinted like opals from within layers of indistinguishable clothing. Their face was partially shielded by a cap, tied tightly under the chin like a tourniquet. While they were silent, their mouth sat twisted in a permanent snarl. A divot in the upper lip extended to their nose, the space between exposing a singular brown tooth. The gap was repeatedly swiped with a fat, globulous tongue, leaving the fleshy gap thick with stringy saliva. These people were in my house. It wasn't right. The seal was broken and rot had been invited in. As I stood at the foot of the stairs, I observed the silent interactions between the visitors and Mrs Curry and believed that, at that very point, it was clear that my mother had truly lost her mind.

Mrs Curry nodded at the two of them: 'Helena. Solomon.'

They both nodded in return, the man smiling warmly and tipping his hat with a small bow.

'Lovely to see you, as always, Agnes,' he said with a gentle lowland croon.

Mrs Curry didn't break a smile, but closed the door behind them. Walking in front of my mother to do so, Mother remained where she stood, wordlessly smiling at the visitors.

I stood unmoving, observing the strange quartet with wide-eyed curiosity. The short, squat figure was still indistinguishable in species, let alone gender, in the lamplight. As the strange visitor stood by the doorway, they remained looking solely at Mrs Curry, as though she were the mistress of the house. I looked on from my perch with growing anger. My mother, however, still bore the excitable expression of a child in summertime.

'I'm sorry about all that, Agnes,' rasped the figure with an old, vaguely female, voice. 'When my feet play up, I can barely move. This weather don't help either. Not that I'm complaining — I know how important this is to you —'

The man that stood beside her suddenly coughed.

'Well —' continued Helena, turning to look at the widow beside the door, still fixed with a rictus grin. 'Young Solomon looks after me well, don't you, dear?'

The man chuckled. 'Well, Helena, you're more precious than gold, aren't you?'

Mrs Curry pursed her lips, clearly perturbed by the lateness of the guests. 'Quite.'

She lowered her voice, leaning a little closer to the man. 'Put a stop to the charmer act,' she hissed. 'This has to be efficient. We don't have time —'

'He's too kind, y'know,' interrupted Helena, addressing Mother with a wet smile.

Mrs Curry said nothing, but wrinkled her nose, checking the time on her chatelaine watch with a deliberate jangle of the chains.

'I'm so sorry to hear about Sir Kenneth, Margaret,' she began. 'My heart goes out to you and wee Elsie. Have you thought of employing any keeners yet? Its only that —'

The young man forced a second cough. Helena fell silent, but smiled at my mother, stroking her widow's hands and receiving strange star-struck smiles in return. The large visitor once again moved her gaze to Mrs Curry.

'Are we all set up then?' Helena questioned.

Before Mrs Curry could respond, I made sure to stride into the group, standing with clenched fists. While this was mostly from fear, rather than rage, I hoped they would not notice my trembling voice.

'I see we have visitors!' I announced, gradually emboldened by the rudeness of Mrs Curry's houseguests. 'Margaret.' I repeated Mother's name, her real name, giddy at my own insolence. I stared into my mother's eyes. 'I would think that introductions are in order, wouldn't you?'

Mother shrank into herself in some approximation of modesty and naivety. The change of character was sudden and frightening.

The visitor Helena slowly turned to meet me. Her head and body seemed impossible to move separately from one another, as though she was one enormous malformed vegetable, with no joints of which to speak. I had been perfectly pleasant in my speech, a little forthright perhaps, but such was my place. I clenched my fists tighter, desperately trying to conceal my racing pulse. The wizened face that met mine seemed disgruntled at my presence. My mother and the tall man, Solomon, both turned towards me, each meeting my eyes with a growing, heavy ringing silence. Mrs Curry exhaled and made merry with her chatelaine, not bothering to look up.

I found myself angered by the group, who remained huddled together like thieves in a tavern. I stood tall and released the tension in my hands, deliberately over-presenting myself with fluid hand movements.

'It is truly a pleasure to see new faces in our estate. I'm —' I began.

'Soon to be Lady Crofton, I hear,' interrupted Solomon.

'It's a matter of paperwork,' I responded meekly, my smile promptly dropping as I closed my mouth.

Something about him was unsettling. He moved slowly, and smoothly, like a snake.

'I wouldn't consider congratulations to be in order. Father's death has devastated us all —' I said quickly, keen to cover any thoughts of unfeeling on my part.

Mrs Curry loudly exhaled.

'It's all just ... paperwork,' I stumbled. 'Is that your area, Mr —?'

'Oh Lord save me, no. All that office clerk business would never settle with my character. I'm a people person, Miss. I love to meet and talk with people. Life would be so dull with such a routine, Miss. A room full of old men at desks? There's far too much beauty in the world to stay in one place. Don't you think?'

His speech was a beat too fast to comfortably process, his voice being too soft and gentle, easing me instantly against my conscious will. I flushed a little at his tone, and a little more when he took my hand and kissed it.

'Yes, yes. I — suppose so.' I blushed scarlet at the visitor, whose hot breath still hung on my hand like a wedding band.

The man moved towards me. 'Bexton, Miss, Solomon Bexton. Sorry about the bad business with your father.'

Something about him was familiar. His gestures perhaps. He had still not removed his hat, which seemed most impertinent, so I focused on its velvet band. It was very similar to that which circled my waist, save for the tiny glass beads that separated them.

I attempted to convey my expression as one of sadness or concern. No one, least of all a handsome and not unwelcome stranger, was to think that I eagerly anticipated a new position or ownership of Duncain House. No one was to think that I was so crass as to grab at status when it presented itself.

'Of course, Miss. Sorry for your loss. Your father meant a lot to all of us,' he said in hushed tones.

I smiled and nodded in return, clasping my hands together, mimicking a piety that my splintered nerves could not process.

'How did you know my —?' I began to ask, a little concerned about the change in company with whom my father had conducted business.

Before finishing my sentence, the man stepped a little closer and gestured to me, his hands moving quickly from head to foot.

'If I had been told of your beauty, I would have dressed a little finer, Miss. The little I have known of you has done you no justice.'

My previous concerns were smothered by a hot blush that rose from my neck like bindweed. I returned a smile to the sudden and, admittedly, unfamiliar words.

'Oh, I've embarrassed you, haven't I? Ha, don't mind me, Miss. I mean no harm.'

He lowered his voice to a whisper, leaning ever closer, 'unless you want me to'. He winked, chuckling at his remarks, and turned to greet my mother.

'Dearest Maggie!' I heard him cry, before I desperately tried to tune out of our strange sycophantic chatter and focus on returning to a regular heartbeat.

He looked a little like the men from the coaching inn by Dungannon, but far better dressed. The inn had been a strange experience, and most visually unusual, being fortified with rough wood panelling, applied with all the skill and care of a reticent drunkard. The flagstones were similarly uneven, which at times seemed to be a deliberate slight against women. When leaving, I had toppled towards the floor, with all the elegance of a cabbage falling from a market stall. As I stumbled, I was roughly caught in the arms of a hawker; it was an experience to be indelibly etched in embarrassment. The man's name escaped me, but his looks lingered in my memory. His mutton chops were daring but well-groomed, following the curve of his jaw with the cradling precision of a lover. His hair was a deep, glossy black, standing stark against his beautiful field-tanned skin. His hands lingered a little too long around my waist, with neither of us keen to move. I had thought of him a little since, at night, at my weakest. I thought of it as a fleeting amnesty from my vows, but one that weighed heavy in my waking mind. My heart unsteady in my chest, my mind lingered on the curious similarities between the men and the softness of the tall stranger's hands.

Without looking directly, I knew that Mrs Curry was watching me, judging. I suddenly became aware of the silliness of my behaviour. The hot flushing, the inability to speak to a man, to hold my own strength in my own house. As handsome as he may have been, the man's niceness slipped away with his lingering wink. I would redeem myself, for my own satisfaction; not Mrs Curry's.

The visitors took off their coats, which were hung on the hat stand by Mrs Curry.

Placing the man's hat on top, she waited a moment to check its security, before moving her hand. I had never seen Mrs Curry treat the finest glassware with such reverence, so I made sure to stay close, curiosity burning holes in my bodice.

Helena scuttled towards me and grabbed at my hands before I had time to consider what was occurring.

'Despite our disagreements,' said Helena, smiling through caverns of wrinkles, 'your father really was a clever man.'

She reached up to touch my face. These people did not seem real, just some cruel play come to life. Helena was close, grotesque, and worst of all, over-familiar. I stood frozen against the cold roughness of the stranger's palm.

'Not clever enough to escape death though, eh?' crooned Helena. 'Not as clever as he thought.'

Helena smiled in queer condolence, while my breath caught in barbs within my chest.

This was a waking nightmare, it had to be.

'Anyway, away with ye, young lady, you shouldn't be so frightened!' chirped Helena, falling back from her tiptoes.

I remained motionless, my mind and body fixed in place.

'Mourning will become you, you know. I know, I feared it when my John died, but I found it so nice, I stuck with it for t' last forty years!' she laughed. ''Tis a pain to start dyeing clothes anyway, and at my age, it hardly seems worth it. Imagine me, ay, running around with these great sleeves!'

She cackled and prodded at my shoulders, making a great joke to herself. 'Ahh...' she exhaled, 'to be young.'

Helena sighed and scuttled back to Mrs Curry, who seemed to be wrangling my mother into a more sedentary state. Occasionally, Solomon would turn away from the three women, who stood hunched around an unseen cauldron, attempting to steal a small smile from me as I slowly adjusted to their twisted dynamic.

I was suddenly conscious of my belt and of the warmer tones that swaddled me. Wrapping my arms around my body, I considered my two paths — upstairs or further into the house. I couldn't align my thoughts into anything consistent, but directed my rage towards my dress. I loved that dress. I loved my clothes. Every stitch was my own, bright and clean. Black was for workers, and for hiding dirt and oil. I had accepted my fate, but would not go into that long, joyless year of mourning without a fight. And with any luck, Algernon would find it unbecoming and forbid it. It was a thought I had not so much entertained as longed for, with all the voraciousness of a lonely wife.

I had long loathed mourning. It was a ritual of little concern in Duncain; my family was small and accounted for. There was no need for ornate drapery and crape-edged skirts that scratched across the floorboards like sandpaper. A few months past, Mrs Dalziel of Camden had lost her husband and refused visitors. Considering that we often shared conversations of fashion and the latest trends, it was an upsetting task to watch my friend through the windows as I passed on my way to the gardens. With the windows open, the horrid scratching of bombazine in motion carried through the air and I found myself useless and feeble, able to do little but look at my friend from afar and pity her blackened, swaddled state.

Following Mrs Dalziel's fate, I would actively cross the road when in the city centre. Regent Street, which would have thrived with beautiful milliners and dressmakers, was flanked by enormous warehouses of grief, which featured widow's weeds in the windows as though they were some great fashionable opportunity for women. Occasionally, old women, draped in enough veiling to furnish a house, would emerge from the doors in clouds of dust, both pleased and miserable with their fate. London had quite enough merry mourners, and I was sure not to join them for as long as possible. I had gone to great superstitious pains to cross roads when meeting anyone in black, avoiding the enormous cemetery parks that had begun to circle the city, and skimming the tiresome time regulations for grief so often repeated in Cassell's.

If Algernon saw fit, I would wear mourning for a year. A full 365 days of black, mauve and other such dull variants awaited; meanwhile the moths would make merry with my silks. The year would be long and lonely. As such, for all of Duncain's murky faults, it would offer a full period of wardrobe enjoyment, before I crossed the sea once more. Chelsea would provide upon my return: a house call, a milliner, and a perusal through a jeweller's catalogue. Admittedly, the latter was not an unpleasant thought; black jewellery offered a few northern indulgences and I was sure to have the finest collection of jet in London. I was not one to take risks lightly, but my journey had been planned and Algernon was a man of his word; the transition would be seamless.

The group began to move and snapped me from my angered reverie. Old Helena moved slowly past, looking at me with a visible sense of pity. The visitor made her way through the house like a mudslide; thick and grimy, staining each board she stepped on. As I peered around the hallway, she seemed to move slower still, more like a slug than the scurrying creature I had spied from the upper windows. She was swaddled in shawls and blankets like some great filthy infant. I could do little to tear my eyes away from the faded and muddied mass of fabrics; they seemed to be held together by dirt and willpower alone. As Solomon continued chatting to my besotted mother, I watched Helena move with tiny, gradual steps, her eyes straying to the upper floors a little too frequently for my liking.

Although I did not turn to see the trio by the door, I knew their eyes were upon me.

I motioned to follow Helena on her path through the house, but soon stopped in my tracks when I was a few mere feet from her. Beneath the shawls came the familiar polished glint of the most beautiful gemstone. From her ears hung enormous teardrop bullets of Whitby jet, polished so brightly they seemed to produce their own light.

Helena caught my eye and smiled at me with pity, as when passing paupers after church.

'You alright there, Miss?' she smiled, through whistling teeth.

'You — you have,' I stuttered, my throat suddenly dry from the hallway's dust.

Helena laughed. 'I thought you'd be liking my jewels, Miss.'

People like Helena weren't supposed to have jet. Certainly not before I had a chance to order any, and certainly not of such quality. She was a tatty Duncain widow. There was no outlet for jet in Duncain; even our meagre bog-oak pieces were eschewed by locals, with tourists outside the county picking the trinkets, but only under the promise of charms and luck. Not even vulcanite, in its fraudulent moulded brooches, had crossed the county border.

I remained transfixed at the pendulums swinging from Helena's ears. They were enormous teardrops; simple and glistening. They were a favourite of Adelina Patti. The great, beautiful, fashionable Adelina. I had seen her sing a few weeks ago in London. Her lithe soprano voice filled the concert hall with more grace and power than I could ever have imagined. Rumour had it that she had trained her pet parrot to shout at any promoters entering the room, demanding payment with a shrill caw of 'Cash!' She was wonderful. But most striking of all, her jewellery was beautiful. She was so weighed down by jet that the music faded away in pockets, such was the beauty of its carving. Jet had no place in Duncain. It was for across the water, and for me. Well, for me in Chelsea.

'What do you think to this then, eh? Bet this'll knock your socks off!' laughed Helena, pulling a shawl from her shoulders.

Jangling beneath her neck was the most enormous jet chain, gleaming bright and beautiful, glorious in the low lamplight. The chain was huge — each link clattering against the next, seamless save for small peg holes I had only recently come to identify through catalogues. From every fourth loop hung a beautifully carved cameo. It had to be vulcanite, or horn perhaps. Jet would be too cruel. Most importantly, I realized, jet would have cost a fortune. No one in Duncain, not even the Croftons, to be truthful, had that kind of money. Her great reveal didn't so much incite envy as fear. Something told me that this was not earned wealth.

Helena turned to me in full light, holding the central, enormous pendant to her face.

'The acorns symbolize truth, you see,' she said, spitting through her lip with each word. 'The empty kernel here, you see it? That symbolizes the cup of truth.' Helena held my eyeline with deliberate cruelty.

'Truth is the most important of all things,' she said, turning away and continuing her slow-footed path. 'Of all things.'

As Helena lumbered across the boards, I thought of the twisted name brooch, brought back from a friend's weekend away on the north coast. I had treasured the piece, not least because it was the first gift from any friend, in all my years. The carving was a little crude, and the 'C' of 'Alice' was a little too small, compared to the other letters. I thought of it, sitting in my jewellery bag upstairs, and my pride fell away with its sheen. The brooch could not possibly be worn in Duncain — not now.

As an afterthought, Helena shouted behind her, rather than turn to face me, 'Oh, and we're sorry your father's away. Did our Sol say that? I think he did…'

Mrs Curry was next to walk the corridor, with Mother and Solomon a few steps behind. Mother was chattering excitedly into his ear, her grieving hand hooked around the crook of his elbow.

Pausing as she passed, Mrs Curry leaned into me with a small, soft smile, her eyes still fixed on Helena. 'Jealousy catches up with us all, Miss. There's no shame in it.'

'Now,' continued Mrs Curry, giving her words little time to be understood. 'Are you staying down here, or are you going to lurk on that landing, cooing at gentlemen like a pigeon all night?' She forced a soft chuckle, as though we were friends and such comments were a gentle joke, but there was no warmth to be felt.

I stared at Mrs Curry, my mind rather too sluggish and weighed down with the curious old visitor to consider my own thoughts. There was no forced laughter or sense of jovial banter between us. There lingered a cutting question, a judgement and a barb that caught in my clothing like a fishing weight.

The strangers had entered the dining room unattended, at least not by me, and my mind flitted to unprotected silverware and the opportunistic hands of salesmen. Mrs Curry's words, once suspended before me, fell like stones and I finally moved towards the open door.

Acclimatized to the darkness, I shielded my eyes from the scene that met me.

From the dining room emanated a low, pulsating, orange light. The drapes were drawn. The drapes should never be drawn. They had always been tied open, for as long as I could recall, each with its faded gold tassels facing towards the room. Never towards each other. The old velvet was tired but thoroughly lined; it would block out any sun, but had never needed to. I had thought in my exhaustion that the house couldn't possibly get darker with its half-burned candles and endless internal cloud, but the environment that met me proved to the contrary. While the sun had set hours ago and candles glinted from several rooms, somehow, inside the walls of Duncain, it was perpetually darker than outside.

Chapter 15

Séance

The grand table that had taken up the dining room had been reduced and pushed against a back wall. Chairs hemmed it in like livestock, the seats stacked high in unsteady towers. Mrs Curry had moved the occasional table, leaving its scuffed footprints awkwardly exposed. The ash from the fire infiltrated the room in soundless clouds. I could taste it, feel the gritty warmth in waves, but kept myself still. Most disconcertingly, I felt it land on my hands, outlining the circle where Solomon's lips had rested. When the urge became too great, I rubbed quickly at the back of my hand, just to be sure that there were no marks, not of man's making, nor from the house.

The state of the room was unsettling; the drop-leaf table was never intended to be used, only to occupy space in its cavernous setting. Since purchase, long before my birth, it had been drably decorative. It existed in a state of permanent disuse, cultivating rings of thick dust around the vases on its surface. The vases sat empty and inelegantly in stacks around the curtains, the circles remaining on the table's surface, immovable in the dark wood. I suppressed my panic a little more and focused on breathing deeply. I assured myself that the strange friends of Mother's were certainly not bailiffs, merely fools. After all, who else would entertain my mother's company so gladly?

The room had been transformed into a curious court. It could have been mistaken for a Quaker meeting house were it not for the horrid smell of damp wood and the presence of Mrs Curry. Without a glance necessary, I could feel the housekeeper behind me, looking over my shoulder like a dirty conscience. If the visitors had arrived to conduct business, I was certainly not about to let them do so without me. At first, I thought to sit, but as my eyes adjusted a little better to the firelight, I found myself with rather more questions than anticipated.

The arrangement around the table looked frankly ridiculous, with an array of mismatched chairs tucked closely against each other. Decorative, wicker woven seats and an offensively squat captain's chair gave the appearance of a great house clearance, or a mothers' meeting where each woman was of drastically differing height. Father would have been incensed by such a display, and Mrs Curry would have certainly not survived another day in service for entertaining it. I can't say that I'd blame him either. The room grew in embarrassment with each moment of my observations. The firelight was dying quickly, reduced to nothing more than glowing coals with occasional grey wisps from trapped kindling. It was not the roaring welcome of the Croftons. Father may have been a cold man, but he would never have allowed visitors into the house — however unusual their appearance — without the formalities of a healthy fire and a tidy parlour. The captain's chair, Father's desk chair, with its meticulously preserved woven back, was set a little too close to the coals for comfort. They would surely scorch the chair, and the sitter's back. If there was a greater sign that Father truly was dead, I could not have thought of one. Some cruel flicker within me hoped for Mrs Curry to take the seat, and scorch her overfamiliar rear.

I supposed the oncoming performance was another means of distracting me from the necessity of solicitors. Instead of resting in bed, beneath clean covers, I found myself in a filthy room with my mother, two clear thieves, and Mrs Curry, who was more beast than servant. Something was wrong with the fire. Dust and soot lodged under my eyelids in a fine, unmovable film. The visitors, although blurred in my vision, seemed unaffected. It was tiredness, of course, and the stresses of such strange arrangements on an overworked mind. I had become accustomed to such lapses in strength during my visit, but feared them all the more when they occurred in company.

The dust of the fire adhered to every pore of my skin and I was sure that my sickened state was obvious to the visitors. The ashes caught in my mouth, muffling my breath and scorching my throat. There was nothing but an impenetrable, ink-black darkness beyond my eyelids as my lashes sewed themselves together beneath my fingertips. The smell of burning was overwhelming, and through my panic, I heard the jabbering of the visitors, their words hammering together in a mishmash of non-speech. Above it all rose the sing-song lilt of Elsie's laughter, as high and light as a piccolo. But the door was locked and she slept in her room. Of that, I was sure. I had heard her reading her books not moments earlier at the top of the stairs, sounding out every word. But things were passing me by, sleeplessly so.

My eyes burned so tight and hot, stretched taut and thin until I felt a tear and a sudden, screaming release of pressure in my head. I screamed, not through pain, but as a reflex that tore my throat raw. Something soft, warm and jellied fell from my useless eyes, and I tried to catch it, but did so blindly, the pieces falling between my fingers. All the while, water fell around me, coating my face in a foul-smelling liquid that ran like tears, but was far greater in volume. Pressing my hands to my cheeks, my eyelids wrinkled and sagged against the void behind them. Doubling over, I gasped for breath, pawing at the hideous wetness.

Suddenly, it passed. My senses returned one by one in quick succession: taste, smell, and lastly, sight. As quickly as it crept upon me, it faded and the room was as it was before. Cool, dark, and dusty. My face was dry to the touch, if a little damp in places. There was a little dampness of oils, or sweat; untroubling and smooth. All was as it should be, yet my body shook against my will, tingling at my fingers with unspent energy.

My mind, however, did not feel my own, as though I were waiting for dizziness to take hold, or some other force beyond my understanding. I took long, deep breaths and readjusted my throbbing vision to the low light of the open doorway.

Mother crooned from across the room, breaking the taut silence with a shrill voice.

'Are you alright, dear?'

They had seen nothing. Rather, there was nothing to see. It was sleeplessness, dirt, and a fancy mind, nestling behind my own. It had lasted minutes, or seconds. A foolish matter to dwell upon. Some strange waking nightmare to firmly keep to myself. I would sleep and never give the strangeness another thought, however much my body might shake.

'You're being very quiet,' pushed Mother.

'I —' I began, hoping to exit without the necessity of conversation.

'Are you feeling poorly?' interjected Mrs Curry, her hardened face betraying her spoken concern.

I held my answer beneath my tongue, resting my body in a little pocket of silence. Each muscle was exhausted, my gums sore and raw to the touch. Duncain would hold me for only a short time longer. *Well, Alice. Treat yourself and count down the days.* I would hold power over the ruin and return home. Home to Algernon. Nothing could remove that comfort.

Nursing my mouth of sores, I reiterated to myself that I couldn't leave Duncain without the paperwork; not for my sake, but for Algernon's. I had never considered having to force such things, but I would find the strength, or would do so to spare my mind.

'She's taken his death hard,' mumbled Mrs Curry from behind.

The housekeeper shielded her voice in a poor approximation of compassion. She had always played tiresome games. I was starting to believe that perhaps my Father grew wise to it. And perhaps I did too, in a way. My mother, however, was a far simpler soul.

'She's had problems all her life, you know...' continued Mrs Curry in hushed tones, stroking my shoulder and seemingly delighting in her new, tiny veiled acts of cruelty.

My mind wandered to Father's body once more, not lying on the carpet, seeping into the fibres, but afterwards; truly in death. Had the undertakers treated him well, or left him to rot in some back room while Mother busied herself with bedside meals and expensive veiling? There had been no talk of his body, no funeral cards, no mason's catalogues or lingering floral tributes. Had anyone but me been told of the old man's demise, as though it were some filthy secret to which few were privy?

'She's a little weak,' announced Mrs Curry, turning to motion to the visitors, her hands clasped in callused concern.

I wanted to snap at her impertinence, but a sudden nausea hit my stomach, twisting my insides like wringing hands.

The fire soared suddenly, breaking the confines of the hearth. There were no shrieks of acknowledgement. It had to be another trick of my mind. I had to leave, to avoid any relished humiliation with this strange temporary loss of my senses. I took a stumbling step towards the door, but immediately realised my painful mistake. It was not the door, but the sideboard. The brass chambersticks rattled as my knees met wood.

Solomon laughed as he turned to meet me. 'Oh dear me, Miss. Do you need a little help?'

At once, I felt his sleeves against my skin, an arm stretch across me, his fingers grasp my shoulder, holding me upwards. I nodded and smiled in a gesture I hoped to say, *I'm perfectly well, goodnight.*

I took a few short, deep breaths and made motion towards the door. The chairs had rearranged again, facing in odd directions, different from before. The door open, a cool breeze flowing beneath the entrance doors. Yet Mother stood in the doorway, blocking my exit with a multitude of mismatched petticoats.

She had been behind me; at the opposite end of the room. Something deep within my twisting stomach urged me to flee, but I barely held the energy to walk. The fatigue flung itself upon me like a cloak, doing little to ease the bile that rose from my stomach.

Mother's eyes were slightly glazed, as though sickness had taken root. Infections came with the winter moths that laid their eggs in her sickbed. Every year, the ailments returned. Having no doctors nearby, she was prone to self-medication with concoctions peddled by women in the village. Of course, all dispensed by Mrs Curry's hand.

'I thought you wanted to sleep,' said Mother through milky eyes.

'I think she may best take a seat,' spoke Mrs Curry from across the room, poorly hiding a wheeze against the gathering dust. 'Take this one, Miss. You won't miss the action then.'

She dragged out a small chair with a wicker base.

'No, I'm quite alright —' I began, motioning to pass Mother. 'I just need a little sleep.'

The door was shut, with no hand to close it. A large white tablecloth had since covered the old ring marks on the table, the enormous sheet edged with heavy crocheted lace.

Another move of Mrs Curry's doing; she showed herself able to work quickly if it served her purposes.

'Welcome our guests, dear,' chirped Mother from the far end of the room.

'I have — we've spoken,' I began, before jumping out of my skin. Behind me were Solomon and old Helena.

'Good evening there, Miss,' chirped Helena. 'We're sorry about the business with your father.'

'This jape stops here,' I said, gathering what meagre strength I could. I had hoped to sound forceful, but my voice fell in a whimper, brushed away with the fire ash.

Helena gave a little wave from behind the table, too comfortable in her environment.

'We didn't think you'd be comin',' she crowed. 'We're glad you are, though, Miss. Nice to have things in place, ain't it, Agnes?'

I forced unwilling breath through my lungs. 'I am tired. You are to let me leave.'

I desperately tried to shout, but it could as well have been a whisper. No twitch of recognition came from the guests, nor my mother.

Solomon stepped out from behind Helena, roughly repositioning his curled mop of thick hair with one hand and tightly grasping a tattered doctor's bag with the other.

'Have we met, Miss?' he crooned, holding out an open hand.

'Yes. Solomon Bexton. Your name is Solomon Bexton,' I said, my arms wrapped tightly around my waist.

'Yes!' he cheered, his face bright with surprise. 'Well, Miss, it's a pleasure to re-make your acquaintance!'

Taking my hand in his, he pressed his lips against it, his eyes flickering up at mine in unspoken, salacious acknowledgement. His lips sat soft and warm against my skin, grown too cold once more.

'Oh,' he muttered, smiling and turning over my hand. 'For later.'

He pressed his lips into my palm, my hand gently tensing around his. Coarse whiskers tickled my thumb and, for a moment, a ripple of desire snaked itself around me.

'It's alright, it will be over soon,' he whispered, placing his lips close to my ear. 'You're not mad, dear. Well —' he laughed, his breath hot against my cheek, 'not yet.'

His whiskers lingered against my skin, his hand squeezing mine with matrimonial familiarity.

'We've met before, Helena!' cheered Solomon, projecting his voice across the room and dashing my hand back towards her.

His voice was too bold, too familiar. Tall and angular, he struck a handsome figure, but unlike any that Duncain had ever produced. The Jubilee Inn. The coaching inn. It was the same man, but slicker. Each hair on his head was curled and oiled to perfection, his face shaved and sculpted as though he was cast bronze.

Joining my exhaustion was a glancing blow of foolishness, and dirt, as though some old sin had sprung back to haunt me. Like a chastised child, I took my seat on the wicker chair, waiting for shame or my mother's cheer to spirit me away.

Mother stood at one end of the table, the guests flanking the other sides. Curiously, they both kept their distance from Helena, as though she were a great box of explosives.

'You — We', chirped Mother, interrupting herself, 'should regard ourselves as lucky. These people are the finest Spiritualists in the whole of the county!'

Such a claim might have been impressive if it did not consider the subjects of both Spiritualism and Duncain. It came as little surprise that Mother had developed new interests in resurrecting the dead. Namely, those who were rested enough not to have to tolerate her company, let alone indulge it. I remained slumped at the table in my exhaustion, holding my head in my hands. My tolerant spirit had been utterly broken. The whole scenario was, at last, too fantastical to entertain.

'I trust you're familiar with Spiritualist practice?' said Mrs Curry through pursed lips, her eyes squinting at mine.

'Of course,' I replied, somewhat resigned to my fate. My hands remained in their place, partially obscuring my vision, but not enough to block out the proud old women before me.

Chapter 16

Before my return to Duncain's cold and indifferent walls, life in London had been a riotous rush of sound and colour. London was a different country; different rules, different rulers, and far too much to learn. London speech leapfrogged itself into unfamiliar patterns, wordless telegrams of changing fashions were delivered to all women of note, and my assimilation was exhaustive and delicious. The fashions, the speech, the theatre and operas were added to my list of conquering triumphs in those first sickly sweet weeks of marriage, but spiritual matters had languished at the bottom of my list.

Spiritualism had blanketed London for long before my arrival. Every woman I crossed had their 'special' reader, their favourite medium in some rented back-alley second-floor room, keen to tell them that their husband really did love them and that children would soon ensue.

I had played a little table-tipping after an afternoon of high tea and pleasant chatter with the Chelsea ladies. A small table would gently rise and fall, tipping and turning at the questioning of the host to squeals of delight. They would ask about balls, gossip, and the weather for their excursions, but nothing more. The table business had made little sense to me and was a source of light enjoyment, and certainly a fine way of closing an afternoon. I often thought of how we should thank the spirits for their wonderful idea of making secondary use of the tea table.

The books and lectures, however, were another matter. At one time, I thought every hall and theatre in England must have entertained some curly-haired child, professing to have knowledge from the other side. And knowledge it was. Mrs Hetfield found herself and her husband trapped in an enormous assembly hall for three long hours as a visiting American girl held them captive with some flimsy, if relentless, gibberish about the structure of the human soul.

I had supposed that by hour two, I would be begging the spirits to take me to join them. I had quite enough religious education from Mrs Curry in her more fearsome moments, without some American upstart preaching about the ghostly nature of eternity. The world free from Duncain was beautiful; eternity was a bonus.

I had given spiritual matters little thought beyond childish attendance certificates from within my bedroom Sunday School. I had, however, cultivated a selection of increasingly elaborate hats for half-listened-to services. Physical attendance at the new church in Chelsea was but another scribble in the attendance book of social necessities. Talk of Spiritism had entered the church, but was swiftly dismissed in sermons with talk of divination and sorcerers confined to fiery pits. Yet it was discussed ferociously in huddles at the church gates, like children stealing snuff from their father's cabinet.

Much like the stacks of unread 'Good Christian' books of boyish adventurers and sweet martyred little girls, spirit play was for decoration, not for serious study. I had little interest in participating in any of the circles in London. Many of the ladies were utterly obsessed and took weekly meetings in Dalston, professing all manner of visions and messages upon their return. Many more of them hoarded periodicals like gemstones, leaving them on side tables in great wedges to boast to visitors of their newly enlightened state.

After a few rejected invitations to the Dalston meetings, the invitations stopped. My interest peaked a little too late for the spiritual gates to reopen and I felt myself foolishly cut from my new ladies' groups. I cursed the spirits for my marginally more open diary. I should have accepted and played along with their games; at least my finest clothes would have had far more outings. I had asked my friends questions in passing, but had certainly not wanted to seem as though I was angling for another invitation. Even though that was the desired effect. Their meetings seemed to grow so popular, with ladies knocking at meeting houses several days a week. The ladies spoke of the amazing things they'd seen at Dalston. Yet, save for a few messages of love, the niceties of death, some strange chatter on slates and trumpets, their stories did not seem fantastical enough to hold my interest, at least when the newest meeting group oversubscribed before I could visit. I would soon make a habit of changing the subject at tea, when talk of mediums and spiritual matters arose. However, a slightly misjudged comment of mine about the quality of a particular medium's spirit art may have been the final nail in the coffin.

Chapter 17

Séance

In Duncain's drawing room, the visiting Spiritualists joined in stilted and uncomfortable chatter. As I watched on in cold frustration, my mother scuttled about the room, addressing the visitors like an excited child.

'I'll sit down,' chirped Mrs Crofton. 'I've a weak constitution, you see. Especially since my dear husband passed —'

As my mother lowered her rear slowly onto a high-backed chair to the side of the table, the squat visitor lunged forward like a yard dog.

'Don't you go sittin' down until I say.'

Mother froze, half bent over the table like a rusted hinge.

'But she —' whined my mother, pointing at me like a naughty schoolchild.

'She doesn't count, as well you know,' snapped Helena, her face visibly changing from that which had shared laughs with Solomon moments before.

'Rules are there as much for protection as they are for conduction,' she continued. 'Stand. Up. Margaret.'

The unwelcome visitor barked her words, slowly revealing herself from her blankets like a worm from compost. Mother silently rose and stood to the side of the table, staring at the floor like a chastised child. I'd be lying if I said that my satisfaction at her dismissal wasn't obnoxiously visible on my face.

Helena busied herself about the room, dragging chairs around the table, the legs producing uncomfortable, protracted honking sounds against the boards. She bore all the traits of a Duncain widow, the likes of which dotted the landscape like standing stones. Ugly, heavy, and stuck in the past.

An unfamiliar voice cut through the candlelit haze, with all the sangfroid and poise of a butter knife through stale bread. Helena's hacking cough and audible spittle was enough to turn my stomach once more, my skin flushing hot and clammy. As I finally, slowly gathered my strength and moved to leave, a wide palm encircled my wrist.

'I think it's best you stay, Miss. It's what your mother wants, and our visit would be somewhat without purpose if we were reduced to a party of four,' whispered Solomon, his lips a little too close to my ear for propriety.

No man had touched me with such control since I left for Duncain, and my body recoiled at such. There was a tone in his voice that forbade question.

'Sit,' hissed the hunched visitor, a globule of greying spit fixing itself to the back of a dining chair.

The Spiritualists of Duncain possessed curious standards, with the purpose of the ramshackle affair becoming as unsettling as it was unclear. In some unwelcome, exhausted reflex, I shrank and sat on the outstretched chair with my mother beside me. There was something within the old visitor's face. Something old and dangerous within her aged, glinting eyes was too cruel and sharp to disobey.

Solomon strolled over to one of the two remaining seats beside Helena. Each step was elegant, his legs arched like that of a dressage horse. To find a man with such natural elegance was astounding and mesmeric in equal measure. His gentle accent was hard to place, but held an authority that unnerved me, even in his silence.

Helena busied herself by rustling beneath her blankets, as though she were following some persistent, elusive flea. No one spoke, save for the occasional crackle of the logs.

'Agnes. You keep your mistress waiting,' wailed the old visitor.

Her nasal voice rang through the room like a shotgun blast. Helena spoke with such authority that my mother and I remained seated in some primal acknowledgement of spoken power.

The name 'Agnes' was unfamiliar in Duncain's walls, and disrupted the air like a fat fly. As my mind wandered to the tragedies of lost etiquette, a woman's figure filled the doorframe, broad enough to blot out any candlelight. From her pocket hung a huge circle of iron keys that swung and glinted as she pushed the door to.

'Some of us have a household to run, Helena,' snapped the housekeeper. 'The spirits will have to learn a little patience, much like yourself, Mrs Watling.'

Mrs Curry sneered, seemingly perturbed at the crass bellowing of her Christian name.

The housekeeper had moved herself in and out of the room once more. For such a large woman to become imperceptible in her movement was nigh attributable to witchcraft.

For all their trickery, her repeated games of hide and seek grew tiresome to comprehend.

With one broad, muscular hand, Mrs Curry dragged my father's old captain's chair back on its brass casters, patted down her skirts, and sat. The springs gently squeaked under the unfamiliar pressure as she sighed and folded her hands on the table top. A housekeeper's place was not in the eyeline of her mistress, yet there sat Mrs Curry, staring as though she herself had gathered her employers into her home. I was not a cruel woman, nor malicious. But something in my gut told me that when the house was mine, Mrs Curry had to go. For all our sakes.

'Shall we begin?' smiled the old medium, each word whistling against her solitary brown tooth.

Expecting a little chatter, I leapt from my skin as Solomon suddenly bellowed in a terrifying baritone. *'Shall we gather at the river?'*

'*Where bright angel feet have trod...*' My mother joined in the song, her voice shrill and piercing.

'*With its crystal tide forever...*'

Mrs Curry's voice grew stronger in accent, but followed the tune. Unlike the others, whose eyes were closed, their faces tilted downwards, her eyes were fixed on mine. With each line, the three of them grew louder in song, Mrs Curry's eyes still piercing mine, in some horribly intense serenade.

The hymn continued for far too many verses, each a little louder than the last. My mother came in a beat too slow for most, exposing that she knew the words far less than the 'professionals'. As they closed with a bellowing, pseudo-rousing couplet, '*Gather with the saints at the river, that flows by the throne of God*', the silence that followed was blissful. To no longer endure the shrieks of godliness was, indeed, a blessing. The silence lingered, my mother's eyes excitedly skipping between the two visitors. Some heavy unspoken rule weighed heavier still and no one dared break the air.

After an age of dull, unblinking silence, Helena — looking quite comfortable at the head of the table — began to move. She extended an ungloved hand from beneath her blankets, and every inch of her skin seemed muddy. Her hand was more like a twisted bird's claw than anything possessed by a human; her palm thick with grime and liver spots, fingers as twisted and gnarled as old tree roots. She flipped a pack of bent cards from an unseen pouch within her layers and proceeded to spread them around the table in a crude circle. Each card bore a different letter in fine, spidery writing. Between her and Mr Bexton sat two larger cards, marked 'YES' and 'NO'.

I chastised myself for not anticipating such things from my mother; I could never experience anything without a sense of performance, so why should my father's death be any different? I saw the odd, tuneful duo through narrowed eyes. They were interlopers poised to ease my mother of her wealth with talk of spirits and ghouls.

I had heard in passing about such financial cruelty in Chelsea; truly respectable people hiring mesmerists and the like to enter their homes and claim to deliver wondrous news from the heavens. I also recalled that Mrs Dunbar lost fifteen pounds to a young woman who assured her that the spirit of her son would grace her day-room, should she only part with a little more cash. I had never attended such silliness, yet could recall the 'unveiling' of Mrs Dunbar's child with such relish at dinner parties and the like. After parting with more of her husband's wealth, she was so overcome with emotion when her dead son did wander about the room that she instantly rose and lunged at the 'apparition'. Instead of embracing the foolish woman as a lost son would, the spectre's gossamer appearance fell from its shoulders, revealing the young medium herself with a crude paper beard affixed to her chin. A cruel part of me wanted to laugh at the time, that some spiritual pantomime had entered their lives and duped her friends, yet there was a real, cruel tragedy in a heartbroken mother who failed to tell the difference between a thirty-year-old soldier and a fraudulent child playing dress-up in her mother's wedding veil.

'Another,' said the old stranger.

I had understood such a play to commence with some call to the heavens, admittedly a painful musical one, but how it could not be enough for any household was a painful thought. Yet from beside the firelight came the low baritone of Mr Bexton, singing 'Son of my soul, thou saviour dear'. I had considered that any spirit, living or dead, would be chased from the room by their choral efforts, rather than welcomed. As Solomon continued, Mrs Curry and old Watling joined the tune. For a few bars longer, I could have thought myself to be in my Sunday School class once more, were it not for the sudden interjection of my mother's shrieking voice, singing a tune not known to God or man.

Following the last discordant bars of the hymn, Solomon retrieved a large velvet bag from beside him, one which he had deftly concealed upon arrival. From it, he retrieved a small brass bell, a ball made from woven rushes, and a smaller, flat velvet bag that clattered as it moved; all of which he placed on the table, a short way from Helena.

'We will ease in today, Madam,' he nodded to my mother. Solomon was aiming for a sense of gentle authority, but spoke as though he had drawn me a bath. I half-expected him to continue with talk of warm towels.

'We do not wish to fully enter the spirit kingdom as I fear it may be a little much for one so delicate such as yourself,' he continued.

He was so comically brazen in his intentions that I awaited a chorus of chuckles. Yet silence remained, Solomon's rehearsed lines acting as a compliment to my mother's susceptibility, and also a get-out clause for him and his companion. The old visitor had sat back in her chair, the pressure from her back eliciting pained creaks through the wooden joints. Her arms were outstretched, her hands wrapped tightly around Solomon's and my mother's.

Solomon continued to hold court. 'We must wait for her to enter spirit. Mrs Watling will travel through the ether, into the Summerland, and locate your husband. I am sure he will be waiting for you.'

He smiled and nodded, as though he were explaining a new sewing technique to a simpleton. I had not expected my mother to hold a great level of scepticism, but watching her simpering responses to Mr Bexton's claims was a further unpleasant experience. Helena, hands still tightly clasped, began to breathe loudly, increasing her exhalations in volume until her calls were indiscernible from those of cattle.

'Are you in spirit, Mrs Watling?' began Solomon.

Mrs Watling returned no answer, save for the whistling of breath against her tooth.

'Spirits, give us a sign of your presence!' he pressed.

Solomon's command was quickly followed by a light ringing of the brass bell. It slid an inch or two to the left, never leaving the table and making very little noise. My mother's fingernails dug hard into my palm, as though the dead had truly awoken and the heavens were poised to empty themselves into the drawing room.

'Spirits!' yelled Bexton, addressing the ceiling and sending my mother's nerves skywards. 'We wish to speak with the departed Mr Kenneth Crofton.'

'*Sir —*' I interjected with sudden, emboldened annoyance.

It seemed to me a little petty, but if Father's spirit was to be crudely impersonated, I would make sure he would not lose his title alongside his dignity. A moment of silence followed, pricked only by the cracking of burning logs. Helena inhaled sharply.

'It is I, Sir Kenneth Crofton.'

'Is it truly you, Kenneth?' mewed Mother, barely missing a beat.

'Yes, dear wife, it is I —'

The old medium's voice was low and forced, no more masculine than before, more of a child's impersonation of my father. Mrs Watling may have been no newcomer to her business, but she was certainly no master. My mother edged forward in her chair, her fast-held hands the only thing tethering her to her seat.

'Are you well?' she chirped.

Mrs Curry, whose eyes had been closed in reverence, opened one eye to stare at Mrs Crofton.

'The spirit realm suits me well,' mumbled the medium.

'Do you think of me still?' continued Mother, oblivious to all else.

'I will forever care for your health. You take to your bed often —'

With those words, Mother interrupted the mundane interchange with a loud sob and sharply raised her hands from the table. She arched towards the old medium's face as though her sagging features covered some spectral window.

'My husband, my love, is it you in there?'

The entirety of Duncain knew of her willingness to succumb to any imagined illness, and a ghostly husband provided no incisive news. Mrs Curry reached across the table and with one enormous palm pushed my mother back down by her shoulder.

'I'm sorry, I grieve,' she whispered, a chastised child once more. 'How is heaven?' she chirped, her grief leaving as quickly as her senses.

'Heaven is beautiful, my love. I am surrounded by my family and those I love. The skies are bright and clear and we live in the most beautiful gardens,' came the answer.

'Who is with him?' My mother had turned to Mrs Curry, her voice strong and accusatory.

'He didn't like his family. He certainly didn't have friends... Are you quite sure, dear?' Mrs Crofton once again pressed herself closer to the medium.

'We let bygones be bygones in the —'

'I just don't see who's there, dear,' she interrupted.

'The ether is clouding my connection. The vapours are too thick. Solomon, the vapours are too thick!'

Helena's voice was breaking; a long way from Kenneth's unconvincing tone.

'Something's wrong. The people, the children upstairs, they —'

Helena's head lolled from side to side like a rabbit caught in a poacher's snare. She spat half-formed words through the tear in her lip, addressing the ceiling and walls; focusing on none of us in particular.

After a series of short, gurgling coughs, a slew of muddy white froth fell from the medium's mouth like a lolling tongue. Mother gasped loudly, freezing before weakly struggling to remove her hands from the grasp of her neighbours'. We all sat staring, fixed and unsure as to what to do, yet Mother fluttered towards the limelight, even during the production of spectres. Solomon and I held her fast, pressing her wrists hard against the table.

Solomon turned, whispering towards me, 'Don't fear, it's proof spirit is with her.'

As the bubbling froth continued to flow across Helena's blankets, I watched on, sitting rigid in terror. It moved, slowly and gently, rolling down her clothes with thoughts of its own. Reaching her lap, it curdled in fat pools, glinting shiny and wet in the firelight. Her face was taut, her mouth open to its fullest, expressing sporadic, small coughs between expressions of the strange material.

At once, it grew, twisting and rising from old Watling's mouth, flowing into the air. It rested heavy on her blouse, but floated a little above her with all the lightness of the finest silk. The higher it turned, spiralling in on itself, the more it appeared to emanate a little glow, glinting like starlight against the blackness of the ceiling.

Helena's hands were clasped in others as the first strand slowly retracted and straightened, projecting from her mouth like a rod. Suddenly, with a great cough, the strange material rose and covered her face, snaking upwards in larger tangles. A portion grew larger, greying and darkening in strange patination.

First, there was an eye, then another, then a portion of beard and balding head. Before my drying eyes grew the likeness of my father. Small and suspended high above our heads. His face hung, unmoving, as he was in life. He looked healthy and far younger. He looked as I had hoped him to be in heaven, if he had indeed reached such a place. He looked as he did in his finest portrait; the one that hung in the entrance way, albeit a little obscured by dust.

The longer my eyes lingered on the strange phantom, the closer the similarities I found. Before I could straighten my senses and make a little more understanding of the affair, he too was enveloped by the whiteness of the medium's froth.

It fell towards her, weighted like swags, disappearing back into her mouth and slipping down her throat like wet leaves down a drain. Slowly, it returned to her, an inch, then a little more. It snagged a little and Helena choked, as though primed to vomit. Instead, spirit flowed back to her, softly and slowly.

With a sudden snap and roar of the fire, the illumination lasted just long enough to show the weave in the strange material; wide and fine. The light was momentary and the remainder soon spooled itself back. If the matter was of the medium's making, if it existed within her at all times, or if all manner of spiritual matter was a literal woven cloth from God was distressingly unclear. My body shook at the strange voyeurism it endured and ached to leave the table.

As the visitor gargled, swallowing the last thick white spirals that had fallen from her mouth, the whole affair left me feeling shaken, unsteady, small, and decidedly grubby.

Chapter 18

Dear Algernon,

I must apologize for the bluntness of my tone, but I have an important matter to discuss with you.

I must return home at once. I was foolish in my insistence to return here and the additional costs of hiring an external solicitor are to be fully justified. I know that you were against such a choice, and ordinarily, I would never concern myself with decisions of monetary matters.

However, I do not feel safe and I must return. The solicitors' fees, however large, can be taken from my estate. You will not owe a penny for the procedures.

I will order a cab as soon as possible and return home by the end of the week. I know my time here was never supposed to be protracted, but I simply cannot remain a day longer.

Yours,

Alice x

Chapter 19

As the slip-slip of Mother's house shoes led the shambling old medium to the door, I strained to hear the familiar clink of silver coins into an open palm.

Of course, they wanted money. In my absence, charlatans had taken root in Duncain's soil. In my youth, it was pegs, charms, and remedies which were easily dismissed with the wave of a hand or shotgun, should the groundsmen be present. I was sure that a gullible widow with a known fondness for remedies and outbursts of unsubstantiated hysteria made the family sitting ducks. My father was not long cooling in his grave while his wife keenly played childish games with my inheritance. The mediums left without looking back. The inner doors swung shut with a grating click of iron bolts, rusted thick from years of disuse.

Looking on, bile burned in my throat.

'I'd suggest you gather the spirit matter for the cook. But I fear our guest has taken her spiritual cheesecloth back to her burrow,' I snapped.

My eyes were wet and hot, holding back tears with burning determination lest my mother gain strength from my outburst.

My mother paused on the lower stair. 'Mrs Curry has quite enough on her hands without you referring to her as a "cook". You'd best become acquainted with the stove.'

I took the stairs slowly, and with a deliberate, practised rhythm. The dining room lay as it had before, the only sign of visitors being the occasional popping of dying embers and the small velvet bag which lay dark and forgotten in the centre of the table.

* * *

My mother wore grief well. It suited her. She sported my father's absence like a new haircut or fashionable sash. She seemed more alive in the weeks since Father's passing than in all the years I could recall. Mother's voice had developed a sing-song lilt, her skin had a glow many women would covet in pregnancy, and she was spending fewer hours confined to her bed. The realization that my old mother could function at some level of normalcy was astounding and frustrating for me to observe. If my mother was losing her mind, it would be pertinent for her to make haste and complete her demise with as little cost as possible. While Father's illness came quickly, at least he was proper enough to keep his chequebook closed and his madness confined within the estate's walls. He certainly didn't outsource for crooks.

Mother had been quiet that morning. The house would've seemed empty were it not for the occasional clanging of copper pans from the scullery and the tell-tale rustlings of starched skirts from below floors. Elsie remained in her room, as always. I'd often thought that a mumble or scuffle from behind Elsie's door could have provided some small comfort through my sleepless days in Duncain. Some semblance of human life might offer a welcome reassurance if I wasn't holed up at world's end and life did indeed await me elsewhere. But Elsie continued her existence in perfected silence. Mrs Curry insisted that Elsie's routines were paramount to retain discipline. She had said Father demanded it so, but as the hours passed, I couldn't help but wonder how much unsupervised work a child could complete between those four walls. Elsie seemed more of a pet, project, or precious cheese than a girl; an existence of rest, silence, and needlework would either create the perfect lady, presentable to society, or a woman more bizarre and unstable than Mother herself. She had grown comfortable in her enforced solitude, overtaken by cabin fever perhaps. I knew she would be thinking of escape, of our journey back to London together. I wasn't going to let her down this time.

It seemed to be a Thursday; certainly past midweek. No one had passed Duncain House for days, not since cattle were clumsily driven along the way, their rumbling lowing ringing through the windows like a death knell. It was an uncomfortably familiar sound I had keenly forgotten in my city life. I'd often wondered if they knew they were being walked to their deaths, if the infernal roar of their transportation was a kind of sad acknowledgement of their fate. Market Day was always a Monday. The gates would rust shut before the post brought news of Algernon to me.

I sat beside my bedroom window a while. I'd had few fortunate experiences during my time in Duncain, but possessing a vantage point free from rot and swathes of spider silk was certainly a blessing, albeit a small one. If I spent further hours watching crows tear through the purpled stalks of rogue bedding plants, it hardly seemed like time wasted. Time spent away from the Spiritualist visitors and Mother's new social circle was something I regarded as time spent a little closer to God. Or London. Or Algernon, for that matter. Or rather, time a little further from their boasts. It was quieter at least, and in Duncain, that seemed to be a state of affairs for which to be thankful. There was still no sign of lawyers.

It struck me that sitting in purposeless silence painted an uncomfortable picture for someone who prided herself on the enjoyment of life, and of time. I reached aimlessly towards the bookshelves, my eyes still fixed upon the destructive crows on the front lawns, half-hoping they'd come to blows during their binge of herbaceous vandalism. A soft spine buckled under the pressure of my fingertip. I tilted the base and slid the book out from its resting place, grating the spine slowly against the rim of the shelf. I rested the green tome on my lap with no real intention of reading it.

Soon, the crows had lost interest in their aimless activity and flew away uttering deep caws, no bird looking back to see if the other was following. Duncain returned to its state of familiar emptiness, leaving me with little to watch other than the occasional gust of dead leaves, scuttling across the gravel pathway. The book seemed heavier somehow. I traced the faded edges of the once-gilt pages. They were greying, powdery, and slightly damp towards the spine, the pages wet like morning grass. More likely rot. The book wouldn't open. It seemed solid suddenly, the pages fused. It became heavier still, unmovable. The cover was leaden; cold and smooth against my knees, pushing my feet hard against the floorboards. My knees grated against one another, my thighs bowing under the weight, my heels forced against the floor so hard, I was sure they'd snap in two. My lungs were airless as I strained against the force on my thighs, pain screaming down my calves in hot darts.

The sound of childish giggling filtered through the cracks of the ceiling like smoke. One voice, then another, then another. At once there were a thousand and none, whistling together, flooding the room in some infantile dirge without beginning or end.

I could feel my knees starting to separate, the muscles straining their last. The laughter softened, lulled, then moved; first it came from above the window, then from the back wall. Between them, I strained and wheezed, trying to pry the book from my skirts, achieving little but lifting my nails from their beds.

A sudden lungful of air took me by surprise. My breath rushed in so quickly it began to feel like drowning. I slammed my palms into the side of the book, sending it skidding across the floor, the spine bouncing end over end in inelegant thuds. It came to a rest at the open doorway, white pages spread wide like a seabird in flight.

The momentary silence pierced the air, my heart pounding with anticipation. The stillness crackled like the space between lightning strikes.

A noise began to build from the beams in the roof, softer, but cruder than before. A gentle rumble was followed by the sudden pat-pat of tiny feet. They were slow at first, as though they were emerging from a deep sleep. Slowly, the footsteps were interspersed with more frenetic bursts, tracking from one end of the ceiling to the other. They seemed to criss-cross, snaking in arcane routes, as though following a maze. It was nothing. My imagination. Old houses make noise; they creak and groan with every rainstorm. Mrs Curry could have employed new staff, or Elsie found friends. My attempts at mental reassurances fell flat.

They certainly sounded like footsteps, light, like a cat's. Yet as the steps came closer, the force of each thud suggested otherwise; as though something larger were up there, running free through Father's rooms.

The steps began to circle above me. With it came a thick, tearing ache down my calves. They were louder, harder, faster, and would surely come through the plaster any minute. I had to leave. Through the pain and breathlessness, I grasped and pushed my palms against the arms of the chair, attempting to rise.

As suddenly as they had started, the footsteps stopped.

Mrs Curry, arms laden with pressed linen, filled the doorway.

'Mrs Curry,' I rasped, panicked, 'you have to —'

'At this moment in time, my child, I have to do little other than press bedsheets. You'd do well to look after yourself. You're looking rather pasty, my dear. Get yourself back under those covers, eh? I'll bring you some soup.'

Mrs Curry turned to leave before twisting back and gently setting the linen down atop a chest of drawers. She knelt, lifting the splayed book from the doorway, and brushed the spine, as though it had accumulated layers of dust as it sat in state.

Slowly, and with mild disinterest, she spoke. '"Conversations on Botany". I'm surprised that such works lead you into fits. Although the written word can be a little straining when you're feeling poorly.'

Mrs Curry tilted her head and smiled, moving forward to put a claw-like hand of reassurance on my shoulder. She wordlessly turned and moved towards the bookcase behind me, pausing only to gently slide the volume back into the gap in the shelf. She deftly moved to return to her sheets, showing little interest in me as I arched uncomfortably in the day chair.

'Upstairs —' I said, quickly.

'Is of little concern to you, Miss. I don't want you wandering when you're looking so pale. Those rooms remain locked at his lordship's demand,' clipped Mrs Curry, still smiling, but with a fierceness rising in her voice.

'There were noises,' I said, insistence rising in my tone.

Mrs Curry exhaled and raised her head with a small smile. 'Don't you go worrying yourself, Miss. I have not allowed rats to flourish under this roof. I may be a staff of one, but I am competent enough to run this household.'

Mrs Curry's smile was joined with a soft resting of her shoulders, as she gently stroked the folded sheets with rough palms.

I paused, rubbing my strained neck. My throat felt raw, torn from breathless screaming.

'No —' I began, stretching my neck. 'Bigger.'

Each word tore through my throat, tracking long, raw lines down my gullet, like swallowing pins.

'Oh, Miss, there's nothing for you to worry about here. There's no beasties in the house, and' — Mrs Curry paused with a raised finger, as though predicting my thoughts — 'I haven't seen a squirrel in a decade or more.'

Mrs Curry, seemingly displeased with my ensuing silence, motioned towards me, bending to examine my face.

'Perhaps you aren't sleeping enough. I can bring you up some tea —' she began.

'No, no — thank you, Mrs Curry. That'll be all.' I tilted my head downwards. A little embarrassed at my impudence.

Yet to meet Mrs Curry's eyes seemed exhausting in itself.

'We don't want you getting feeble now, do we?' crooned Mrs Curry, unmoving from her position.

'We?' I questioned.

'The family, Miss. Now you rest up.' Mrs Curry paused at the doorway. 'If I happen upon any rogue packs of cats, dogs, or wolves upstairs, I'll be sure to bring them down for your inspection.'

She left with a smile, one of banter between friends, of knowing. She had turned on her heels, the floorboards creaking beneath her in some cruel punctuation of intent. The jovial interaction was one-sided and I remained pained and exhausted in my chair, the arteries and muscles of my knees throbbing with each heavy pulse within me.

I sat a while longer. I stroked my throat and willed the crows to return to the garden.

I'd suffer anything; pigeons, starlings, even a gust of leaves would be welcomed with opened arms. But Duncain stayed silent. As mist began to roll across the northern hills, Duncain's iron gates dissipated into the haze, the flowerbeds following shortly thereafter. It was only when the haze engulfed the last of the lamp-posts that I realized my fingers were covered in blood.

Chapter 20

From below floors came the familiar juddering clunk of the great doors swinging shut with misplaced, unsuccessful gentleness. The metal latch hung loosely beneath the keyhole and rattled like a penny in a jar when the wind was strong enough. A storm some years before had dislodged the old iron keyhole cover from the front doors, sending it skittering across the gravel pathway. Since then, the cover had sat on the window ledge outside, waiting for attention it would never receive. With wind building, the latch took up its insane dance, tapping wildly against its cradle.

The echo of the door was followed by an irregular tap-tap of leather-soled boots. The layer of dry mud dust that gathered by the door was a consistently growing project. When the grime had dried and the sun was right, walking across the tiles kicked up brown plumes like hooves on a bridle path.

My mother, among her many new vestments, had acquired several pairs of laced leather boots that hugged her feet so tightly, her ankles seemed to spill over the top like broth on a rolling boil.

Father's absence continued to hang over the house like a heavy drape, filling the corners with a thick velvety grief that spread like a comfortable mould. The environment of the house hadn't changed at all; I had read stories of great, aching absences after a death. The noticeable absence of laughter and conversation; a physical pain, leaving one unable to heal.

Yet Duncain remained unmoved.

My mother had not so much integrated her mourning into her identity as climbed into its skin. She was no longer a Lady, nor a Crofton, but a widow. Her very breaths were decorated in black crape, her words carved from jet. Her garments were so opulent, so beautifully finished and decorated that she might as well have been carved from black gold for all it must have cost her.

This was not the mother I was accustomed to, and certainly not the mother who took to her bed at the merest excuse. She'd worn the same muddied, heavy skirts for years, the twist fraying with every week that passed. If she'd been a more active woman, more prone to perambulating, she'd have spent decades draped in rags. Mother's faded and muddied day dress was a source of constant embarrassment. The fine blue brocade had long been reduced to a murky grey, the bodice spotted with tattered black patches of lining, pushing out like boils. It seemed the foul day dress was consigned to a familiar, dwindling past. And I would have bet all my wealth on Elsie enduring the same dresses of my youth, had the house not turned itself, and its pockets, upside down since Father's departure.

From the upstairs landing, I could track my mother's path through sound alone. The reverberations from any footsteps jumped across the house like fleas, allowing anyone with a keen ear to track the movements of any unfortunate visitors to Duncain. The carpets had become approximations of their former selves, long pale threads snaking across the corridor, like vines waiting to wrap around some unfortunate soul's heel and pull them back towards the entrance.

Mother tap-tapped into the drawing room, her heel catching roughly against the door's metal threshold. The rugs were smattered in threadbare patches that fell like puddles above the tiling, each clunk signalling a misstep as fresh soles wore down further threads.

Each of Mother's movements was accompanied by a new unfamiliar symphony of rustling and 'shricks' of silk crape against doorframes. She ascended the staircase slowly, her bustle pad hanging awkwardly behind her like an anchor, as layers of fringe slowed her ascent even further. Mother was beginning to take on the appearance of some macabre occasion cake; each layer more elaborate and unnecessary than the last. Silks weren't cheap, especially in Duncain. The very fact that Mother had found someone competent and 'connected' enough to stock them seemed unimaginable. If it wasn't for the source of the funds being of concern to me, I'd consider myself impressed.

Mother stumbled into my room like a clumsy eclipse, the ruffles of her caplet catching the meagre glow of sunlight like crow's wings.

'I'm taking a walk into the town,' she declared.

'You've just been out. Do you have an obligation to parade your grief in front of more poor strangers?' I chimed, a little too unfriendly for any bolstering of our relationship.

I was cold, exhausted, and frustrated at my ever-lengthening stay within the walls. Mother had made no mention of legal counsel, and dodged any questions not to her liking with frustrating ease. It was her parade of squandered wealth that finally tore my frayed nerves.

In death, widows were supposed to withdraw from society, not discover it. Her cape, dresses, and beaded accoutrements were moulded into one almighty insult. A groaning mother in a sickbed was tiresome, but a spendthrift was infuriating. If my sleeplessness had not sapped most of my strength, I'd have risen to my feet and chastised her in far stronger words.

Yet I remained slumped in my reading chair, half-needing matchsticks to keep my eyes open.

'I'm going to the post office to collect a parcel sent by Mr Bexton. He'll be visiting me later, you see.'

I released the rest of my breath with an empty sigh.

'He's been most kind to this family,' continued Mother. 'I can't say you've been as helpful; I've had little comfort in my widowhood. You have certainly made no effort.'

I examined Mother the way a sergeant major pores over uniforms on parade. It was evident that she wasn't used to the great billowing sleeves of modern dress, let alone mourning ephemera. That was clear for all to see; her clothes were fast becoming a map of sorts. Tracks of dust and crumbs wound their way across the weave of the cuffs like greying veins, carrying a silent testimony to her snacking routine.

A widow's cap sat awkwardly atop her head; a mass of mesh and velvet that came to a peak on her forehead, giving the appearance of a huge beak. I remembered the picture-books I had cherished as a child, before they were torn to pieces in a rage born of 'almost-adulthood'. There were pictures of American natives and fearsome hunters who wore animal hides as capes, the splayed pelt of a wolf or bear worn like a hooded raincoat. My mother, however, was no hunter; seeming as though a jackdaw had come to nest and met an untimely end among her unkempt curls.

'Mr Bexton's going to need a lot of room tonight,' began Mrs Crofton, chattering with ill-fitting excitement, 'so I need you to get up and help Mrs Curry. Mr Bexton needs the table cleared, so make sure to polish it and ask Mrs Curry where the best tablecloths are kept. Mr Bexton might get thirsty too, so make sure to leave the best crystal on the drop-leaf.'

Her repetition surrounded me like a chant, sending me deeper into the realms of exhaustion. Her comments were dull and unrelenting, but with one hand, she continually fumbled the crinkling contents of a pouch bag, the diamond-shaped clasp opening and closing with the firm, continual click of a metronome. After noticing my eyes boring into her bag, she swiftly swung it behind her and began to fidget with the thick crape edging on her overskirt. She began to jabber excitedly. Something was awry.

'Mr Bexton says... No, Solomon. He keeps telling me to call him Solomon, but I feel so dreadful calling him so. After all, he's a gentleman, a professional. We're very lucky to have him, you understand? He told me he doesn't do this for everyone...' Her voice petered out weakly.

Modern grief was fickle and bore no loyalties. My father's absence seemed to concern my mother less and less. Indeed, the promise of a young visitor appeared to have a miraculous restorative effect upon her. If only I could have bottled such a power and sold it to the empire's grieving widows, we might finally have enough money to redress the rest of this awful house. By the current state of affairs, Mr Bexton would be retained, honoured and idolized like some bloated golden calf. He'd be moved in to freshly gilded quarters, we sisters reduced to bunking with Mrs Curry as my mother continued in her parade of mourning. At least, it seemed as such.

I certainly did not feel fortunate to have the arrival of the eponymous Mr Bexton hanging over Duncain. Now I knew he wasn't a local man, so whatever had drawn him was not of the cultural or social persuasion. He was well dressed, perhaps even educated; to some level at least. But his accent was impossible to place, a little like Algernon's.

Mother's voice chipped back in, piercing the air like rat squeals. 'He says our Elsie's got a gift; I knew it, all these years. I knew she was special. Your father didn't believe me, told me I was mad, but ha! He's wrong! Maybe Elsie can tell him herself! Imagine it! It's all true — our Elsie's a mag-magnet, you see. She attracts these —'

'Silk's a bold move on a woman of your size. There's little stretch when you sit.'

I wasn't aware where the cruel jibe originated from, but some part of me was tired of being riled. Each sleepless night, each day without progress, and each repeated statement of someone else's brilliance chipped away at my tolerance, like fingernails picking at my skin.

'I knew you'd be jealous. This house will welcome who I see fit, and I will not have you ruining my and Elsie's chances of —'

Mother's voice petered out, her eyes tracing patterns on the ceiling. I watched her a while, savouring the short window of silence.

'Mother?'

Nothing.

'Mother!'

Mother returned to look at me with a swift intake of breath. 'I should return in a few hours. Mr Bexton is expected at six. I trust you'll behave in a manner more becoming to someone of your station.'

She turned on her heels with unexpected speed, almost losing her balance in the process. I followed the quickened sounds of her footsteps as they pattered downstairs and across the corridor. I couldn't help but break a small smile when a sudden slip and thud indicated that my mother's new leather investments had little purchase on dining-room floors.

Chapter 21

Pacing upstairs, I found that my old bedroom regained its cruel familiarity in little time at all. The muddy wallpaper that had been a long and discomforting presence in my youth remained in a familiar state of perpetual decay; torn at the edges, peeling, ugly, refusing to move or change through damp or heat. The painted vines had yellowed and curled in the time between my stays at Duncain, but the pattern remained the same. The twists of each printed stem continually jack-knifed in faded interlocking swathes. The bedsheets lay as they always did; heavy and coarse, offensively grey and perpetually covered in a fresh layer of fibrous dust that constantly regrew in a cyclical insult.

My time in Duncain had not been dissimilar to that of my youth in most ways, although I was loath to admit it. The curving walls of my bedroom were like beech trees, hanging ever closer, hugging my shoulders as I paced. It was uncomfortable, claustrophobic at times, but it had always been territory outside of Mrs Curry's dominion and was cherished as such. The walls were shot with bare nails, aching for some long-forgotten frame. The rusted spike beside the door once held a print of Christ with children. It had been torn from a child's picture-book, one that I had never actually seen myself. Christ's eyes, rough black blobs against the crisp white of the paper, would follow me around the room, unblinking. Christ had indeed been everywhere, but no longer. The tell-tale bleached and mottled outline of sun-starved wallpaper hung beneath, an icon in itself.

The childhood Christ had spirited itself away. It was unlikely to have been repurposed in Elsie's room. In Duncain, each object's purpose was set. For a piece to exist for decorative purposes alone was an unfamiliar state.

I spent a moment tracing the outlines of former pictures. I rubbed my fingertips roughly against the brown stains that fanned out like scorch marks. The grime transferred to my fingers in a gritty film. The house was always surprising me in its new ways to rot.

A heavy metallic 'shrick' and muffled bang carried up from the rotten floorboards below. Thereafter came a busy burst of ringing clinks, like scuffling horseshoes atop stone. I approached the window to peer down, expecting some disgruntled visitor's pony to be straining against its reins. Instead stood an amorphous mass of black, the edges rippling in the wind. My breath caught in my throat, my sleepless, sticky eyes adjusting to the dull glinting of the phantom beside the great door.

As the mass turned back towards the door, I hunched closer to the sill, hiding my face behind the heavy drapes.

A fine curtain of rain began to drip from above, like some arcane theatre cue. With that, the mass twitched, turned upwards, and revealed the familiar bloated face of my mother.

Mother hadn't tarried at all, rather wasted time, adding layers of wool and gloss until she resembled some monolithic rain beetle.

She must have tried to drop the latch gently, unsuccessful in her attempt at secrecy. However, the frenzied clattering of taut shoes on gravel would have alerted the whole household regardless. As my mother scuttled down the path, she appeared to be making sure not to look back, as though she were running from Gomorrah and meeting my eyes would transform her into a pillar of salt. As she ran down the long gravel path to the gates, I feared sunblindness from the glare of Mother's jet beads in the afternoon's brightness.

As the last tremors of her shoes faded into the caws of gathering crows, the dust in my room began to gather again. If I focused, I swore I could feel it matting mid-air, falling in clumps all around me.

Time passed twice as slowly in Duncain. If I could, I'd burn through it like touchpaper. All that would be left would be to seal the accounts, protect my assets, and return to society and surfaces that didn't require a hurricane to sanitize.

The fibres of damp wood continued to catch against my slippers, their shards shattering the silk toes. They had been beautiful little boudoir slippers in a pale peach with floral beadwork and a tiny bow to the front. They had been immaculate, and quite the investment. They were everything I should have been — lithe, delicate, beloved. The house couldn't even let me keep the smallest vestige of my Chelsea life before tearing at its seams. Of course I was upset. At first, such wear was an irritant, but as the long days crept ever onwards, I entertained their need for contact. There would always be new slippers in London. I had to reassure myself of something. If only Algernon would respond to my letters, send a little money, then I could return home and rest my mind. Anxieties would be thrown to the wind and I could be a society lady, a proper lady. I could be dull, beautiful, and simplistic. No worries, no concerns, just a fleeting interest in dresses and tiny cakes with friends. Most importantly, I could rest. Dressmakers would know of the finest fashions and bring catalogues of slippers for all occasions. My feet would look like rich, polished, ivory beads against the new dresses I'd order upon my return.

I had been particularly weary over the last few days. My mind wandered for hours at a time, returning only when my aching body was sure it had entered some backstreet fist fight. I was sure to attribute it to tiredness. There were sicknesses caused by little sleep and little stimulation. I had heard rumours of women losing their minds through rest alone and I was sure not to become one of them, as much for Algernon's sake as for mine. With each day passing, the house grew in its animosity towards me, I was sure of it. My hands were perpetually tired from shaking, and I tried so desperately to keep hold of all the mental threads I could.

The faded decor seemed increasingly offensive, as though reacquainting oneself with a school bully. But all was the same in Duncain. The only changes came with the splintered floorboards that bore fresh stains and creaks with the dawn of each day; a welcome sign of time passing.

The atmosphere for Mr Solomon Bexton's arrival was not as I had anticipated. No storm clouds had gathered, nor had lamplights flickered and died at the mention of his name. Instead, the dining room was warm. Cosy, even. Through the windows filtered a pinkish mist that grew from the sunset, the soft hues blending together like paint-water.

Mrs Curry had cleared the table. The place settings and tarnished silverware now rested in organized peaks below the far windowsill, the handles catching the evening's light like a mountain range at dusk. Were it not for the presence of the housekeeper trotting between rooms, Duncain, at least looking out, could seem rather pleasant.

I rested downstairs for a while, sitting by the dining-room window and watching the light dance across the split inlay of the side tables. Mrs Curry continued to dash between rooms, never pausing to look at anything but her job in hand, her small legs almost comically out of proportion with her body. Eyes fixed firmly, she dragged the table closer to the centre of the room with a strength that had long eluded me. I watched as the old maid went about her duties for a while, her clockwork movements proving mesmeric in the half-light.

Mrs Curry re-entered the room quickly, paused, and walked to a small pile of linen laid flat across the dresser. She pushed one gnarled fingertip between the crisp folds in a deliberate performance to prove her efficiency.

'Tablecloth,' she muttered before turning and scuttling from the room.

The pink sky had faded in the moments between. The sky was grey, rotten, broken only by the occasional caws of bored crows. I lifted myself away from the wall, my hands sticky and cold against the plaster. As I moved, sliding chunks of plaster crumbled to the floor, coming to a slumped rest between the floorboards and wall like a drunk at closing time. The exposed lats stood stark against the plaster like a ribcage. When I was small, I had found a deer in the river behind the house. Its legs seemed impossibly thin and tangled, like a dried spider's. Something had wounded it; I couldn't tell which struck first — an animal or a gun. But there it lay, half-moored to the bottom of the jetty, its milky eyes bobbing up and down with the swell. Its ribs glistened a bright white like piano keys against its sodden fur. It was only when it began to float further up the bank that I ran home. I had forgotten about the deer, but the house seemed to remember.

Chapter 22

Early morning and my mother was in the parlour again. Silver clattered with tell-tale metallic inelegance against unseen hard surfaces. The best silver was stored upstairs, safe from her clutches. Despite Duncain's best efforts, life still afforded me occasional, meagre blessings.

Thankfully, Mother's destruction had failed to continue its dizzy ascent since the visitation of her Spiritualists. Her joyful melancholy proved to be a perpetual mild irritant, like children playing noisily above stairs. She had plateaued in her acquisition of new pastimes, yet busied herself all hours of the day with handicrafts and samples for memorial arts to which she was loath to commit. When wandering one sleepless night, I had found that my mother had lacquered my father's card table with thick ridges of gum arabic in her efforts at palette hair work. I had grown to expect chaos from Mother; and, had I little concern for Algernon's belief in my ability to claim my inheritance, I might have begun guessing games as to my mother's daily methods of destruction. The same evening, Mother attempted draping lampshades with a thick crape that filled the house with the smell of burning hair.

I was unable to spy her from my vantage point. From the level of noise, she could be equally enraged, excited, or comatose. Ferocity and noise levels were the only accepted constant within her recent behaviour. Had I slept at all, I would have berated her clumsiness. Tiredness had begun to suit me, bringing new confidence in my exhaustion. There was a certain freedom in speaking out of turn, in no longer filtering my words through kindness and consideration. It changed little of my environment, and certainly didn't rouse Elsie from her chambers, or ease my frustration at not seeing her, but lit a small fire that warmed me through the cold evenings.

My morning routine provided some semblance of comfort in the dragging early hours. As always, I rolled my stockings to my knees, which sat like purpled balls against my bruised and mottled skin. One pair, then another, making sure the embroidery was in line behind my ankles. My swaddled feet still fitted into my house slippers, but judging by their swelling and soreness, such a privilege was not to last much longer. They were beautiful stockings of French silk; pale blue shot with gold. In the light of Duncain, they shimmered a muddied blue, but I knew of their beauty. As I motioned to stand, weighting myself on my tired limbs, even the little heels provided me with a steady ache, where they had once brought me pleasure.

Beneath me, Mother's shuffling had paused in a strained silence. My muscles tensed to their utmost peak as I waited for Mother to signal a return to normality. Mother was forever muttering. She muffled her speech in bile, releasing slithering insults under her breath. She was fond of conducting muttered speeches between courses at dinner. By the time she was presented with her sweet, she had often conducted an entire conversation with herself in crumb-filled grumbles.

I had questioned her on it once, asking her, 'If you are so keen to talk so often, let us hear so that we may at least turn it into a dialogue.'

She responded with a further string of nonsensical murmuring.

'Child!' she snapped, gripping her fork aloft like a trident. 'You have no comprehension of adulthood. I am wrestling with the very fibres of...'

She stirred the air with her utensil, as though the right stroke would tear intellect from the ether and fall into her lap.

'God! The Heavens!'

The air in the room paused as my father and I had. The silence rotted and swelled. Mother eventually relented, and returned the fork to the slivers of grouse before her. Father, who had been reading his paper, pulled it taut, peering wordlessly over his crescent glasses.

'You never speak of God,' I grumbled, in a tone not dissimilar to my mother's.

The boldness of youth, Father had called it in less than complimentary terms. Yet the truth stood. My mother spoke more of the irritations of the yard hens than of our souls' well-being. My mother didn't respond, but tapped her fork against the rim of the plate with dull clinks.

'We don't go to church,' my childish self continued, bolder than before.

I had received no response. My father continued as he did, reading a broadsheet so large, the pages could be used as baby blankets.

'Is that a pastry fork, Mother?' I goaded.

Like a crop to a horse's rear, my mother became suddenly rigid. Father didn't so much as blink in response. His listed mouth rested in a clenched tight line, his eyes unflinching from his paper.

'Child, that's quite enough,' Mother hissed.

As though a puppeteer had pulled her strings taut, Mother had thumped the table with a clenched fist, while, with the other hand, deftly concealing the small fork within her napkin.

'No one speaks of God here. Not unless Father's business associates pass by,' I goaded.

'Child!' barked my mother, her hand pressed hard, fanning across her napkin concealment.

My mother's mind appeared unable to function without accompaniment, choosing the word 'child' in repeated, hushed tones until her brain agreed to function.

I had become accustomed to such an address from a young age. I had often believed that Mother had consciously foregone the arduous task of memorizing my birth name, as she chose to address both of her daughters and the hunter's dogs similarly, by their species. Still, she persisted, her garbled chanting syncopating with the heavy rain. 'Child', a thud on the sill, 'child', a crack on the pane. The dining table had cultivated its own meagre percussion.

Mother was not so much a conductor as an ignorant participant, and Father? Father was another matter.

Father never noticed such little things as the sound of rain. Nor did he pay heed to the wider wants of his wife and daughters. He responded to affairs of money and land; everything else was a disposable 'frippery'. The mesmeric thudding of Mother and the rainclouds ended abruptly with a short outburst from between my mother's sticky, stringy lips.

'To — to the yard with you!' she yelped.

Her eyes bulged, in some deliberate attempt at menace. To my childish gaze, she appeared strained, filled with the internal menace that only horseradish or overeating can provide. I had thought to respond, but my bafflement sat more comfortably in silence.

Mother made a noise somewhere between a cough and a whimper. She was like a hare trapped in a snare, the wire tightening with each strained movement.

'To the yard — If you act like a dog, then you shall join them,' she spluttered, her face flushed in anger.

Mother's eyes shot to the window pane, confirming to herself that yes, indeed, the house was in possession of a yard.

In her fury, words spluttered from her mouth, half-formed. 'Your indolent-insolen — insolation must be punished!'

With each touch of her lips, the strings of spittle thickened, increasing like spider's webs, filling the void between her brain and jaw. Her words floated by as of little consequence. My mind remained primed on the spun slop between her lips. My father, however, had begun to rub his forehead, as he so often did when his wife spoke with parental demands.

'Mrs Curry!' Mrs Crofton wailed, piercing the air with her needling shriek.

Father was pinching the bridge of his nose, stemming an imagined nosebleed. His shoulders were rounded like a boulder, while his beard jutted forwards, cascading over his shirt buttons in tangled grey wisps. From the right angle, I could see him as a rotund wading bird with a great curved beak. From others, the extreme angle looked like a scaffold. The images lonely children create to entertain themselves continued to baffle me long into my adult recollections.

Father had cleared his throat with a rasping hack. His stirrings were always preceded by an announcement of sorts. He moved by not so much springing into life as groaning into existence. He swallowed hard, his throat irritant returning to its settlement. His Adam's apple juddered up and down like a ladder toy, as though rhythmically gaining its own sentience. He laid his broadsheet flat, one overlong fingernail marking his position in the report. He grew his index nail long, but never told me why. Even then, I knew enough of manners to know it would be untoward to ask.

'The child will stay in its room,' he began, with a drawl. 'I'll not have the groundsmen interrupted by such idiocies.'

My mother pressed her arms into each other, her head turned to the wall. If there had been anything hanging there, she could have been inconspicuous in her aggravation. However, all there was to examine was some water-stained cornicing and a beheaded porcelain cherub, whose fate was dealt at the hands of maternal tantrums past.

'Besides, it appears to be raining. Her slippers will tear up the lawn. I, for one, will certainly not be paying to have it relaid,' muttered Father.

Responding to Mother's wails, footsteps tracked to the dining room, waiting for commands in rehearsed silence. Mrs

Curry stood in the doorway, her eyes purposefully flitting to the long-handled service bell that my mother was determined to ignore. Before Mother had chance to vocalize the demands her outstretched arm was poised to convey, the tapping of Mrs Curry's house shoes commanded the room's attention. Father folded his broadsheet with unnecessary precision, sealing the fold in the sheet with a spit-slicked fingertip, having completed another hour of failed eye contact. He chose to eat his meal later in the day, in the dark nest of his study. As always. I had long envied my father's cold authority; his tiny acts of oppression. In Chelsea, I would have sooner cried than disturb an unused napkin and longed for the day my mind would develop as his. As a woman, it was never to come, but in tiredness, I regained a little hope.

As he rose, Father's eyes passed mine, not stopping to focus. As a child, I was to him as great an inconvenience as the rats that made their home in the coal shed. As I sat as a lone child, before Elsie's arrival, I was categorically informed that there were too many girls.

Mother waited for him to pass by the threshold before exhaling her contrived irritancy.

'Well!' she gasped.

The rain had worsened, becoming sheets of water that near rattled the glass from its frame. Elsie had not yet been born, and my rudimentary toys had held little interest. For several formative years, my mother was a toy; a spinning top of disinterest.

'Are we really followers of Christ, Mother? I have seen Mrs Curry using the Family Bible to reach to top shelves in the kitchen,' I goaded, angling for a little more excitement in the day.

Mother dragged the side of her fork against the china; a pig squeal emanating from the last flecks of decimated grouse. Her lips were so tightly pursed that they turned white. To me, they were tiresome and a red rag for further probing.

'Mother —' I chirped, in a sing-song affectation. 'There is no Protestant church in Duncain, so are we Ca —?'

My childish jibes lit my mother's fuse with immediate ferocity and she exploded in a mass of spit, sauce, and patched linen.

'Well we shall build one!' Mother bellowed, eyes fixed forwards.

My mother's hands were shaking, her chubby fingers leaving patchy sweat marks on the tablecloth.

'Father won't —' I began, eager to continue our bizarre dialogue.

'Mrs Curry!' my mother commanded, eyes still fixed in the middle distance.

Mrs Curry was at the door. Her expression fixed with a perpetual, practised mix of resignation and annoyance.

'Yes, Madam,' groaned the housekeeper with worn anticipation.

Mother replied with all the concern of a diner requesting to be passed the salt. 'See to it that a chapel is built within the grounds.'

Mrs Curry paused at the door, thick eyebrows raised like hedgerows, awaiting details that my mother had yet to contemplate.

'Well, well, go about it,' my mother muttered, her hands ushering the housekeeper away.

'Of course, Madam,' replied Mrs Curry, curtseying and smoothing her apron to leave. Her readjustments sent a waft of old naphthalene across the table. The taste stuck to my tongue, a coarseness I could conjure long into adulthood. My appetite, although meagre at the beginning of the meal, was truly quashed. Mrs Curry turned and left, her chatelaine swinging like a miniature guillotine.

'Mrs Curry!' Mother bellowed, spittle dappling the table linen in a sprawling crescent.

Mother's back was arched like a hawk poised to strike; her eyes — which now were firmly affixed to the old housekeeper — flickered with visible intensity.

The two women locked eyes as my mother prepared to speak.

'What have you prepared for sweet?'

'Blancmange,' responded Mrs Curry, barely missing a beat.

'Ooh, delightful,' giggled Mrs Crofton. She tugged at her cuffs, exposing the swell of eager wrists.

She shuffled back in her chair, clapping her palms together in quick bursts. Grabbing her napkin, the offending cake fork was sent scuttling across the floorboards, but my mother's hearing was otherwise engaged. She had grasped her soup spoon like a huntsman's axe and waited for the old maid's return.

Chapter 23

My mother's church, a folly built precariously at the top of the jetty, lasted a summer before the back wall collapsed, sending her devotion crumbling into the lough.

I could just about see the crumbling carcass of the folly from the upper window. The windowsill itself was scattered with ugly clutter and a thick wedge of dust that inched and listed in the breeze. My time in the house had not been long at all, but I missed my beautiful things terribly. I missed the smell of polish and yearned for the pungent tang of freshly polished silverware; the sound of beaten carpets; the shine of heavily waxed furniture whose patina glinted in the window's morning sunlight. In Duncain, a long-dead fern slumped in its pot, blotting the sun's menial warmth with its crisp fronds.

I hadn't thought about the chapel for years. It had been a ruin for so long, it was barely noticeable in the craggy landscape of the grounds. Duncain House was the largest in the county by far; at least, the only one of note. In any rational society with predictable criminality, it would have groundsmen chasing away poachers with a blast of a shotgun. Here in Duncain, the house attracted little interest. No interest, to be precise. I could not recall trespassers of any kind; even to inquisitive children, Duncain House held little interest. Jealousy and the straying hands of local children had made light work of any structure in my youth, loose or anchored down. I had watched men pull apart their own father's outhouses to construct their own. The boggy earth was an ideal assistant, clinging on to little placed upon its surface. But the folly still stood, a skeletal knot of my mother's imagined faith.

My mother stifled a sneeze below stairs. It sounded wet.

If I strained my hearing and closed my eyes, I could hear the whispers of the lough. Its swell rolled with a tidal intent, as though the waves were searching the pebbled shore. For ten years, its green tongues had lapped the back wall of the crippled chapel. Yet the lake never seemed committed to reclaiming the stone; the water stretched and swallowed, but always returned its rocks. She was an old woman spitting the stones out of damsons, slopping froth where it was unwelcome.

My mother sneezed again. Unstifled.

Clouds smothered the sun in time for my mother's variation in route. To watch her had become somewhat of a novelty, as though she were a toy train free from its rails. But she continued, circling, mumbling, hauling clattering hulks of detritus between rooms. Her lips moved with the ferocity of a flag in high wind, but she could not distinguish a clear word. Sound travelled by its own laws in Duncain, yet the conversations one wished to hear were the ones the walls kept for themselves.

I crept further down the stairs, my slippers tight on my layered stockings, yet blissfully silent in movement. Mother continued her dizzy ritual, her excessive petticoats leaving Mrs Curry's efforts at sweeping the entrance hall utterly obsolete.

I waited a moment as she reached the final turn in the staircase. My mother's pace had changed, the clinking of crockery and tin diminished into wheezing silence.

I peered around the corner, another desiccated fern frond obscuring my vision. My mother slid herself from the parlour, her back pressed flush to the wall, her skirts making a louder noise than ever. She moved slowly, switching her head from side to side like a pantomime villain. She moved to the small cupboard beside the entrance, turning the brass knob with exaggerated delicacy. She held her face close to the handle as though it might impart some arcane wisdom. Rather, her bones cracked as she moved downwards in an unsettling nod to her age. She leaned into the cupboard's depths, her efforts at muffled rustling awakening every sleeping soul within the county. She backed out from the doorway, her voluminous skirts peeking out and retracting, like Jonah escaping the mouth of the whale. Mother slammed the door, clutching a paper-wrapped parcel close to her chest. With both hands adhered to the packaging, she ran to the parlour in a clatter of taffeta and wheezing.

I hadn't noticed the cold affect me; I had felt little of temperature in recent days. My swollen knees had locked solid. Feeling them through my dress, they were very cold, unfeeling, colder than the house itself. My arms and hands were waxy, as though I were to become a devotional effigy of myself. I returned to my room for a thicker robe and descended the stairs, as quietly as my tightly bound feet would allow, wincing with each step, and slipped into the parlour. Secrecy proved as infuriating as it was compelling.

'Good morning, Mother!' I chirped, with frozen effort, timed with a shriek of feigned enthusiasm.

Mother's hands shot from the drawer. She jutted her hip to one side, slamming it across like a pendulum. The cracking of her hip against the brass handles of the bureau slammed the door shut with a solid bang. In so deftly concealing the overfilled drawer, the drawer itself was surely embedded in the wall plaster behind it.

Mother turned her face to meet mine. We were separated by a gulf. Between us, a tangle of furniture. Yet, through the distance, I could feel my mother's cheeks burn a throbbing crimson.

'Yes?' asked Mother, her head tilted in mock relaxation.

My mother had forgotten how to stand, and slumped awkwardly against the desktop.

'I was tidying... checking the quality of Mrs Curry's work,' she stumbled.

To justify her yelping, Mother dragged an elongated finger against the moulding beside the desk. She raised it close to her head, the tip covered in a wet sludge of dust, coal ash and unbuffed wax. She and I stared at one another, furrowed brow to furrowed brow.

Mother nodded her head, 'Well.'

I watched her, and her finger, in curious silence. After weighing my options, my mother briefly tucked the offending finger beneath her bodice trim.

'Good morning,' she quipped after an achingly long pause.

A thud rattled the wall from the dining room beside us. My mother's eyes widened, her mouth tensed to a fine line. The entertainment value gained from my adventures in concealment had long run dry. Another muffled bang came fast.

'I wasn't aware we are hosting unattended guests. Or workmen, for that matter,' I said, sucking at my teeth.

As I turned to leave the room, my mother was upon me. Her widow's hand circled my wrist, the fingertip smear of gunk tracing my flesh like an unwashed bracelet. She held her face close to mine, grey twists of hair shaking above her head like a storm cloud.

'Nonsense, child. It was most probably dear Mrs Curry preparing the room for the evening,' said Mother, her speech stilted and delivered with a fine smile.

Again, a muffled bang, a clatter, and a culmination in the winced exhalations of a child.

'Where is Elsie, Mother?' I pressed.

'Oh, I see. Concern for your sister at last?' Mother said, inciting my old propensity for teasing.

Mother stood poised with pursed lips, as though she had crafted a most troubling insult.

I made a gesture to leave once more, but my mother scuttled towards the window seat. She moved with such fearsome intent that her bustle, which protruded from her lower back like an occasional table, came close to removing the few displayed ceramics that had survived her previous outpourings.

'Tea! We must have tea! Yes. Elsie is well. Otherwise engaged. Sit!' Mother shrieked.

With a practised flourish, my mother removed the huge white cloth that had draped like a pyramid atop the window table. Mother's cake stand was a culinary Tower of Babel. Rock cakes sat piled high, like boulders prepped to fall, crushing unsuspecting visitors. Below it lay shrivelled sandwiches hewn from Duncain rock.

'The sandwiches are filled with provisions from the gardens,' she chirped with discomforting cheer.

I cast an eye over the illusive gardens, as Mother tilted her head towards the window. Thick reeds blotted out the view of the lake behind. They allowed a hazy light that flickered as branches arched in the breeze. There were no provisions within the grounds, merely reeds, long grasses, and mosses that grew their own cultures on the garden walls.

I sat at the gestured chair. I would have uttered my discomfort at its overstuffed pad, but the sudden severity of the aches prevented me. Fresh bruises bloomed on my skin at the gentlest touch, leaving my thighs painfully tender, aching with each gentle movement. In retaliation, I pushed my fingertips into the crunching seat. It was too hard and, with such sunfading, would fetch little at auction. It would burn well.

Chapter 24

30th October 1877

Dear Diary,

I have never known such exhaustion. As I write here, in the afternoon light, my arms ache with leaden weight. Heavy purple bruises have tried to grow around my forearm like gaudy bangles. I have tried to strangle their growth by sporting tight lace sleeves that I also hope to warm me. I heard once that pressure may reduce swelling, and hope it to be true. However, judging by the tenderness of the flesh beneath, I find myself to be waning in optimism.

Algernon has still not written and I am terrified of every moment within these walls.

The nights are cold and unrelenting. To think I ascribed my fitful sleep to a change in linen, then to a change in air. My state is deliberate. I do not know how or why, but something is happening to me.

My stomach rejects my body almost daily, and I am sure it wants to leave this place as much as I. In these sleepless twilight hours, my mind swims with images of little beetles nipping at my fingertips, boring through my nails, gorging themselves down to the bone as I sleep.

My dreams have been fitful and linger uncomfortably afterwards. My body is too weak, too blanketed in aches, pains, and swollen joints to forget them. I am so terrified Algernon will not accept me. I have shrunk so unattractively, so suddenly, and I can't be sure how. My bones are too big for my body, I am grey, and walk with less grace than Mrs Curry. I am sure that London sun would help, but each day brings no news.

Alice x

* * *

I went to bed as usual. The house possessed few working clocks to establish a routine, yet the crows had ceased their cawing and the outer reaches of the garden were fast dissolving into darkness. I drew myself below the covers, taking pains to pin my nightshirt closely to my ankles. I had taken to counting knots in the wardrobe, tight black balls that seemed to scatter like fat little spiders. I never noticed how much I relied on the lives of others to punctuate my day, but Duncain's emptiness has brought it to the fore.

Sleep was sudden, sharp and hard, like slipping into an ice bath. I lingered in darkness a while, in some kind of hazy half-sleep. When I woke, it was as though dawn was gently rousing me. But when my eyes adjusted, my room was not my own. The furniture lay where it did before, but it was different, as though each had been replaced by a charred approximation of itself. The wallpaper moved in seasick swirls, twisting and contorting in ever-descending spirals. I tried to touch the wall, but the house was crumbling and reassembling itself in deft circles around me. My stomach lurched and I was sure I would be violently ill, yet I found I could not move.

The footsteps that plagued my waking hours began again, but they were somewhat lighter, like a child's. They began at the corridor beside my bedchamber and continued circling on the landing. I was sure it wasn't Mother or Elsie, rather spurned country-folk or debtors to my father, come to frighten women for spiteful entertainment. More footsteps joined and soon there were thunderous clatters across all the upper floors. They continued building in ferocity until I was sure the whole house would awaken.

'Hello! There — there are guards, there are men here! Leave!' I weakly shrieked.

They stopped as swiftly as they began. At once, my body sank against the sheets, every muscle aching from exertion. There was no one. No interlopers, no children, nothing. It was a figment of my imagination. A cruel trick of the mind. For a blissful period, there were no footsteps nor untoward movements to unnerve or distract me from my own exhaustion. I believe I slept a little, although I cannot be sure if that was imagined too. When I half-woke for the last time, it was from an unfamiliar hand. My forearms were encircled by many tiny cold bands, pressing with unfamiliar strength, painfully stinging my skin.

I found my eyes failing me as I searched for the faces of my captors. I strained to focus; the candle had somehow made its way to the windowsill, casting the room in a flickering half-light. Beside me stood three small figures on each side. They were smaller in stature than little Elsie, but stood with long, outstretched, sinewy arms and skin so dark it blotted out the shadows. I tried to release myself from their grasp, but with each pull of my arms, their fingers sank deeper with such gentle violence, until I was sure they were removing my arms at the bone. I screamed with such fervour that I could feel my lungs fill with the bitter tang of blood, but no sound emerged.

The creatures that surrounded me in the cruel guise of children had faces that were not their own. In the space where expression should lie grew an ever-changing mass that twisted and knotted in endless threads. Their eyeless faces were all turned towards me, expectantly awaiting some reaction I could not satisfy.

I tried to scream, partially in pain, but mainly through primal desperation.

'Father!' I screamed, my throat burning. 'Father, please!' No one came.

I closed my eyes. It was a dream, it wasn't real. It was my mind. Dear God, it had to be my mind. Instead, I made the situation worse. When I reopened my eyes, the children were gone, leaving no sign of their visitation. I struggled, but their hands remained without them, silently holding me against my bedframe.

'Oh sweet Jesus,' I wept, desperation overtaking my body.

I hadn't thought to look up; my eyes were too focused on the aching bands that continued to circle my arms. I strained a while, but became entranced by the rhythmic thudding of the clock. The chronometer kept its time with tell-tale inelegance. It was always too grand for Duncain. The case, lacquered black, stretched up to the ceiling, casting a shadow greater than the tree from which it was sawn. Between its familiarity came another pulse, a softer tapping I could not place. The knocks were slower than that of the long case in the corridor; the beats became syncopated, tripping over one another. I looked to the doorway to find the cold candlelight of the corridor blocked by an enormous shape.

'Mrs Curry?' I whispered. 'Oh thank the Lord, please, light the room.'

There was no response from the figure. Instead it grew, stretching to the ceiling in silent threat.

It took my mind a moment to recognize features, until I noticed the horror of certain familiarity. In the doorway hung the heavy, wearied figure of a man, his leather shoes swinging against the doorframe, out of time with the house.

With it came the too-familiar stench of black tobacco and the hacking cough of a snuff-taker. The shoes that tapped against the frame were not only my father's, but moved several inches above the floor. He stared at me with the twisted face of the children that preceded him. His eyes, masses of black twists that I couldn't bear to meet with my own.

Great clods of earth fell from his clothing, rolling to the floor in wet cascades. His suit was the last that I had seen him wear, but stained in wide puddles of discolouration, his old sack coat brushing his knees. His waistcoat seemed to slowly tighten, as though he were bloating before my eyes. All the while, his sagging body gently swung in time with the heavy ticking of the chronometer.

I tried to speak, but all that came from my dry mouth was a croaked 'Father?'

Eventually, behind his legs, a smaller figure grew from the shadows. Step by step, a small white shape came forward, as though compelled by the moonlight that illuminated it. The crisp paleness that sheltered beneath Father's hanging form raised my terror to fever pitch as I recognized the guipure lace circling the hem of the nightdress. Elsie stood behind him. I knew it was her.

Her room must have been left unlocked and she had been disturbed by my shouting. The sight of Father would kill her with fear. She had to leave. I had to save her.

Yet as Elsie approached the doorway, she showed no wavering. Her tiny hands clasped around Father's knees as she used to when Father was alive.

She stepped from behind his legs, her bare feet sticking to the floorboards' mildewed sheen.

'Father's here to help me. Solomon sent him,' she whispered, a smile twisting at the corners of her mouth.

Panicked, I knew of little else to do than beckon her away from him. Although I had no strength to move, I could speak, but she ignored my words as though they had never been spoken.

'Elsie, come here,' I said, my voice faltering.

She stood beside the hanging body, his shoes tapping gently against her nightdress. I repeated myself, louder this time.

'Elsie, come.'

Father's body continued its arc. As it swung, his shoes brushed Elsie's nightdress. At first, the contact left only a small brown scuff. As she remained where she stood, the scuff grew, the shoes grinding layer of dirt on layer of dirt. The circle of filth grew with each swing of his shoes. The stain grew quickly, spreading through the threads like water, or blood.

I forced my voice harder. 'Please.'

My eyes were stinging. She was in such danger, but seemed clueless as to all that surrounded her. Her nightdress had become sodden, thick with a reddish-brown slime that pooled on the floor, staining her toes.

'My friends are coming back soon,' began Elsie. 'So you'd better be quiet.'

Elsie's arms were folded, her lips pursed in petulant cruelty. Father groaned. I hadn't looked at him since Elsie's arrival. He had grown bloated, his skin was painted like a riverbank; mottled in browns and greens that seemed to slip from his frame.

'If they know you're here, they'll come for you. They don't like you,' sneered Elsie.

I knew Elsie was still staring at me, but I couldn't tear my gaze away. Father was rotting before me, black pockmarks spreading to holes as big as ink blots across his hands and neck.

'They know you're jealous,' shouted Elsie, her hot breath close and hard against my cheek.

She was beside my bed. She was *wrong*. A trail of viscous brown slime stretched behind her. She pressed her face close to mine, her breath reeking of moulding fruit and dirt.

Her lips touched my ear, cold and wet.

'They know your mind has gone,' she spat, baring tiny pin-like teeth.

Elsie bent back to her position beside my bed, grinning through her yellowed smile. Father was silent, but for the steady drip-drip of murky fluid hitting the floor. As I returned my gaze to Elsie, she had stopped smiling. Her face was turned to mine, seeing and not seeing at once. She stood, waiting in ringing silence, before emitting a scream so loud, I was sure she would wake the masses of heaven and hell. Her eyes bulged, her lips peeled tightly back to the gums. The foetid reek poisoned the air around me like a noxious cloud.

At once, her head snapped backwards, her screaming replaced with horrid rattling. With one hacking wheeze, a white fibrous knot protruded from her mouth. It slowly grew, folding forward like a warped, pale tongue. Wet gurgles emanated from her throat, bubbling up between her teeth. The mass grew still, slithering across her cheek, hanging across her throat; a great snake erupting in hot white froth.

Her body was rigid, but the twisting creation continued to grow. It spread outwards, unobstructed by weight, bridging the gap between Elsie and my mattress like a sodden swag. It rested across my hand, soaking my paralysed wrists with chilled smears. It continued its route, rearing, inching closer to my head until I could see the fraying fibrous nature of its innards.

Elsie remained at the side of my bed, my gaze switching between my child sister and the plasmic wretch of her own creation. She returned to look at me, her masticating jaw thick with dripping spittle and bile.

She bared her teeth once more. Stifled giggles emanated from the corridor, at which her serpentine expulsion fell across my face in a sodden curtain.

I woke with the ache of the springs against by back. The thick sheen of my own sweat was stinging my eyes, while my bedsheets lay knotted at my feet.

I am so scared. I am scared of the children, and scared of my silence. In truth, I am scared of Elsie. No one can know. Algernon would not suffer the shame of sending me to a doctor's, and I daren't linger long on the alternative, in fear of inciting such a thing. I am unsure why I'm entrusting these horrid things within these pages, but I have to write. If no one else can, I must know it was real.

Chapter 25

Séance

I succeeded in four hours of bedrest before the noises from beneath my bedroom woke me. It was some small relief that it was chatter, rather than strange nocturnal happenings, that dragged me from my sleep. After dressing, examining the same sodden lawns from my window, my mind returned to my travel bag. I had never finished the last of Elsie's letters. They no longer felt like a sweet reminder of home. But not knowing their contents frightened me with each passing day. She may have been frightened, pleaded with me to bring her to London. And I had abandoned her. She may have warned me. Or told me of Father's health.

The possibilities sickened me.

Retrieving the final letters was an unpleasant task; the damp of Duncain had seeped into the bag and the envelopes sat wet and flush against the leather. Peeling back the musty seals, I wiggled out the papers and read where I stood.

Dear Alice,

I saw Father on the landing last night. I shouted through the lock, but he didn't say anything. When I woke up, he was lying flat on the floor and I think he had been there all night. I thought he was dead, but no one heard me shout, so I waited and watched him so he wasn't alone. Mother came eventually, and ran back to her room screaming again. I don't think she checked to see if he was breathing, but everything was well. Mrs Curry looked after him. She cleaned him up and removed the strange white sick from his face. Mrs Curry looks after us. She cares for us, Alice, all of us.

You should bring her presents too.

Elsie x

'Lord have mercy,' I muttered.

Elsie had watched our father die and barely considered it. It was little wonder that her character seemed to have changed of late. But the sick. Something was wrong with all this talk of white vomit. It plagued my dreams, and seemed to plague hers too.

Alice,

The undertakers took Father away today. When Mrs Curry walked me to the jetty for air, his office door was open. It was such a mess and not like him at all. His mind had left him. You must know that, Sissy. We both must remember that.

You must come home now. Mrs Curry won't like it if you don't.

E x

The last envelope was saturated and nearly fell apart in my hand. The lip of the envelope tore away in my fingers, falling to the floor like confetti. The letter sank into the rolls of my palm like pastry. Browning, filthy.

Alice,

If you get this letter in time, run. It is not safe here. You must not come to Duncain. I am taking a huge risk writing this and fear the consequences if I am caught. The children are Father's visitors and they never left.

Please don't think me silly, but I think they killed him. Mrs Curry said they don't want to hurt me and that I'm special, but she's lying to make me feel better. She doesn't want me to write to you any longer. Please don't come. Something very bad is happening here. The visitors came back and they took lots of Father's things away. They said the house is theirs.

Elsie xx

I flipped over the paper, searching, hoping, for some sardonic 'P.S.', some sign of a childish jape, but as the letter turned, it tore. Ripping into strange shapes through fault lines in the paper, the writing smeared, illegible and mangled. Sticking to my fingers like bandages, I flicked the remnants onto the windowsill, feeling the filth of the mouldy paper burrowing beneath my fingernails. I had to get Elsie out. She would not be in a house where her mind was filled with such corruptive nonsense. She would come to London to be a proper lady, and be free of Duncain.

I stood by my washstand a while, scrubbing at my hands with a fat bar of soap taken from the kitchen. Only when my hands throbbed red did I put down the coarse brush and think of leaving the room. Father had been ill, nothing more. Elsie was scared. That was all. I repeated the statements in my head, but they failed to take root, slipping out as the familiar sickness of fear rose within me.

Reaching the door, I heard chatter beneath the floors, with Elsie's voice dancing above the others like birdsong. Beneath it, rumbling with a baritone smoothness, was Solomon. Of course the Spiritualists were there. I imagined them creeping through the door at the crack of dawn, making strange little nests in the dining room like spiders. To leave them unmonitored was to invite an infestation.

Quickly descending the stairs, I was met at the threshold of the dining room by a very disinterested Mrs Curry. Leaning on the frame, she idly cleaned a candlestick on her apron, as though the strange meeting behind her was but another regular feature of her cleaning routine.

'Ah, we thought you might join us,' cheered Solomon.

'Hmm,' murmured Mrs Curry in agreement, roughly shoving the candlestick onto the nearest surface.

I could do little but stand by, wordless and slack-jawed as the Spiritualists continued their chatter with Elsie. Meanwhile, I remained by the door, dismissed as another piece of ill-fitting furniture. After sharing some words with Solomon, Mrs Curry turned slightly and gestured at an old chair.

'There's a seat, Alice dear. You look tired,' mumbled the housekeeper, pointing at a stool.

'I beg your pardon?' I replied breathlessly. I couldn't move for the ache in my legs, but remained by the parlour entrance way, the ringing in my ears churning my stomach.

'Your chair's there, dear,' repeated Mrs Curry, jabbing at the air with a spiked finger.

'There.'

Mrs Curry smiled and sighed in exasperation, throwing up her hands as if to say 'These girls!' before returning her interest to Solomon and Elsie. The chair of which she spoke was an old dining chair, sun-bleached and unsteady, clearly dragged from some shadowed corner of the upper rooms.

'Elsie, come on!' commanded Solomon, although she was hidden from sight.

She emerged slowly. Elsie was dressed smartly, but far older than her years, and far simpler than she deserved. She tottered into the light wearing a white blouse, long skirt and strange little brown boots, the likes of which I had never seen before.

I was so taken with confusion at Elsie's dress that I had not thought to take in the carnage of the room. Beside the fireplace, where a gallery table once stood, was a large frame, about the height of a bookshelf, but looking far more like an enormous cabinet. In the place of doors hung a huge wool curtain from the pole above, creating a closed, private room.

Craning my neck into the open structure, I could see that inside lay only a stool, a child's tambourine, and a length of rope. I couldn't hide my bafflement at the strange contraption and promised myself that my eyes would remain trained on the rope, just in case anything untoward was planned. From what I had seen of their works, Solomon's hands-on approach knew no proper boundaries.

Mrs Curry caught my eyes and strolled to meet me, leering over me.

'Hello, dear. I do believe you said that you were acquainted with fashionable Spiritualist practice?' she smiled.

She looked me up and down, like a tailor sizing a client.

'You're looking a little thin. Are you sure you wouldn't like to take a stroll of the grounds?' she crooned in concern.

I was sure the housekeeper knew I would not leave such a strange farce unmonitored and I responded to her wittering with stony silence, settling my eyes on hers. Fixed in a staring stand-off, Mrs Curry finally broke and scuttled about the room, humming an off-key tune, closing curtains, and lighting two small candles. By the time she finished, I could barely see my hand in front of my face, but the candles provided enough illumination to see Elsie walking into the strange cabinet. Solomon took Elsie's hand, at which I sucked against my teeth. The impropriety of the man knew no bounds. The familiarity was followed by Mrs Curry, who tottered behind, leaning into the cabinet as Elsie sat in her odd, ill-fitting clothes. Pulling lengths of rope from the cabinet, it was clear that Elsie was trussed. I would have stood and commanded them to leave, were it not for Elsie's gentle laughter and my own shameful curiosity. Like any mirth in Duncain, it was quashed almost instantly by Mrs Curry's hissed commands for silence.

After a short time of tightened knots and rattled chair legs, they both professed Elsie to be 'secure' and drew the curtain on the child. Solomon pulled up a seat beside Mrs Curry and addressed the empty room with mock reverence.

'She has entered the cabinet,' he stated, addressing no one.

We sat in strained silence for a while, the air sporadically broken by Solomon's repetitive commands of 'Spirits, come to us... Spirits, we are gathered to receive your wisdom.'

The latter statement tickled me. I sat with a poorly hidden smile, hardening my convictions that indeed there was no wisdom to be found within Duncain's walls. Twenty minutes must have passed before a gentle rattling of the tambourine could be heard. It paused, before cyclically jingling, louder and softer, before pausing and starting again.

Considering that Elsie was bound, it was an unusual feat, but I sat with no fear in my heart.

'They are with us,' whispered Solomon, narrating the rather uneventful performance.

Suddenly, with a crack and a metallic rattle, the tambourine hit the floor with a muffled thud. In response, Solomon's exhalations of frustration were not half as hidden as he intended. Cracking the air once more, with a sudden shriek, the tambourine skidded across the floor, coming to rest at Mrs Curry's feet.

I thought to ask if the spirits were displeased, for little reason other than to rile the deceptive pair. Elsie's mediumistic powers had certainly not grown to encompass grace. I waited for Curry and Bexton to end the strange dark séance, but they remained in their places, somehow satisfied with the outcome. As they sat in communal silence, nothing made a sound, besides the occasional flicker and crack of the candle. After a short while, a little subdued rustling was heard from inside the cabinet.

First crept a pale hand; then a face, then one tiny foot emerged from beneath the curtain. Each peeking, then disappearing back into the cabinet. Each was white, small, and disappeared soon after its emergence.

'Good, now —' began Solomon, motioning that the performance was over.

Before he could finish his sentence, a whole leg stepped from the cabinet, followed by a thigh, then, standing in the low light, a pale figure. I couldn't help but gasp. Before me stood Elsie, shivering and small, dressed in nothing but her underwear.

Solomon's lips grew thinner, his hand reaching to rub his forehead. 'Ah,' he exhaled, 'this is...'

'Grizelda!' sang the child. 'Miss Elsie's spirit guide.'

Solomon spoke under his breath, although whether the words were 'Oh God' or 'Oh good' was lost in the gathering sounds of Elsie's gentle warbling. Elsie appeared, dancing in her lacy combinations, her flesh translucent and milky white. She spun about the darkened room with the imitated grace of a ballerina.

Solomon spoke, stumbling over his words. 'Grizelda has come to... tell us of the spirit world.'

I crossed my arms, shaking my head in disbelief. 'It's Elsie.'

'Ssshhh,' hissed Mrs Curry.

'This is inappropriate, she is a child,' I whispered to Mrs Curry, lowering my tone.

'I am no child, I am a spirit,' sang Grizelda, twirling across the floor.

I watched and thought it bold for such a spirit to go barefoot on the floorboards. The damp had made the houses' wood susceptible to splitting. I fought against asking the spirit if splinters affected those who had passed over, but thought better of it.

'Heaven is in eternal Spring,' chimed Elsie, spinning on wiry legs.

Tiring of their claims and with a fierceness growing in my aching chest, I outstretched my foot to trip the 'spirit' as it danced by. With reflexes far younger than her years, Mrs Curry saw and deftly kicked the foot back under my seat with a sudden swing.

Naïve to growing tension around her, Grizelda danced about in her combinations, placing little buds of forget-me-nots beside the silverware.

Frustrated, but growing in confidence, I slowly stood up from my chair. I clenched my fists and moved towards the cabinet, reaching the curtain in three strides. I thought that I'd have to fight away Solomon or Mrs Curry's lunges, but they only looked on with mild irritation, slowly standing from their chairs as I grabbed at the curtain's edge. They appeared more perturbed that their comfort had been interrupted, rather than possessing any concern for their imminent exposure.

I hurled the curtain back with the gusto of a ringmaster, and prepared a shriek of victory for unveiling the empty room. Instead, slumped in the chair, sat Elsie. She had sunk forward, her breathing low and ragged, her body tightly bound with fist-sized knots. She was dressed as before, sitting in her blouse and skirt, gasping with exhaustion. She could not have moved.

I studied Elsie with panic. I peered behind myself, as though the spirit might still linger, but all that looked back were the piercing eyes of Solomon and Mrs Curry, their arms folded in displeasure. Elsie's shoes were on her feet, but unbuttoned; her legs bare, her stockings nowhere to be seen. Solomon and Curry maintained their stance, saying nothing, but watching my face, as though to say 'See?'

'You shouldn't have interrupted her. Look what you've done,' sighed the housekeeper, moving to untie Elsie.

'The poor girl is exhausted. You severed the connection. This can be very dangerous for a woman as young and inexperienced as our Elsie,' continued Mrs Curry, groaning as she bent to untie the knots at Elsie's ankles.

I threw up my arms in exasperation, regretting the movement as sharp pains pierced my shoulders. 'She's not *your* Elsie!'

Forcing myself closer to the hunched figure of Mrs Curry, I spoke with insistence. 'And she's not a woman, she's a child, not some mystic.'

'Then what did you see here?' interrogated Solomon.

'I saw a child. I saw a child dance in her underwear. Have you no shame?' I snapped, incensed by his boldness.

Speaking slowly, he insisted, 'I saw a woman, Miss. I saw the spirit of a woman —'

'No,' I interrupted.

'I saw the spirit of a woman, and I saw a child in the cabinet.' He spoke in slow, gentle words, smiling, as though talking to a simpleton.

My body burned with rage.

'That — that performance — was wholly inappropriate. Teaching a child to dance about like an actress? A... a... street girl?' I flustered.

Solomon watched me in silence, his head turned, questioning.

'Are you envying her trim little body, Miss?' said Solomon, his breath souring the air.

'Beast,' I hissed. 'How dare you.'

Solomon spoke quickly, blocking my path.

'Oh hush, Miss, I mean no insult to you!' he chuckled. 'I think Grizelda had a dreamy look in her eyes, far, far different from Elsie's. Grizelda is a' — he paused, mulling over his words — 'sensual spirit.'

His smile was soft and affable, but his eyes flickered with the cruel enjoyment of a thug at a cock fight.

'Her nose was pointed, not like Elsie's button nose, and her Cupid's bow was far more pronounced. Don't you think?'

He continued to smile, keeping his eyes fixed on mine, leaving no space for a response.

'She may look a little like Elsie,' he began, 'but such a likeness is unavoidable when Elsie is the vessel for the manifestation.'

Solomon walked closer, forcing me to move away from the cabinet. Edging forwards, we moved in synchronization until the hard ridge of a sideboard signalled that I had hit the back wall. He spoke quickly, his words flying clipped and sharp against my skin.

'I don't mean to be so forward, Miss, but in my line of work, we really do value respect. Mutually, you see. I'm a very modern man, as I'm sure you've noticed.'

He smiled and stroked my arm. He was tender and gentle, his smile kinder and warmer than Algernon's.

'I told you she was gifted, and you've seen it yourself. Don't try to clip our little bird's wings,' he chuckled and stroked my cheek. He paused and exhaled, examining my face as my skin burned with embarrassment at his closeness.

'I don't want to pry into your relationship with Elsie,' he said quietly. 'I know how dear sisters can be to one another. But remember that jealousy is such an ugly trait.'

He sighed and tapped the tip of my nose with his finger, grinning like a lapdog. 'How goes your embroidery?'

He smiled, teeth bared, then backed away and returned to Elsie's cabinet. From across the room, I heard him spit at her, 'I told you to wait. You're not ready for full manifestations.'

Sudden fear rose against my will, my eyelids stinging with unspent tears. I shook as I struggled to walk from the room, but stopped in my tracks when disquiet rose behind me.

Mrs Curry and Solomon were hissing over Elsie's slumped form, like foxes fighting over a carcass.

'She needs a little more training,' he barked.

Mrs Curry cut him off with a gruff shout. 'What she needs is bed. I'll take her now.'

'I think this is my realm, not yours,' snapped Solomon.

'I will tell you when she's ready. It's too soon,' insisted Mrs Curry.

With her final words, she grabbed at Elsie, who stumbled like a drunkard, too exhausted to hold her own weight. Hand in hand, Mrs Curry led Elsie from the room with neither of them giving so much as a backwards glance.

Chapter 26

The thudding from the dining room was rhythmic. Bursts of light taps were followed by a heavy bang that rattled the china cabinets on the far wall. Precisely what Mrs Curry was doing, as with all things, appeared to be on a need-to-know basis.

The incessant noises would suggest she was undertaking major building work, heading a passing-out parade, or carrying out a heavy-handed and conspicuous burglary. Mother and I sat in the drawing room, both of us uncomfortable in our chairs, and each other's company. Mother had insisted we bond. *Or rather, I was being kept within sight.* Her attention was grasped by the murmurings from the dining room beside us, noises that she had not long deemed 'disinteresting'. She grasped the tray cloth in a rictus grip, eyes fixed on the panelling between the rooms. I turned to my tea, hoping steam would appear where warmth had ceased to be. The cup was overfull. To sip, even politely, would be a task beyond my shaking hands' abilities. Still, Mother clutched her cloth.

I spoke quietly into my teacup. 'If you plan to weep or dance with that rag, make your choice quickly.'

I rotated the handle, motioned to lift the tea, before returning the cup to its saucer. Mother had failed to grace me with the daily maladies, which alarmed me greatly. There had similarly been no sign of fresh crape in several days. We were speaking at least, and this was a development I was sure not to take for granted.

'You know, in London I have heard of countless grief-stricken women collapsing in their households,' I said, somewhat intrigued at her sudden improvements. 'You must be feeling a little better?'

My mother, still grasping a teacup between her fingertips, jumped at my voice. I pulled the standing tray closer to my chair in a poor attempt to protect it from her roughness.

The china clinked, rocking in its footing as the tray came to a rest.

'Well!' Mother exclaimed to the panelling. 'I thought we could enjoy tea together.' She quickly turned to the sideboard, teasing out a troublesome drawer.

'And here we are,' I said inanely, surveying the strange spread before me.

Surreptitiously peeking between sandwiches while Mother's back was turned, I quickly removed the top slice, which proved as heavy and dense as a pie lid. What lay within was indiscernible. Seeing it did little for my hunger pangs; neither did it inspire any optimism for my own future health. Mother returned and sat at the opposite side of the window. Draping a single-cream fat square of fabric across her knees, she extended a gloved hand towards the tower of pastries.

'Ooh, such choices,' she cooed.

Her crocheted fingertips rolled across the sandwiches, collecting heavy crumbs in their divots. She raised an offering to her mouth, prised apart her thinning lips, and devoured it in its entirety.

'We are so fortunate to have Mrs Curry to treat us so well,' she said through sprays of spit-dampened loaf. 'All this at such short notice too.'

The banging resumed, punctuated by bursts of muffled conversation.

'We'll have half of the empire coming to our door with such service! Won't we, Mrs Curry? Haha! Yes, yes we will,' she shrieked with strange, sharp enthusiasm.

I watched my mother entranced as she dug a teaspoon up to the handle in brown preserve, flopping it wetly onto a finger of sweating cheese. My single sandwich remained obnoxiously firm between my fingertips. I hadn't eaten and had to keep up my strength. The lawyers would come soon, and I had to be strong enough for the journey home. I inhaled deeply and bit. It bore a resistance unlike any bread I had encountered. It smelled of soil and clung to my teeth like overbaked potato.

The bread was just bread. I repeated it in cycles inside my head. *The bread is just bread.* Mother busied herself with tart-smelling slop and I kept my eyes at close focus on my task. I pulled the sandwich away and felt resistance; a tongue of wilted greenery refused to break, and flopped like a rotted handkerchief onto my chin. My stomach twisted and I quickly returned to focusing on my breathing.

'Eat up, child. You're terribly thin. It doesn't suit you.'

Mother leaned back into her chair, raising the empty cup to her lips.

'Yes, I am aware,' I muttered.

'Plenty of women can carry it off, but you look awfully grey. You should be wary of leaving the house; you'll remind people of the Blight.'

I sat breathless and wordless.

'The Blight, child. Have a little thought for others. You've grown so selfish,' my mother chuckled, the sharpness in her voice poorly concealed with a smile.

'Do you mean the Famine, Mother?' I gently pressed.

'So now you taunt a widow! You delight in my pain! You think your mother uneducated! Uncaring!'

I remained seated, unsurprised that her brief foray into motherly concern had crumbled so soon. I knew to wait for the inevitable outburst that would send vases, lamps, or occasional tables slamming into the plasterwork.

'I am overflowing with care!'

Mother's nostrils flared. She threw her arm forwards, wrenching apart the shoulder seams of her dress with an audible rip, and hurled an offending scone at the panelling behind me. It promptly rolled back towards my slipper, resting at the foot of the tea tray, intact. As I opened my mouth, an almighty clatter came from the dining room. It was the sound of shattering wood. Mother's eyes widened in alarm.

She reached across, pulling the trolley in front of my path.

'Sit,' she barked.

I pushed the trolley once more with one chapped, bony hand, the empty slops bowl teetering dangerously.

'What have you got her doing? Mrs Curry!' Anger rose in uncomfortable waves. It was a rage too great for me to house, threatening to spill from my eyes in the ugly tears of a weakened body.

I pushed the tray, but Mother's unexpected strength held fast. Avoiding my gaze, she mumbled, addressing the crockery, 'Mrs Curry isn't alone.'

'Then who's with her? What are they doing?' I snapped.

Then came another bang, louder than before.

'Mrs Curry!' I bellowed, louder than expected, my stays shifting uncomfortably against my ribs.

A door clicked open from within the house.

'You're ridiculous,' I spat, pushing the trolley out of Mother's grasp.

I moved with all the speed I could muster, taking a few quick steps towards the door.

Suddenly, the enormous frame swung open, unveiling a stocky black blot in its place. Mrs Curry stepped forwards, her boot nails clinking against the floorboards with each heavy step. Her elbows were bent, hands raised and sheathed in long leather gloves. She slowly lumbered into the light, her arms glistening in the meagre afternoon sun.

'Yes?'

Mother and I were silent. Mrs Curry's glove cuffs showed signs of once being a warm brown, yet their entirety was swathed in a thick layer of burgundy-coloured gloop that slowly traced itself in droplets down her forearm.

I tried to speak, my words catching in my drying throat. 'Could you —'

'Could you be quick, Miss,' sighed the housekeeper. 'I've just been slaughtering a pig.'

The smell began to waft in, following Mrs Curry like a bridal train.

'In the kitchen?' I stuttered.

Mrs Curry rolled her eyes in practised facetiousness. 'No, in the attic, Miss.'

Mrs Curry pursed her lips together, her heavy breathing punctuated by occasional drops of viscera hitting her shoes. She tilted her head to the side, to meet my mother's eyes.

'I'll be removing the tray later, Ma'am. Mr Bexton has asked to stay for dinner so he can focus on his work. I took the liberty of accepting his proposal on your behalf,' she said, her words hard and authoritative.

Mrs Curry raised her eyebrows expectantly, her brow folding into a thousand speckled rolls.

'That will be quite lovely,' my mother responded with sudden perkiness.

Mrs Curry nodded and turned, her sodden apron flaring out before flopping back and adhering itself to her skirts.

'And be wary of the knob if you decide to make a run for it, Miss; the brass is covered in blood and is awfully slippery,' she cheerfully shouted behind her.

Mrs Curry turned and left, the echoes of her boots ringing long after she'd exited the room.

* * *

Slaughtered livestock and destruction of the dining furniture didn't seem to be such a horrific concept in comparison to another night with Solomon Bexton. If Algernon had the slightest idea of the company I was forced to keep, let alone the conflicting thoughts I was having, he would undoubtedly be ruthless in his punishment. Rumours from situations such as mine would spread like cholera through the social set.

A nagging pain began to bubble behind my eye. The evening's options were troublesome; I could starve and avoid Solomon's company at dinner, but conversation might flow a little too freely in my absence. Conversely, I could eat and join them. A thought which terrified me. Algernon would come. I would keep reminding myself that I would not be alone for long. With little thought, I returned to my seat, the raffia crunching as the base sagged.

'Well,' sighed Mother, 'I hope you're happy with your little performance.'

I dismissed her sneers and leaned towards her. 'How long has he been in the house?'

Mother poured the tea to the brim of both cups.

'Oh, Solomon?' she asked, her eyebrows raised too high.

'Who else, Mother?' I sighed, forcing a smile.

Mother retorted with a silent glare under heavy eyelids.

'Unless your need for male company is suddenly so great that you've started an employment line?' I muttered under my breath.

'Solomon has been here a little while. He's doing wonderful work with Elsie,' said Mother softly.

I closed my eyes tightly, pinching my nose and willing my looming headache to slip away. I managed to mumble a feeble 'Hmm' in place of the snide retort that hung on my tongue.

'She's such a fast learner, you see, and he's such a wonderful mentor,' she simpered, her lips puckering. 'He's found qualities in her that are really rather special. She has the *sight*, you see.

She needs training, but she could be very successful, really pull it in.'

'Oh I see,' I said, nodding. I didn't understand at all, save for her relentless desire for attention and pocket money.

I was surprised my mother had taken so long to consider the money-making possibilities of Elsie and her new friends. The house had long crumbled around the Croftons, and it was evident that my mother was not in the business of spending her money on family matters.

'And help so many people, of course,' she quickly added.

'Of course,' I echoed, too tired to feel anything like disgust, only resignation.

Mother sipped at her tea.

'And none of us appreciate your interference in your sister's success. Jealousy is a sin, my dear,' she said quickly, addressing an argument I did not have the strength to contest.

Mother had always been selfish, and snide at times, but never truly cruel. Something poisonous seemed to have taken root in my absence, and considering her newly widowed state, I was rather loath to address such a change.

Mother upended the contents of the cup into her mouth and placed it on the windowsill. The leaves lingered in her mouth, despite a small inadvertent cough she tried to muffle with a napkin. The dark flakes decorated the already blackened crevices between her teeth.

'None of us,' she repeated. 'We are not alone in this house, child. Your father was keen to forget that too, but it comes to us all.'

I sat puzzled. Mother hadn't spoken of my father in days without shrieking, let alone in passing. But as the old woman finished her speech, she uncomfortably rearranged her bustle and stood beside the window. As she stood away from the light, the tea service was fully visible. It was a jumble of sets and designs, all beautiful once, but now fading and worn.

I supposed it didn't matter any more; broken things have no value to anyone. Was Mother trying to be mystical? She would tire of it soon. I hoped so.

The banging in the room beside us subsided to muffled clatter. Behind me came a gradual scratching, like claws against the grain. The panelling seemed to rattle gently, before resting and resuming. There was silence, a scream, and a crash. This was quickly followed by a bellowed cheer and the sound of heavy dragging, like furniture being righted.

Mother gently knocked, squeaked, and exchanged murmurings with a mellow-toned Solomon at the door of the dining room. His voice carried like a church bell, bouncing from wall to wall, infesting ears with the reverberations of his drawl. My mother's voice was lower and coarse, like the sound of a thresher. Their chattering continued like commands in a distant hunt until the mumbles died out, the door clicked, and light tapping began.

* * *

I had never considered myself a lonely person. My whole life was not spent alone, but waiting. It was instilled, by me, and by my father, that when an opportunity of marriage and movement came, my waiting would end and life was permitted to begin; those were the rules to which all life adhered.

Mother was a different beast, being all grief, illness, and solitude; the things that terrified me above all else. Algernon could calm all my concerns, all my pains, if he were to find time to write. In his absence, if Mother could allow me to see Father's papers, I would sign my mark and leave with the nearest carriage.

Father was never an affectionate man, but lost the last of his interest in familial matters after my mother stated that her ability to bear children had passed. His ambivalence turned to contempt, resentment, and, as Elsie and I grew, disappointment. As little as he was interested in his daughters, I remained his firstborn and I was sure that my father would do his duty by me in matters of inheritance. *After all, his contempt for my mother was too great to dismiss.* Mother's reticence to show me the papers spoke far louder than any probate.

'I feel that I need to know what happened with Father,' I sighed.

Mother stroked her hands across the black beading of her apron, refusing to look up.

'Father is no longer with us. Let that be the end of it,' she answered, curtly.

Mother ploughed towards her seat, twisted and sat, lifting her cold cup to her lips. She held it so roughly, with her hands in a rictus grip around the handle. She held everything with such little care. She rarely held Elsie in infanthood; and to that I credited her survival.

'He is with God now. And, as you know,' she nodded, using the pause to scramble in the recesses of her mind, 'blessed are those who mourn.'

Of course my mother remembered that verse. The old Family Bible had been both a kitchen step and a draft excluder in my youth, yet it seemed to have been promoted in recent months. It was of little surprise that the house seemed colder without that tome blocking the chill.

Before I could respond, a large bang ricocheted from the back wall.

'I hear summer may reach us early this year,' shrieked Mother, a beat too late to cover the chaos.

Two large bangs rang out. They vibrated with such force, the house felt a shiver in its foundations.

'I believe the flowers are budding?' she whimpered.

Exhausted, I turned my head towards the window. The reeds that grew like tufts of hair around the perimeter had grown brown and brittle. The flowerbeds had long been overgrown by the thick bracken that blighted all of Duncain. The garden was dead. The grounds were all dead. The lake was the only part that changed, and that was at the will of itself.

The rushes moved like a great metronome, keeping time with an ancient pulse of their own. Between sways, a tuft of reeds twisted against itself, parting. A shadow moved between them; grey at first, before darkening like a spreading ink blot. It moved closer, leaving the reeds. Duncain's keen dusk was setting, and the figure had grown to at least three feet in height before my eyes had settled upon its shape.

I had to get out of the drawing room. Solomon had free rein of the house while I sat, slumped and subdued like a budgerigar with a blanket over its cage. Meanwhile, the wind was plucking birds from their flight paths; the reeds were unremarkable and were swaying with the slightest breeze. Elsie was categorically, affirmatively inside the house. There was nothing and no one in the garden.

I had to move. I would take a walk, and embedded the thought in my head. I would wander the grounds but not outside its gates. Times were not so desperate. The scones, the bread, the air, all of it was stale. The windowsill was grey, the table was grey, and the air was thick with grit, cloying with each protracted minute I lingered by the window. Every breath tasted old and dead. The scones, still teetering on their ceramic plinth, would soon gather a layer of dust. They were part of the house now; part of Mother and her reticence to join the world outside her own.

'You haven't eaten.'

I looked back at my plate, which stood stark and threatening in its porcelain glaze.

Mother's eyes widened as she nodded towards the abandoned spread, her lips thinning in the approximation of an encouraging smile. Some vague sense of familial loyalty tricked my wits as I moved my hand back to the table. Edging forwards, she extended a finger to touch an unthreatening leaf peeking from the closest sandwich. It was wet. It wasn't damp, like freshly picked or washed lettuce, but wet like rotting leaves. The edges of the leaves were dark, soft, and jagged like teeth. Like nettles. My fingertips soured, as did my tongue. The leaf slipped from my hand with a faint, wet flop. Nettles.

A voice cut through from the corner.

'Pickled nettles,' said my mother with a smile.

The smell hit me a little slower than I would have hoped. My fingers stank like a tart pomander. Extending my punishment, I found that my sense of disgust and rising sickness left me fixed to the table.

'Pickled nettles,' I echoed weakly.

'Pickled nettles,' repeated Mother.

Mother brought the offending bread to her lips, the nettles stringy and limp between her pegged teeth. She bit and pulled away, green mulch sticking to the fine lines around her lips. Her breath stank of vinegar and rot.

'Delicious,' she whispered, her glove doing little to remove the fibres that adhered to her lips.

Mother swallowed and set down the sandwich with slow precision. She cleared her throat, returned her gaze to mine, and addressed me from behind damp gloves.

'From the kitchen garden.'

Mother's bulbous eyes, toad-like in their protrusion, closed in some hideous approximation of ecstasy as she took another bite from an expectant, greying sandwich. Something caught in her throat, eliciting a grating cough. She coughed again, failing to dislodge the offending crumb. Another cough, and another. Her coughing became deeper, rasping, and yet suddenly, wet. The sandwich, now a mangled shadow of its triangular self, dropped to the floor. With two fingers, still wrapped in crocheted gloves, she tried to save herself, thrusting them down her throat, her hand narrowed and flanked by tiny teeth. She choked, sending snailtracks of spit down her hands. I watched her, frozen in uncertain anticipation. Her coughing ended abruptly with a protracted wet hack. As the fingertips left her lips, they were followed by the visceral squelch of a long, green ribbon. A nettle leaf. She flung it against the rim of a saucer before falling backwards into her chair, gripping at her throat like some wounded knight.

Her gasps were replaced by protracted sobs, her gloves pressed into the corners of her eyes, holding them shut. As her sobbing subsided, a series of loudening taps floated through from between the wood panelling. I finally motioned to leave.

'Won't you at least help your poor mother, I've had such a fright!' whispered my mother, in a coarse approximation of her voice.

I passed her a napkin, which was swiftly grabbed and pressed to Mother's face like a shroud. I moved a few steps towards the door, the unsteady creaks of the floorboards giving away my location to the hunched wreck of my mother.

'Stay!' she commanded. 'Sit with me. There is... so much good food. Such a spread, you see.'

I carried on towards the door, the smell of spittle still hanging in the air. My mother raised her head and voice, beckoning. 'Mrs Curry will tell you about wastage.'

'Mrs Curry will do well to know her place,' I spat.

I continued my stride towards the door, turning to meet my mother as I reached the suspiciously wet knob.

'Your picnics will be the end of us all. You try to send me the way of Father,' I hissed.

I left at speed, quickly closing the door behind me. I pinched the brass knob with the tips of my fingers, mindful that some of Mrs Curry's gristle still lingered. No sooner had the mechanism clicked than the door rattled with the sudden thud and familiar crumble of hurled pastry against wood.

Chapter 27

The outer door of the orangery was always open. The hinges had snapped in high winds and the old frames were pinned back with half-rotted wisteria vines that refused to bloom. I sought to revive myself in my walk, going in search of the country air of which everyone spoke so fondly in London. Yet despite my strides, the country air of England was undoubtedly different from that of Duncain. The old path was still somewhat visible through the grassy mulch that surrounded it. The wind was low, the rain at bay, and I would stroll, breathe, and reclaim myself. My slippers would almost certainly not survive their journey outside, but such things were of little consequence now.

Before I had chance to consider further fashions, I found that I had walked half the perimeter of the house. Beside the largest window to the dining room, across the way, was the old entrance to the rose garden. Father had it planted when he was young, long before he married my mother. The brick archway remained, but the gates were all but swallowed by riots of thorns and twisted stalks; there were never many flowers in Duncain.

Few farmers remained in the county. There were more than enough houses, thanks to my grandfather's foresight, but no jobs, and no one to maintain them. It was a queer sight to see swathes of untended, muddled fields, overseen by doorless houses. Peeking beyond the garden's walls, a square, grey structure peered back. I remembered a Mr McCray who used to rent the cottage, him and his two huge hunting dogs. He was long gone, and the dogs too.

Something rustled in the rose garden. At first, a twitch, soon escalating into a manic fluttering. I thought it to be a trapped bird. At first sight, it could have been anything; a blackbird, a crow. It moved with such ferocity, but was all a feathered blur.

It thrashed more, appearing then disappearing behind the thick stalks. As quickly as it began, the noise stopped.

A few lonely feathers settled on nearby leaves, but the bird was gone.

The wind had picked up around the side of the house; I could hear it whistling as soon as I stepped outside, but the inlet beside the drawing room caused it to howl. It was my father's side; the upper floors at least. His room, his study, his bathroom all overlooked where I stood. Glancing upwards, it seemed so odd to think those rooms were at last free from purpose. His office, when I was a child at least, was a mausoleum of ledgers and towers of matching leather-bound books, read by no one. I had never been bookish enough to show interest; even if I had, the office was a boundary not to be crossed. I couldn't understand why the office window was so troubling. At first, it was the strange emanating light, then the filth. Then, after concerning myself with the trivial point for far too long, I saw lines through the grime. The windows were pasted with newsprint. Layers of criss-crossing text stuck with yellow paste — all from the inside.

The house had never been a riot of life, but it seemed quieter and larger, darker without my father's presence. His office door remained closed as it did in life; but without the rustling of papers and the crackling of his fire, even the clearing of his throat, there was a strange void. The smell of his tobacco smoke hung loosely around the house, absorbed into the woodwork with the help of the estate's perpetual damp. He was never kind as such, nor sentimental, but he was a man of conviction and logic. If a horse was lame, he would have it shot. If a tenant did not pay, he would have them evicted. His life was a simple wheel of black and white decisions, breaking only for the entertainment of necessary house activities: food, adequate bathing facilities. Yet when the introduction of gas into Duncain was proposed, he protested it with the same vehemence as a preacher would incite to ward off the devil. Kenneth Crofton was not a man of change, neither physical, nor mental. Of this, I was sure. How my mother and father met was a fact so baffling that I had never given it any thought. It seemed to be an arrangement into which they both fell, and never thought to leave. Mother married into the Croftons, and Father, mentally at least, married out. Their interactions were a long lesson in bored tolerance.

My mother had always little interest in me, save for the little sympathy incited after my birth. The disappointment that they had, indeed, produced a girl lingered well past Elsie's arrival, as though her survival was an insult to the Crofton name. When my mother was expecting Elsie, I had followed her growing bump with hawk-like interest. It was no secret that she had hoped for a male heir; she ate glossy berries throughout the night, with strange broths appearing at her door at all hours, concocted in Mrs Curry's cauldron. Her night-time prayers were so loud and filled with hatred for the daughter that listened, but they had little effect. I would follow Mrs Curry's errands, sprinkling a little salt on my mother's bread when the housekeeper's back was turned, spitting in her tea, and professing to the staff that, 'If she has a boy child, I shall drown it in the lake and not feel an ounce of regret.'

When Elsie emerged on a late spring evening, the house was torn apart with screams that lasted long after the baby emerged. But there was another pregnancy, one I half-remembered, when I was very small. Long before Elsie, when the rose bushes still bloomed with scarlet flowers, my mother swelled one summer. The season was the hottest for years, and I remembered it only in a hazy delirium. As a toddling child, I had become ill, sleeping away the summer months in a lingering sweat, staining my blankets with blood and bile. Mrs Curry used to tell me that I 'was supposed to die'. She never worded it pleasantly, but meant well, stroking my arm as she spoke. However, I was never 'nearly called to Jesus' or 'nearly passed'. Always 'supposed to die'. I remembered small parts of those months: a cup of water, a nibble on some bread, the trim on Mrs Curry's apron, brushing by. At one point, in breaks of fever, I remembered someone screaming — high, shrieking screams that cut the air like broken glass. I thought it was a baby at first, but it never stopped. When I recovered, snow was falling. The staff remained in their crofts for the season and the gardens remained as flat and white as dinnerplates. It was also the year that my mother stopped caring for the state of the rose gardens. By the arches, a smooth slab of granite glinted against the snowdrift. There was a name, a birth date; some chiselled proof of existence. In the years that passed, it was swallowed into the tangle of greenery. Occasionally the littlest corner caught the light on summer mornings, but such moments lessened over time. It was never mentioned by my father, and I returned to my toys the next year. My mother and I barely spoke after the long winter, while Father filed away the matter like another business expense. Yet the silence that filled the house was heavy with the stench of lost masculinity.

My father and I spoke at length only once, with the conversation being more akin to a lecture than a dialogue. It was the safest way, and I was not one to force an engagement with the man. I was to listen, then leave. To make conversation was an act of insurrection, not to be tolerated. For the first and only time, I had sat in my father's office the day before I left for London. Perched awkwardly in a captain's chair, I sat across from the man who examined me as though I were interviewing for a position in his office.

From early morning to late afternoon, he brought out reams of paper, explaining the boundaries of each croft with another; yellowing, rolled-up indenture. From his shelves and bureau, he brought endless papers, covered in spidery writing and enormous gothic letters, too elaborate to read.

I watched boxes upended and listened as their content was recited in meticulous detail; wax seals of long-dead grandfathers with only the shortest of breaks to test my recollection. My father's throat never ran dry.

'As my firstborn,' he began, 'it is paramount that you understand this.'

His face was not one of anger or aggression, but an unfamiliar sincerity that disarmed me.

'Upon my death, all of this will be yours,' he said. 'It must *not* go to Margaret.'

I responded with a nod of my head, reticent to push him on his reasoning for cutting my mother out.

'Do you understand?' he insisted, leaning closer. 'Under no circumstances must the estate be hers.'

He sighed and gathered his papers, rolling contracts into tight tubes.

'She is… not well.'

He sounded uncomfortable somehow, as though someone was pulling at his tongue.

'She has served her purpose,' he said, pausing to gesture to me. 'But *never* turn your back to her. She is not so great a fool as you think.'

I sat, nodding in agreement, my head spinning with questions never to be posed. My father paced the room before stopping suddenly and looking to the ceiling. He remained transfixed, straining at something far away. He flinched, rubbing his ears as if thunder had cracked beside him, then returned his gaze to me.

'I have never trusted anything that was not leather bound, and I am imploring you to do the same.'

'Yes, Father.' The response was glib, but I had little else to hand.

He straightened his back, cracking his knuckles and clearing his throat with the practised air of a Lord.

'Can you write, girl?' he asked.

I responded quickly. 'Yes, Sir.'

He sighed in gentle relief. 'That Curry woman did one thing right then.'

He moved across his desk, lifting an enormous brass inkwell from its spot, and, placing it close, he picked the pen from its cradle and extended it towards me.

'Sign your name here,' he insisted, his demeanour suddenly rushed. 'You have one?' he pressed, hissing his words.

'Yes, yes,' I affirmed, flustered at the strange interrogation.

'Make haste,' he whispered.

I did as I was told, signing my name on the paperwork before me. Duncain's fate was to lie with me, but the reasons why were known to my father alone. With the clink of crockery and the thuds of a weighty gait, it was clear that Mrs Curry was stirring from below stairs. The high-pitched clinking of porcelain grew louder as she ascended the steps from the kitchen, at which my father rolled away the last of his papers, secreting them in his towering archive.

'Now leave, we're done here,' he hissed.

I moved to leave, with my lips still in no rush to speak. I pushed the chair back on its castors and turned to leave, only a little wiser than when I entered. Before reaching the door, Father ran up to me once more, speaking in hard, low tones.

'Do not speak of this to anyone, do you understand? Not to family or —' He paused to quickly return papers to his desk drawers. He returned, frantic. 'No one. Not a living soul until I am dead. Do you understand?'

'Yes, Father,' I whispered.

'You must swear!' he insisted, holding my arm.

'Father, I —'

He gripped my arm harder, his eyes wide and frightened.

'I swear, I swear, Father. Not a soul,' I whimpered in return.

'This land, this house, holds more than you know, child. Many will try to take it from you, or steal it. With a sympathetic handshake or an agreement with the wrong man, you could lose it all. This house is older than it seems. It's older than words, child.' His breath was hot and acrid on my face, his eyes wild and desperate.

I stood frozen and wordless as my proud father scrabbled at my shoulder like a frightened child, speaking into my ear in stranger tones. 'People will lie, cheat, and curse you for this land. It must always be safe. And if I die before your mother, as I am sure I will, watch for visitors.'

He strode to the large inlaid cabinet at the side of the room and roughly threw in a handful of papers as though hiding sweets from his governess. Locking it with the tiniest gold key, hanging from his fob, he returned to the door, dramatically calmer than before. His face had changed; he looked tired, disinterested, with his pallor greyer than moments earlier.

He opened the door and dismissed me with a flick of his wrist. 'You are dismissed. Return to your sewing, or books, or whatever it is that you do.'

I nodded and left. We would speak only once more before I left. Early the next morning, I was called back to his office, where I met a cold and tired old man. He had received a request for my hand in marriage. It was a simple affair: a question, a statement of finances, and a small photograph of a not unhandsome man, mounted on card stock with unanswered requests for enlargements. The response had been written and posted before I rose from my bed. Within days, I was in London, married at St Luke's church with a wedding party of five, four of whom I had never seen before. A week later, I sat on my chaise longue with a furniture catalogue at hand, decorating my three-storey homestead, drinking in the fumes of freedom. Or so it seemed.

Chapter 28

My walk had stalled. For such a disinteresting place, the house held perpetual mundane distractions. To my weakened mind, I was sure that the day would come when a wooden spoon would hold my interest for a whole evening.

My side of the house was furthest from the jetty. Yet the clay was still sodden and waterlogged. It hadn't been turned over in years, but the grass still grew in miniature hillocks beside long-dead flowerbeds. I would have suggested it to be a sign of moles if I hadn't thought they would drown in their burrows. The ground took all it could, the water pooling on top in muddy pools. Grime would float on the surface like a thick soup. My thoughts ended abruptly with visions of Mrs Curry and her stove.

Beneath my father's window, and beneath the parlour shutters, lay a small patch of pink. The colour was faint, but seemed so alien, so unnatural. There were six small flowers, weak and delicate with frayed, thin petals; tiny things. Their petals looked so soft, so welcoming, that I could have popped them into my mouth like bonbons. I knelt to touch them — to see if they were as gentle as they felt — but a clatter from behind caused me to turn quickly. Something in my back snapped, something that wasn't my stays. A hot streak of pain shot down my leg. My mind scrambled wildly; I had been shot, or stabbed. My body convulsed forwards, my knees and slippers several inches deep into the earth. Ruined. Each breath was accompanied by a yelp as the pain refused to subside. My leg was on fire, my back broken in two. I was going to die.

'You need to watch yourself there, Miss.' Beside me stood Mrs Curry, as tall as a building.

She was cast in her own shadow, darker than the rest. Her apron was smeared with dried blood and dark-green streaks that cross-hatched the linen. The crows were silent. She looked me up and down. In silence, I waited, for anything.

'Dinner's at six.'

The housekeeper turned and left. Beside her, a wicker basket swung like a weapon. From it spilled an indistinguishable mess of greenery. I watched her slink into the rose garden, crackling beneath a wall of dried leaves.

I remained hunched, my knees slowly freezing in place, more swollen than before. The pain reduced itself to a dull throb, but something was definitely wrong. I waited a while, expecting to see the housekeeper return in a tangle of thorns, but she had disappeared into the ether. The grounds had many overgrown paths, and only Mrs Curry would be foolish enough to try and navigate them.

I had to get back inside. My body ached and stung in so many places that it felt as though my skeleton was trying to escape my body. I only knew of basic needs through the pain: I had to get warm and out of the grounds. After some deep breaths and words I had never uttered to another, I was upright. I had smeared the windowsill in mud in the process, but I was up.

I was about to begin my shuffling to the servants' door when chatter floated from the house. Elsie was giggling, her garbled chatter escaping through the window pane. I hadn't realized that I had walked that far around the house. I was directly beside the window where the rhododendrons had grown in a perfect 'U', generously permitting light into the dining room. I had fallen by the parlour, or so I thought. My mind was untrustworthy as my leg throbbed with an uneasy heartbeat.

But there they were, directly through the window. Elsie was seated by a card table and behind her stood Solomon in full tails. Elsie looked so small beside him. She sat in her pinafore, her hands spread before her, surrounded by a ring of white cards. They were marked, but with what, I could not be sure.

Even through the murky pane, I could see the crinkle of laughter around her eyes. Her cheeks rising as she tried to stifle a laugh. Mother's new interests aside, Elsie seemed happy.

A child, enjoying childish things. For her to have a hobby outside of Duncain's walls would not be so awful. In truth, I barely knew my sister, but the likenesses in our fine hair and grey eyes left me with a certain warmth I had been unable to define. It was not a conventional sisterly love as such, but a sense of shared experience, and of fierce protections. It was a love nonetheless, and the only one I could truly say to have known. To see her smile was... nice. I watched a little longer as Elsie spread her hands wider over the green baize. She kept peeking with one eye and giggling, before trying to calm herself, before bursting into fits of giggles again. Something caught the light in the centre of the table; from afar, it seemed to be cutlery, but Elsie didn't touch it. The whole set-up began to strike me as rather odd. Elsie calmed herself and glanced towards the window. Her eyes widened as she saw me, her smile growing until she was gleefully baring all her teeth. She removed one hand from the table and began to wave at me, seeming so flushed, so happy. I had forgotten to wave in return and quickly raised my hand.

The silverware was no longer on the table. Solomon's arm reached behind Elsie and held up a large pair of dressmaking scissors. They seemed huge beside her little frame, and she continued to wave. I glanced down at my filthy dress, to check Elsie wouldn't see me in such a state.

I looked back up and was met with the heavy crunch of metal against bone. Solomon was gripping the shears, raining blows down on Elsie's tiny neck and shoulders. She crumpled forwards, but he didn't stop, stabbing again and again until they both were soaked in her blood. I didn't move. I couldn't make a sound.

The back of Elsie's head was a tangled mess of tissue; blonde hair and great slugs of fleshy pulp. Her forehead head hit the table with a wet thud. The felt was red, the floor was red, blood had covered everything. He wrenched the blade from between her shoulders with a slopping crunch.

Solomon reached into his jacket with one hand, picked out a handkerchief, and proceeded to wipe his hands, the scissors, and his brow. He tossed both onto the table, turned to the window, and waved.

Chapter 29

The grounds were endless. Gardens became fields and each reed delighted in blocking my path. I ran in great clumsy strides, weak and uncertain like a newborn deer. My body was not my own, my muscles burned in unfamiliar places, plants and unseen hands tugged at my clothing as I lunged towards the back stairs. My shoes surrendered to snaking vines that twisted and tripped me as I ran. The back steps were in reach, the latch slowly clinking against its hold. It rattled faster, screaming against the wind, piercing my ears and pushing time forward.

Reaching the steps, my foot lost its hold. My legs crumpled and fell back beneath me, slamming my body against the stone like some cruel jack-in-a-box. My head caught the side of the step, bursting my eyebrow open like a ripe peach. It was hot, sticky, and stung my eye when I blinked. I had to get inside.

The wind had picked up; the door opened and slammed against my fingers, whistling across the doorframe. For a moment, it could have been laughter, or some muffled chortle from beyond the jetty. But the weather is cruel in Duncain; it throws rain sideways and blots out the sunlight when it chooses. I pushed myself up, pain screaming through my blackened legs, and stumbled through the kitchen, making the final set of stairs on my hands and knees.

Reaching the dining-room door, I hammered my fists against the panelling, slamming my knuckles into the grain like a pendulum. I had to get in, but the door stood fast. I hurled myself against the wood, my shoulder meeting the edge of the frame with a heavy crunch.

Something cracked and split like fracturing grain, something within *me*.

The door refused to bow, my body arching against it with each bang. I was sure I heard faint murmuring from behind the door. Solomon was mocking me. Those blasted women brought him into my house and he would kill us all. I screamed that I knew Elsie would live; I would get through and would stop him, I would get a doctor, somehow. It couldn't end like this.

I threw myself against the door in hard thuds, my mind empty of any other thoughts.

My breath burned in my chest, my voice tearing into some inhuman shriek.

The knob suddenly snapped to the left. I fell through the doorway, stumbling forwards before righting myself, my eyes slowly adjusting to the blinding daylight. Everything was white, my ears ringing from the silence.

My vision returned. I was standing beside the table, looking straight at Elsie. Behind her stood Solomon.

I stared at them, my mind swimming. I had tried to scream again, but couldn't. I stood there for years, Solomon's eyes boring into mine.

'Well,' exhaled Solomon, rubbing his hands against his face. 'That was quite the entrance.'

Elsie sat staring at me. Her little legs were swinging beneath the chair; eyes as wide as dinner plates. Her cheeks were pink. She was breathing. She was alive. Pristine, in fact.

My mind ached from exhaustion. I had seen him, I had seen what he did to Elsie, as clear as day. But there she was, alive, breathing, and intact. It didn't happen; none of it, it couldn't have. Her dress was clean and crisp; there were no marks, no cuts, no blood on her person at all. I had been fooled. Some cruel game. Solomon had used some magician's trickery, all under my mother's guidance, it had to be. Neither of them could bear that a woman held status above them. Similarly, Solomon clearly couldn't bear that he was outranked by a grander name. Throughout all of his silly performances within the house, I had been foolish enough to believe him to be a harmless entertainer, helping me to tread water until I could make my own exit. I had been crowned a dunce and had torn myself apart in the process. Foolish, foolish woman. But, most importantly, Elsie was fine.

The room was colder than it had been outside. The wind flitted through the cracks in muted screams and I was suddenly aware that my hands were warm and wet. With my realizations came the pain. Slowly at first, then as a screaming, tearing agony that pulsed across my arms and through my legs. I had little time to consider what I had done, to myself, my clothes, and my reputation. All were in tatters. There was blood across the door, blood on the hinges, and blood on the floor. The pool grew with steady drips, growing and disappearing between the floorboards. Each falling drop landing with a light 'tick', at odds with the hands of the clock. Blood and old varnish, mingling together. All of it was mine. The creeping scent of raw meat and metal filled the air. Elsie screamed.

The piercing cry tore through the house like a coal blast. Wall panels stretched against their seating; I could hear each splinter crack, each floorboard snap like breaking bones. The house contracted around me, tightening its grip.

Black smears floated before my eyes, swooping and darting like blackbirds. My ears rang with the high-pitched whistle of directionless screams. Yet beneath the ringing came a rumbling. It was quiet at first, but grew louder, like the thudding of cart wheels. It was laughter, but grew without joy. It was a cruel, creeping giggle that snaked like smoke, curling around my thoughts. It multiplied, loud enough to hear, but too muffled to understand. It grew, with the screaming and rattling growing louder and blacker until all my sensations were blotted and cloying. Breath escaped me, and my body burned with searing pain. Until it stopped.

The air returned to its musty self. The smell of mould and lavender water, and the short, inhaled sobs of Elsie, all was clear. Turning the corner of the dining room with a handkerchief pressed to her forehead, Mother's voice announced her arrival.

'What on earth is that racket?' she wailed. 'My girl isn't causing you any problems, is she, dear Sol —?'

The clip-clopping of her shoes stopped. The rustling of starched cotton signalling the end of her parade.

'Oh my life! Mrs Curry! Mrs Curry!'

My mother's shrieks disappeared into the bowels of the house, twisting into wordless screams, and I was left to examine my hands. My beautiful lithe hands. They were broken and thin, little more than a skeleton, but throbbing and swollen, cracked and bloodied like burst sausages.

'Should I call a doctor, Miss?' whispered Solomon.

He placed one hand on Elsie's head, making a vague gesture of comfort. The other remained on his watch pocket. Solomon stood as a pinnacle of order. Each crisp fold and lapel followed the angle of his body until the fabric merged into his flesh. His head remained still, his eyes tracing the line from my ankle to hip.

'Or a seamstress, perhaps?' he muttered under his breath.

I half-heard him, the few tatters of my lingering senses focusing on anything I could hook onto.

My dress was ruined. The embroidery was not so much undone as obliterated, my stockings little more than torn bands. My right leg jutted from beneath my skirts, soaking wet and crimson, streaked with smears of grey mud. Solomon remained steadfast, staring. I pulled the back of my skirts across my leg, suddenly aware of my naked flesh.

The nearest chair was towards the back wall of the room. It was small, sunken, and shrouded in the shadow of the dresser. It would take five steps at a good pace, around nine at my own. The dress was torn at the front, intact at the back. Turning towards the chair, steps could be slow. There would be no need to rush and cover. I simply had to get to the chair.

'Miss?' he reiterated, Solomon's voice strong and unwavering.

His mouth was still, yet somehow smirking. Unkind through his forced concern.

Two steps became three, then four, then five. Each stretch of my knee hurt. My stockings were stuck to my legs; tightly adhered like bandages that stretched and pulled at my skin. My left leg brought me forward, the right dragging and raw with each movement. My movements were slow, my body unkind, yet I reached the chair. A tattered, threadbare creation whose horsehair crunched as I lowered myself onto the pad. It was faded and torn with peeling marquetry that scratched at my palms. It had a seat, and that was all I required. I was cradled like a newborn, the gentle release of pressure on my legs being little short of blissful.

Elsie had grabbed at Solomon's wrist, her legs no longer swinging. In its place, her bottom lip wiggled against itself, her eyes welling with tears.

'No. Thank you. I will,' I began, desperately hoping to buy a moment away from the attention of the room.

A tooth rattled against my tongue. It rocked in its socket as I lost my words in my bloodied saliva. It had to be a dream; all of it was a foul dream. I was sure that I simply had to blink and would wake up. I had fallen asleep by my embroidery, or perhaps a cold draught had sent my mind awry. I blinked once, then twice, harder, the tension causing my eyes to throb even more. Solomon remained in his position, moving only to brush Elsie's hand from his.

'We really must continue, Miss, if you don't mind,' smiled Solomon, my presence addressed as a mild inconvenience.

A pain tore through my jaw. I lurched forwards, my leg grinding beneath me. I was terrified that my tooth would escape should I speak. Instead, I gestured to the table, imploring him to redirect his attention to anything but my nakedness.

My mother returned with a leap across the threshold, falling towards Solomon like a spent mare.

'Oh, Mr Bexton! Oh, my chair! Oh!' she wailed.

Her sentence was punctuated by the heavy bang of wood against wood. The end of Mrs Curry's mop met the floor with a purposeful thud. With each wide swipe, she edged closer into the room. Through each step, she forced the widow against the wall with unspoken, unseen force.

Mother fluttered. 'Thank you, Mrs Curry. Thank you.'

'No need, Madam. I'm well versed in such spillages,' smiled Mrs Curry, her eyes looking downwards.

In silence, she continued to mop the trail of blood and filth that I had left. Her expression was strange. Were I in better control of my senses, I could have known, but it looked like delight. Distracted by the searing pains in my legs, I could swear I saw some long-faded life and vigour return to Mrs Curry's jowled face.

My mother leaned towards Solomon, her whisper far louder than my speaking voice.

'She used to prick her finger, you know?' she chuckled.

Solomon looked disinterested. Both his hands remained affixed to the back of Elsie's chair.

'Did it for attention,' she continued. 'Never completed a sampler in her life.'

My mother nodded towards me. Mrs Curry's mop approached and Solomon's glare was fixed upon my bloodied face. The vast expanse of the dining room suddenly seemed very small.

'I knew something like this was brewing. Mother's intuition, I believe. I could sense it. Now look at the house —' My mother flung an arm out, blindly tossing her shawl across the fireplace.

'The stress of it all used to send me to bed for weeks, Mr Bexton.' Her arm stroked his quickly, as though he were a sleeping cat she couldn't permit to rest. 'The pricking, you understand. Not this. Not this moment at least. But with my nerves —' She paused to interrupt herself. 'Why must young women be so selfish?'

I sat, half waking, my mind tied up in knots of pain that threatened to never be undone. I kept my tongue pressed against my tooth, the warm metallic mix of blood and spittle sliding down my throat.

'I don't know, Madam. But I must say, you look quite well from such a tiring life,' crooned Solomon.

Mother's eyes brightened, blind to her bloodied daughter not five feet away. 'Do you think so, Mr Bexton?' — she paused — 'Solomon?'

The gathering of bile in my throat was so great that my mouth was under its own command, opening and emptying a string of deep-red slime onto my thighs. My tooth followed suit, clattering onto the floorboards and disappearing between the cracks. I tried to scream, but an empty void had grown where my lungs used to be.

Elsie, who had quickly abandoned her game of distress, had become preoccupied with a stack of cards. She lifted her head from her close study.

'You're part of the house now,' she chirped.

Elsie let out a burst of giggles before her cards regained her attention. She never met my eyes, but spoke above me. As though I were standing, or someone was standing behind me. Spittle still hung from my lips, too foul to swallow; but with no means of wiping it, I resigned myself to my shambolic performance as tears ran freely, tracing lines in the dried blood and soil.

'Oh, oh, my children, what have I done to deserve this affliction?' Mother wailed, clutching at an approximation of her breast. 'I feel so very faint — someone may well have to catch me!'

Mother was met with silence and averted eyes.

'I'm afraid I must be taking to my bed,' she mumbled, shrugging her layers of shawls and beaded drapes back over her shoulders.

She tied layer after layer around herself, adjusting scarves like onion skins. Leaving in a flounce, her skirts darkened across each wet floorboard. Halfway up the stairs, she paused and called back through the doorway, 'Do call if Mr Bexton needs me.'

'I shall, Madam, but you need your rest. Your girls are safe with me,' Solomon shouted, his words firm, eyes fixed to the ceiling.

With her exit, the heavy thunk-thunk of Mother's feet ascended the stairs, ready to make their home above her bedspread — until her desire for attention was satiated. I had little doubt that her emotional exhaustion would abate when her stomach began to grumble, or when boredom's grey fingers began to roam.

Mrs Curry had mopped a snaking route past my resting spot, missing the growing puddle at the foot of the chair. I watched her route, trying desperately to ignore the pain throbbing up my legs, arms, and warming through my jaw.

With a heavy bang of mop against board, Mrs Curry commanded the room.

'I'm redundant now, am I, Mr Bexton? You going to cook her tea too? Or just shout the ingredients downstairs?'

She pushed the mop handle against the table, sighing with each movement, as though her very existence was exhausting her.

Mrs Curry yanked a drawer from the dresser, unfurled a napkin, and handed it to me, while still staring at Solomon. The embroidery in the corner was immaculate; each laurel leaf precise in every stitch. The scrolling 'A' hooked between the leaves in muted silk. I could have sworn they were mine.

My stitches. A thick red blob landed onto the cotton, tracking through the fibres like spider's legs. Perfectly stained.

My skin was stuck to the floorboards, my stockings black and ruined; the embroidered flowers lost to the pits of the garden. The room was darker since I sat down; the clouds had rolled in, leaving everything illuminated in a cold half-light.

'You should take to bed,' said Solomon, 'and wash.' He spoke to me, but motioned his hands towards the table, re-centring its contents before me.

I could not speak, but coughed. My blood ran slower and was beginning to cool, mingled with the mud that clung to my skin.

Mrs Curry stepped between us, beating her apron with her hands. 'But you won't, will you? You tire us all.'

Mrs Curry spat her words, grabbed her mop, and left.

'This is a house of few surprises. I was told to expect such destructive behaviours. She said it was a family trait, yet I believe it to be little more than frustration at circumstance. Wouldn't you agree?' Solomon's words were strange and crooned, as though fulfilling some unspecified purpose.

'It's a terrible weakness,' he added.

Solomon angled his head towards Elsie's, but clearly had little intention of engaging her.

The dining table was so dark that he failed to cast a shadow as he stooped. He arched from behind Elsie, his clothes expertly avoiding contact with those around him. His hands scooped the cards from before her, his fingers moving slowly and deftly between the paper. He ran his thumb across the corners of the stack, before returning them to his pocket. Holding his lapel steady, he threaded one hand between his clothing, removing a smaller pack of cards from an inside pocket.

I stared at Solomon, as though memorizing each crease of fabric and each curved fingernail would distract me from my clotting sores and rising exhaustion.

He returned his hands to his person, deftly flicked the tails of his coat behind him, and gently moved one hand beneath them. From beneath the tails, from some unseen compartment or band, he slowly drew a large pair of silver scissors. They glinted in the half-light of the near window. Those shears, they were the same ones. From my position, I could see the curl of each cast rose by the handles. I could see the over-polished shine of the rivet between the blades, the reflection of Elsie's eyes in the handles; the reflection of Solomon's in the blade. The smell of blood was cloying, growing stagnant and old with each dragging moment of his movement. I watched him swirl the scissors, slicing the air before setting them in front of Elsie. I could not move. I remained still and found myself only able to wait.

'Are you going to stare at little bird's tutoring for the whole afternoon, or should I ask Mrs Curry to retrieve your needlework, or a book perhaps?'

He had turned to face me without my noticing. He looked warm; a little flushed. His brow crinkled. It was a little too furrowed for a man of his age.

'Or you could wash? You're very off-putting. Presuming you possess that skill at least...'

His words passed like whispers from another room. I took little notice, having no choice but to follow my body's instruction to remain stone-still, lest another wave of pain approach.

My throat was dry and airless and I found that I could not swallow. Elsie giggled, her eyes flitting back and forth between Solomon and the table.

Solomon patted her shoulder and took the stack of cards from her hand. He leaned forwards, rolling the cards between his fingers before spreading them in a smooth circle in one deft motion.

'Focus,' he barked, his fingers uncomfortably tight around Elsie's shoulders.

Solomon made his way across the room, his dancer's legs crossing one another in perfect rhythm.

'You really should consider resting elsewhere,' he whispered across the room, hissing the words between his lips. He crouched in front of my chair, his hands spanning his kneecaps, broad, pink, and spiderlike. 'It really will be terribly dull for you.' He paused. His breath adhered to my face like steam.

'Especially for a girl who lives such a... colourful life' — he waited a beat, gesturing towards the window — 'out here.'

I counted the pulses through my legs. The pain was so great that with each minute consumed by Solomon's words, the likelihood of removing myself upstairs faded, and I feared asking for help at such a late stage. Being inside the room meant that Elsie was alive, Solomon was watched, and I could fool myself into thinking that I could control what was left of their hideous charade. The pain grew with each beat; one, two, three.

'Ladies of breeding like comfort. Maybe one day you'll meet one,' he laughed, forcefully, and seeming somewhat rehearsed in his affectation.

Algernon would come to meet me. If I asked, he would come. He would arrive in anger, but he would come. I began to worry that, should the journey home be arranged, I would not survive it. I had used so much of my energy in remaining seated and holding in the fat sobs that threatened to rise that I had taken little notice of the hand that was slowly circling my ankle. His fingertips traced the curve of my leg, smooth and serpentine. A shiver chased my spine, tangling in the arch of my neck. His cheekbones, shadowed in the half-light of the gathering clouds, leaned towards my own.

He edged closer, so close that I could soon smell the stench of rotten meat, see the clods of grime between his teeth. He hadn't shaved.

'Go home, Mr Bexton.'

The words hurt my gums; the sharp strike of air against their soreness was unavoidable.

'Are you behaving so cruelly because of your father? Is this your grief? Your mother... none of us understand your passivity. She says you weren't close. Curry would say the same. Well, if she could bear to keep your name in her mouth.'

He paused only to swallow his spit.

'Begin your focus, Elsie,' he shouted, without glancing backwards. 'You *should* mourn. What was this? Yellow, pink? Was it "peach"?' he sniggered, repeating the word in an affected voice. 'It looks to be a cheerful colour. Did you do the embroidery yourself?' he mocked, pulling at the hem of my dress. He turned to Elsie, while lifting my skirts like some circus amusement. Elsie giggled, before quickly turning her head back to the table.

Scared to be seen.

In limp exhaustion, I let him lift them. I had been foolish before, but to allow such an invasion under the excuse of exhaustion was a new low. My stomach twisted. Too late for propriety, I removed my skirts from his hand, to which he only smiled further.

'Women are most sensitive about their virtue when they know it is lost.'

He paused, taking his hands closer, deliberately aligning torn pieces of skirt trim. He pressed them between his thumb and forefinger, as though pressure might adhere them.

'That is, if they ever possessed it at all,' he smirked.

My gums were raw, my legs aching, my tongue burning with unspoken hatred for the well-suited charlatan. Our eyes met. With one hand, he circled my ankle once more. Gentle at first, almost soothing. Then, without warning, he plunged the side of his thumbnail into the open cut beside my heel. It slipped through like a razor, a wordless ache catching in my voice. In a moment, he abated, removing his nail, his hand still aimlessly circling my skin.

It was soft and coarse and the room shrank to nothing but the two of us. If the room were darker, I could have mistaken his touch for Algernon's. His hand reached higher; to my calf, my knee, before coming to rest on the soft flesh of my thigh. I did not reach for him, nor bat him away. I wanted to; it was past improper. I should have screamed, but did not know to what end. His hand continued its journey, melting into my skin, airless.

He moved his head towards mine, his breath hot against my ear. His tongue gently met my neck; soft and warm.

My legs prickled, flushed through their pain.

His breath was sweet. 'You taste like fresh berries.'

He was not my husband. He was not Algernon. Solomon moved backwards, his black eyes meeting mine, full of bulbous pride.

'Go to Hell,' I spat, specks of fresh blood hitting his shirt.

He slowly stood, his hands once again his own. He turned to Elsie, rapt in her studies, and turned back to me. From behind his shoulder, I saw Elsie's face. Curious, distracted, and hopelessly young.

'You should be wearing black,' he said.

'It doesn't suit me,' I spat back, my gums raw and tender.

Solomon smiled. 'Black suits everyone. It comes for us all.'

'Black is Mother's colour,' I hissed.

He bent closer, his breath hot and sour, his voice between a bark and a whisper.

'Black is the colour of us all, Miss. Black is the colour of life and death. Of the sky and shadows, of sadness and burial. Black is the colour of your eyes as you sleep. Believe me, Madam, black will be your colour.'

Chapter 30

I couldn't sleep. There was no respite from the thundering roar of footsteps above me. Up the stairs, past my room, back into the attic, they circled and circled for hours, building a rhythm of thuds, taps, and clicks so distinct that it seared into my brain. They weren't real. Of course they weren't real. It was the tiredness. That had been established long ago. With my thoughts lingering on death so heavily and with the house invaded by Solomon, my mind had no respite. And yet the feet circled. Fast, loud, as clear as day. My fingers tapped along on the bedframe. The nails that remained clicked along, a little at first, just the tapping of my fingertips; then my knuckles rapped along.

I didn't know how long they ran, or how long I had lain transfixed by their strange beat. I may have slept, I may have dreamed, but I couldn't know for certain. All I could be sure of was that I woke with sore palms, taut with dried blood and covered in cross-hatched scratches. The splinters were the worst. Yet I was so painfully tired that as I tried to pick at them with my nails, my skin swirled, the room span, and a horrible feeling of sickness grew with each feeble attempt to grasp them.

Although a little weak, I knew the time of day to be early. The sun rose a little, but all was not yet illuminated, giving me more than enough time to speak to Mrs Curry, free from the ever-present gaze of Mr Bexton. The man was poison, but crept around the house like some awful seaside puppet, peeking over every shoulder and around every doorframe, passing comment and judgement on all that didn't concern him. There was no humour in the man, his body a hollow void of cold, deceptive darkness. My mother was smitten, Elsie too, but I was sure that they would see his true self in time. Without my presence in Duncain, I was sure that his feet would be firmly beneath the table. I was also sure that as soon as I returned to

London, Algernon would be sure to rain Hell down upon him. The finest lawyers in the commonwealth couldn't save his skin then. Every penny, every panel in the estate was mine. I knew that Solomon and Mrs Curry thought I was clueless, but I knew their game. They would sell Elsie like some actress for hire, and steal her wealth. If I had not been married before, I was sure that Solomon would have tried to take my hand in marriage if some coins lay at the end of the arrangement. He could not want Duncain, as it was not Elsie's, nor her mother's, to give. Yet something lingered in my mind, some nagging concern about a fire left unattended. Duncain might be grim, but it was vast. In the wrong, or right hands, it could make someone their fortune.

Solomon looked on Elsie like a predator; a tomcat waiting to strike at the mouse foolish enough to entertain him. She had the folly of youth to blame; she had been softened and sculpted by his hand. He had darkened her mind with promises of fame and fortune he could never provide. A sister of mine would sooner be a chorus girl than a damned medium.

Chapter 31

Séance

I stood and dressed. Some dress, some shoes, I can't recall. I left my chambers, moving quickly and quietly to Mrs Curry's bedroom, where I was sure to find her resting. She would have the paperwork. I would sign it, deliver it, then Elsie and I would leave. No one could stop us.

Finding her door curiously open for the hour of day, I stepped inside, my senses prickling and primed for confrontation. I was sure to have the old woman to myself. She would be tired, disorientated, and the upper ground would be mine. My heart leapt with triumph before I had crossed the threshold. I could almost smell the air of Chelsea and hear the rumble of the cab, ready to take me back home.

Entering the room, blinding sunlight burst through the window. Crows cawed from the window-ledge and my eyes burned with the sudden whiteout. Slowly adjusting to the brightness, it became very clear that Mrs Curry had surfaced long ago. I was only then that I realized I had never entered her room before. It was small, as expected, dark and simple. Her bed seemed fluffy at first, as though covered with a woollen blanket. Only with a tentative touch did I realize it was dust. The whole room was thick with spiderwebs. Not little webs, but enormous thick flags of spider silk, stretching from cupboard to wall, up to the ceiling, impenetrable and undisturbed. No man could have lived in there. Not for propriety's sake, but a physical impossibility. But the room was Mrs Curry's. It always had been. I would have entered further if the room allowed, but save for the curve cleared by the door, I would rather have waded through peat bog than taken a tour of her chambers.

As I turned to leave, a patch of her washstand caught my eye. Polished and far cleaner than the rest, it held the only meagre evidence of the room's use. On the corner lay a silver-topped pencil, a small pile of filled notebooks, and a pile of envelopes. I peered a little closer, without intention of touching any of the old woman's grubby things. The writing on the envelopes was mine. The addresses all the same: Chelsea, Chelsea, Chelsea... The entire stack were my letters to Algernon. Each one unposted. But not unread. The seals hung limply from the back of the envelopes, the letters roughly replaced inside. The damned witch stole them all. Her journeys to the postal office a fraud; her trips to the village, all lies. This was all her doing; these games of madness and trickery. Mother was just a pawn to her and Solomon's lies. I would leave and I would expose them all. Mrs Curry would spend the last of her days in a workhouse; Solomon too.

I grabbed the letters, the rage rising in me like wildfire. I would expose Curry, prove their deception for all to see; I would take Elsie and go. I would not leave the poor girl to rot between these walls as I had. Duncain was poison.

I strode from the room, slamming the door with such deliberate ferocity that I swear I could hear the wood splinter off its hinges. Reaching the stairs, I grasped the letters tighter, the paper arching within my palms. I took a step, then another. Then darkness fell.

* * *

The dining room emanated a gentle, warm glow. The table was set for the circle with Elsie at the head. I sat opposite, sinking deeply into Father's old captain's chair. I did not recall sitting, nor entering the room, nor the time of day or the purpose of my movements. The letters, I had the letters. Somewhere. My hands clenched around the arms of the chair, but the letters were gone. I rummaged for a pocket, for a chatelaine, a bag, anything; some sign I possessed more than the clothes I rested in. Somewhere I could have secreted the letters. All that I found was the rustling of moth-eaten taffeta, horrible, crude pleats hanging coarsely against my bare legs.

Looking up, Elsie sat in a trance, one eyelid flickering restlessly. Mrs Curry sat to my left, Solomon to my right. Mother sat between Elsie and Mrs Curry, shaking; although whether it was through fear or eagerness was yet to be seen. All were silent. The candles kept their constant light, the shutters filtering in a little sunlight from behind my sister's head. She looked different. Older, somehow. Like a woman.

Elsie raised her head and spoke, her eyes still jittering, heavy in trance. 'She doesn't know.'

Mother responded, her voice strangely low and reverential. 'Who doesn't know, and what, Elsie?'

'She doesn't know she's leaving,' she replied, her eyes wide and staring.

She closed her eyes, breathing heavily. I could only watch. I tried to stand, but my body was so weak, my legs barely able to move, however much I strained. I would wait, I would watch, and then we would leave; Elsie and I. Together, safe at last.

Elsie suddenly leaned forwards, hunched over the table and coughing hideously, her back arched and at right angles, as though her spine was about to escape from her skin.

Convulsing against her own coarse breaths, she kept her hands clasped with the sitters', her knuckles glowing white hot in the shuttered sunlight.

She continued gasping for breath, hacking and spluttering against a blocked throat.

Her eyes streamed as she thrashed for air. She needed help, she needed help or she'd die.

From the discolouring of her face, it was clear she didn't have long before fainting, or worse. Her eyes bulged, her jaw stretched wide, lips blue, mouth close to tearing.

I wrenched my arms from their clasping hands, but I barely made an inch of movement, just a sudden sharp pain in my wrists that anchored them to their spot.

I had never felt such anger. Elsie had to be protected; she was a child. I thought it was Solomon who would hurt her the most, but it was clearly my own mother, the same woman who proudly held her hand, as though watching her perform a piano recital. They had all hurt her, and trained her to hurt herself. Elsie was too precious, too important to go any further into their murky world. Solomon was no benefactor, nor manager, nor tutor. He was a leech. Elsie would understand. One day, when she was grown, she would look back on all this and feel nothing but relief. But first, I had to get her out. I would get her to London. To safety.

With a guttural retch, Elsie's body smashed against the table, her face hitting the cloth with a sickening thud.

All was quiet. She didn't move; neither did her chest rise and fall with breath. Mother remained watching and no one motioned to move. As the skies darkened behind her, Elsie suddenly arched from the table. Her jaw sank downwards, her tongue lolling and black as coal.

With a low groan, the first stone rolled from her mouth. It clattered across the table, coming to rest by Solomon's arm. A pause, then another. This one was slightly larger, and clinked against her teeth as it fell. Another soon followed, then another, until they fell from her mouth in great clusters, loosely connected with strings of stinking bile. The coughing seemed endless, with each retch bringing more stones and shards from her tiny throat. Soon came the leaves, petals, and sharp, fat sticks. With the sticks came proud thorns, and blood. Her throat and tongue bloomed from torn fine ribbons of flesh, as blood dripped slowly from her mouth, from slits in her lips, until it streamed down her chin in open rivers.

Her lips pulled back to reveal tiny black teeth. Her mouth was a mess of a tar pit, her body producing a constant, low groan like dying livestock. I knew she was dying. We were sitting watching a child's death. We were encouraging it. Every one of us.

Slowly, Solomon spoke. 'Elsie. Prove to her.'

Elsie was soon screaming in pain, thrashing in her chair. Her face smeared in blood and tears, she threw her head in wide circles, fighting against the room's heavy air. The candles flickered and, with a dry scream, Elsie burst from her bindings and mounted the table. Shaking and blind, she tore her fingers into the cloth, ripping the fibres apart and burrowing her nails into the wood beneath. Suddenly rigid in her stance, she slowly opened her mouth. In silence, she held her position on the table, the house as still as the dead. Slowly, blackness emerged. At first a feather, then another, then a wing. Juddering with small movements, claws scratched across her teeth, looping their knuckles across her lips.

The crow hit the table with a gentle thud, rustling its feathers and cawing. It screamed, high and loud, like nails across glass. It stumbled across the table, hopping and shaking its feathers with wet discomfort. Elsie fell to the table slowly, rolling onto her side, her arms spread wide, Christ-like.

Solomon broke the air, saying, 'It is ended.'

He stood and walked towards Elsie. Opening the window behind her, out flew the crow with timed precision.

I never realized I was crying. I never felt a single tear fall, but my collar was sodden.

After the realization came relief; Elsie lived.

'Very good, Elsie. They were strong today. You must learn to relax a little, yes?'

Elsie's face, while bloodied, nodded and grinned wide, the dried blood flaking from her cheeks. While blood still fell from her lips, she seemed unaware, but filled with the energy and excitement of a kitten. She span on her bottom, dismounting the table with a little jump, with the aid of Solomon's outstretched hand. It was madness. He had enchanted her, drugged her, or at worst, seduced her. Such a thought brought bile into my throat and I fought to stand from my chair.

'Have some water, Elsie,' crooned Solomon as he held a glass to her lips.

Watching the interactions between them was enough to turn anyone's stomach. She was ill, needing help.

Solomon turned to face me, his face disgustingly smug. 'I told you she was special.'

I believe Elsie would have blushed, were it not for the blood coating her face and neck. She retained her smile, nodding at every whispered word Solomon passed her way. Looking a little downcast, she rubbed at her stained cheek and slipped from the room. The patter of Elsie's feet to Mrs Curry's kitchen and washstand spoke for her.

Struggling to stand, I mustered all the strength within me to rise from my chair. I burned with desire to say my piece, to unveil Solomon as the fraud he truly was, and Elsie and I would escape. There would be carriages in the town. My name would be good for money, and Algernon would see to the rest; he just had to know we were on our way.

Mrs Curry's voice cut through the room like an axe. 'What'll you be wanting now?'

'This stops now,' I choked.

'Jealousy's so very ugly, child. Go back to bed. Be no hindrance to us.'

'The letters!' I shouted, the words falling from me like hail.

'Letters?' repeated Mrs Curry, dully.

My eyes burned hot with frustration. 'Every damned letter. You didn't post a single one of my letters.'

Mrs Curry sighed, placing a hand on my mother's shoulder. Looking at her, sunken into her chair, I hopelessly waited for a flicker of recognition. Instead, she turned away, moving her hands to her face in anticipation of wiping future streams of mock tears.

'Miss, don't go upsetting your mother now. Stop this foolishness,' she crooned.

'Mrs Curry, I am not a Miss, I am a married woman, and —'

'What are you planning on doing exactly? And where was I supposed to be sending these "*letters*"?' she questioned, eyebrows forcefully raised.

I found myself forcing back tears, speaking slowly through the knot in my throat. 'I want to go home.'

'You are home, Miss. Please don't be startin' this silliness again.'

Her face folded in cruel, patronizing expressions. They wanted to twist my mind, to take everything from me. I was sure not to let them.

I screamed, my arm aloft at Mrs Curry's vile words. 'You will never work again!'

My breaths were short and shallow and I fought to keep my mind free from dizziness.

'You just wait, Algernon will —'

'Miss, you need to stop with this Algernon talk. It's worrying your mother.'

'Damn my mother!' The words cruel, my mind harnessed the worst it could find. 'He will come, and he will *beat* you for your insolence.'

Mrs Curry stood unperturbed, resting her fists on her hips. 'And who exactly is this Algernon?'

'My damned husband!' I spat, my sense of propriety long gone.

Mother, as expected, buried her head in her hands, weeping loudly.

'That'll be your husband. Right. That'll be quite the achievement,' said Mrs Curry.

'My husband. My husband in Chelsea. I'll get back there if I have to walk in my own bare feet.'

Mrs Curry looked on with pursed lips. 'Go where, Miss?'

I screamed, losing myself. '*London*, are you deaf? I will return to London!'

Mrs Curry spoke forcefully. 'Miss, you have never been to London. There is no Algernon.'

'Yes there is and he will come!' I shrieked. Her cruelty was a familiarity, but her cold insistence sent me into a frenzy.

'You have never left this house, Miss,' she began. 'There is no Algernon.'

'He is my husband!' I shouted, my voice wild and unsteady.

Mrs Curry sighed and began to gather and fold the tablecloth. Pushing the curtains aside, she barrelled up the cloth and turned her head to Solomon. He remained standing by the table, sly as a fox, relishing the disquiet with a wry smile.

'Do you know an Algernon?' she asked Solomon, who replied with a shake of his head. She turned to Mother. 'Do you know an Algernon?'

She received no reply from her but the expected dramatic weeping.

She returned to face me and spoke with satisfaction. 'None of us know an Algernon, Miss. There is no Algernon.'

Anger rose in me like wildfire. These horrid games and this performance with Elsie was too much. Something in the house was playing with me, and the hideous visitors within it relished the chaos; that much was clear. Nothing was wrong with me. Something was wrong with the house. I would get out, get past the grounds, and I could get help. The house was the problem, not me.

I forced myself to move, against the will of my frozen joints, and pushed the chair away with all my might. Stumbling towards the door, my head became heavy and drunk.

Before I could leave, I caught my toe on the foot of Solomon's shoe. He stood across the doorway; somehow he moved faster than he should. He stood stoic, his nose high and knowing.

'No one will have you,' he spat. 'And I cannot say that I blame them.'

They circled me like wildcats, my vision fading and refocusing as they passed by.

'You're doing this,' I stuttered. 'I don't know what you're doing but it stops now.'

'We're doing something. You don't know what, but we're doing something. Something bad. And you... can't enlighten us as to what?' echoed Mrs Curry, mocking me with every inch of her flesh.

'Well, Miss, I bow down to your clarity,' she hissed.

Their game was over; their cruel manipulation had to end. They had been playing me for a fool since my arrival. They kept me sleepless, kept me cold, playing out little scenes from the corner of my eye; all to leave my head a tangle. God, I was tired; for every word of their lies, my head grew tired and sickly, aching for the respite of a safe, warm bed. The tiredness — the cold, dragging tiredness — weighed heavy on me like a cloak. They would explain themselves, explain the crude employment of strangers in their work. I couldn't leave without knowing, I simply couldn't.

'The children, the horrid running at night, the tricks, the hiding and dragging Elsie into it — it stops now!' I yelled.

Mother wept a little, the cruel hag forcing a little water from her dry eyes.

'Miss, you are ill,' said Solomon, softening his voice.

'I am ill?' I yelled, the anger flowing from me in waves. 'I am ill? You are making me ill, just like you've wanted!' I jabbed my finger at the three of them, my body filled with a wave of righteousness. If the dining room were a courtroom, they knew they had been exposed.

'What children, Miss? Please, you need to think of your words. You need to rest.' He snarled with fake concern.

I pounded my fist against my chest, insistent that they would accept and admit their deception. To leave the house without a confession would be the worst defeat of all. I had made too many allowances in Duncain.

'I want to sleep, I want the paperwork, and I will go. You will never see me again and I will relish every blasted second of silence without you.' My words stumbled over themselves, catching in the tears in my throat.

'And just where will you go, Miss?' crooned Mrs Curry. 'This is your home.'

'No it isn't!' I yelled.

'Alice. You have *never* left this house. You have *never* left these four walls. You will *never* leave. You are *ill.*'

Mrs Curry stashed away the tablecloth and began to rearrange the candlesticks with strange and idle interest. She moved as though this were some tiresome irritant in her workday, a thousand times endured.

'She', began Mrs Curry, pointing at Mother with one gnarled finger, 'wanted to keep you here and I have tried my best to keep you contained, but you have problems we cannot control. You are *sick.*'

'Silence, silence!' I screamed. 'I am going, and I am taking Elsie.'

'*You are sick, stop this!*' Mother bellowed, phlegm and mucus flying with each wet syllable.

She turned to me, glaring across the table with bared teeth. 'It was fine as diaries. The doctor encouraged it. But these letters, and all this business at night. We thought you were getting better.'

'What, who's "we"?' But my words were snared in their path.

'All of us, Miss. Your family.' Solomon leaned into me, his hand clasping my shoulder. 'You're getting worse. You must accept these are but delusions.'

'The Jubilee, we met at the coaching inn!' I grabbed Solomon's lapels with both hands. He would not take me for a fool, not after all this.

He mumbled, arching his head further away from mine. 'Miss?'

'We met at the inn, that night,' I said.

'An inn,' he repeated. 'And just why would you be visiting an ale house, Miss?'

'Stop calling me Miss, please! And I, I wasn't. I was coming here and there was a storm.'

'And you went for ale?' he interrupted.

'No, of course not,' I stuttered.

'So you didn't go to an ale house for ale. Can you see —'

I forced myself between his lying lips. 'Listen! Stop tripping me!' I took a deep breath and tried desperately to steady my thoughts.

'We met at a coaching inn. It was called The Jubilee, about an hour or so from here. You cannot deny that. We met on the morning of my departure where you sat with friends. Remember?'

I chose my words calmly, taking short pauses, so as not to give them any ground for any claims of hysterics. I remembered, and so did he.

'Miss, I have never been in such an establishment. I have not left Duncain since the weeks before your father passed. I'm sorry.'

'Lies!' I shouted, forgetting myself.

'I am sorry, Miss,' he began, shaking his head. 'It was not me. There was no meeting, there was no inn.'

I softened my voice, insistent still. He would remember; he couldn't hold in his lies any longer.

'Miss, there is no Jubilee and I am certainly not the sort to enter ale houses.'

From above came the foreboding rumble of little feet. One set, then another. They quickly made circuits across the landing, before coming to rest at a point directly above where we stood.

'See — you hear that? I know you hear that. You did this. Who are they?' I yelled.

Solomon continued his mumblings, readjusting his collar as my hands hung by my sides, my eyes fixed at the ceiling rose. I scanned the faces of Solomon and Mrs Curry, but neither had so much as shivered at the sounds. It was clear they were expecting them. The footsteps were too loud to miss. The louder they grew, the more they seemed to emanate from inside my own head, as though my skull bore its own staircase. Solomon's chatter brought me from my watchtower, although I made sure to keep one eye on the ceiling. 'Miss, if you knew my name, my reputation would —'

'I know your damned name, Bexton,' I spat.

However, my reply seemed to take him aback somewhat, as though it were some wild revelation. I may well have been upset, but I had grasp of all my senses, and his poor acting only succeeded in tiring me further. God, I was tired. My body grew so heavy against the weight of my bones. I rested on the table a little, feeling close to falling. A fire suddenly raged in the hearth and the room filled with the stench of burning wool. There had been a fire before. There had to be. My eyes stung. I tried to keep them open, but it hurt. It hurt so much.

As I supported myself, my fingers ran across the edges of papers. Arching my hands, I grabbed the stack of letters stashed beneath the leaves of the table. I knew they were real, I knew

I wrote them. Each one was as I remembered, written with the delicate writing of a lady, not a lunatic. Each had the same address; my home. Not some rough jotted address, not some imagined street name; my address. The place Algernon and I called home.

I dragged myself towards Mrs Curry, using the table edge for support. Holding them high, she would be sure of my sanity, of the reality in which we all found ourselves.

Readying for Curry to lunge, I grasped the letters tight. I sucked against my teeth and watched her eyes, waiting for a flicker of recognition or panic.

Suddenly, with claws drawn, before I could swing against her reach, Mrs Curry grabbed the letters from my grasp, carving long red divots across the back of my hand.

Hurling the papers like salt, the housekeeper cast them into the fire, the edges of the envelopes spinning against the logs with an audible crack.

'There is no Algernon,' she hissed, her eyes sparking across the room like a cat.

Mrs Curry was insane. All she had dreamed was to destroy the family and it was my pride that allowed her. Every word spoken was another second wasted. I ran towards the door, fruitlessly reaching for the brass knob, but was pulled back by Solomon's arms.

'She's past help!' yelped Mother from her shadows. 'You're dangerous!'

Solomon held me fast and I screamed back at my mother. 'Mother, please!'

'I do not want you near my family any longer!' she yelled, throwing her arms wide with unexpected force.

I struggled towards her, yelling to get the mad woman to listen. '*I am your family!*'

'All of this is mine,' I continued. 'Father left it to me, not you, never you!'

Mother was immersed in her performance, shrieking and crying with all the control of a drowning cat. If she broke from her disgusting ego, she would listen and she would understand reason, just as Father did. Her wailing was loud, the fire crackled with the fuel of my letters, and the growing noises from above deafened me, the room roaring with all the volume of a thousand horses.

Gradually, Mother's sobs subsided and I thought she had realized her deception, and the cruelty of Mrs Curry and her cronies. Yet as she sat, dabbing at her face, her lips grew wet with vitriol.

'You're insane. I didn't want to believe it, but you're truly mad. You can't be trusted to care for yourself, let alone an estate. You've made that very clear,' Mother spat.

I could do little but look on, confused. Mother was weak and pathetic, but never cruel, never truly nasty.

'First to lose my husband to the madness, now my daughter!'

I was not ill, and nor was Father. He knew what awaited us and he tried to save the estate; all the Croftons stood for. Father would have lived, that much was clear. Curry and her trickery had been laying roots far longer than I thought. A part of me was resigned to my fate. I would leave, but I would lose Duncain. But still, I needed answers.

'And where is he then?' I pressed.

'What?' wept Mother.

I continued, clear and crisp. 'Where is Father's body?'

Mother responded with silence.

'As you can see, I am not the mad woman refusing to commit his body,' I continued.

'He's by the chapel. You know this,' said Mrs Curry. 'You took it badly.'

'Lies!' I snapped.

'We couldn't drag you to the funeral, Miss. You spent all day in bed,' insisted Mrs Curry.

'You lie!' I shouted. 'There was no funeral — there has been no funeral!'

'Stop this, you're upsetting your mother.'

Solomon's voice echoed from behind me. Standing beside Elsie, who barely looked all of her thirteen years, he loomed over her like an obelisk. She looked at him like a God.

Elsie, clean-faced, smiled. 'The funeral was a week ago, Sissy.'

'No, Elsie, please,' I whispered.

She looked up at Solomon, smiling.

'Elsie, please,' I insisted, taking her hand. 'Come with me. It's not safe here. We can... we can decorate your room however you want and I will buy you all the pretty dresses in England. Please, Elsie. Come now.' I spoke gently, but shook with each word. She would not be tainted by them.

'You lie,' she hissed.

'Elsie, please. Please don't believe them. I don't know what they've said about me, but —'

Elsie's voice cut through mine like a razor.

'Oh they haven't said anything. They haven't had to.' Her face wrinkled with disgust.

'Please. Elsie —' I began. Solomon wrapped his arm across her shoulders like one enormous wing, claiming her.

'No! Stop lying!' I shouted, boring my eyes into Solomon's.

His angular face glinted like flint, proud and fox-like. I tried to bring her back, back to reality, and safety.

'He's lying to you, Elsie, they all are. He doesn't care about you. None of them do.'

Elsie pursed her lips, leaning into Solomon. 'And you do? You're *mad*.'

'Yes, yes of course I do —' I began, before stopping myself. I had neglected her. I had abandoned her in London, dismissed her with the house, and left her to suffer.

'Your letters. I know, I'm sorry.'

'More letters, Miss? Really,' said the housekeeper.

I kept my eyes fixed on my sister. 'I'm sorry, Elsie. Please, listen to me.'

She wrapped one slender arm across Solomon's breast, pushing her cheek into his coat. 'Go away.' She paused, sniffing invisible tears with a glint in her eye. 'She's frightening me, Sol.'

'Please, Elsie, please, tell them,' I pleaded. 'Tell them about the children, about the children in the attic.'

Solomon looked to Elsie, who responded with a shake of her head and a tighter grasp on his body.

'We can't have you here, this is too much!' wailed Mother, her ego momentarily deflated.

'Be thankful Duncain has no asylum,' hissed Curry, who tapped her toes, as if waiting for commands.

'She cannot be allowed to remain. Why must God curse our family?' wailed Mother, addressing the sky in a wild performance. 'I hoped it wouldn't come to this. But it was the only way to deal with Kenneth, to keep us safe.'

The room crackled with stillness, breaking only when Elsie ran to confront Mother.

'Mother? What did you do to him?' I needed to know. I couldn't leave, not yet. 'Mother?'

Mother did not respond, but shook her handkerchief and whispered to Elsie. Solomon and Mrs Curry stared, waiting, poised. Standing tall against the sunlight, Elsie looked like an angel. So beautiful. So pure.

Elsie spoke with an unshaking voice. 'Take her.'

Epilogue

I moved, tried to run, but my feet were too slow, my dress too heavy, and Solomon grabbed me by the door. Mrs Curry came forwards like a wave, sweeping beneath my arms with enormous strength. I kicked and thrashed with every fibre of strength within me, but they would not yield.

They carried me like a naughty child, bound tightly, light as air. I bent my knees, threw about my elbows, but they held me fast.

They took me across one flight of stairs with ease. My joints clicked in and out of their cradles from my thrashing, my back arching in violent angles, but they held me fast. I was angry, so angry, to be taken to my room like a child. Then they passed my room. Moving towards the small stairs at the back of the house, they approached the attic.

I roared with everything I had, quickly regaining my right leg from Solomon's grasp. He reached for my ankle and I firmly brought down all my strength on my heel, forcing it into his cheek with a wet snap.

'You *whore!*' he yelled, grabbing my foot from the air.

Blood fell from his nose like a stream and I held fast in the thought that I could already see his broken cheekbone swell.

'I'll tell you one thing,' he spat. 'You lot deserve each other.'

His foaming spittle landed on my lips, dripping across my chin in one last insulting kiss. Only a few struggling steps later did I realize they were taking me up.

'*No! No!*' I screamed.

The children were waiting. Their little blurred bodies and tiny teeth. They scurried in the darkness, their little hands wandering, tearing, ripping, breaking.

My throat bled raw. 'No! Please! I'll do anything, please!'

'Bit late for that, eh?' huffed Mrs Curry, backing herself into the room.

Held tightly, they carried me further into the room, where the beams flashed above, roughly glowing through holes in the roof.

'*No! Please! Please!*' I hated my mouth for betraying me, for spilling out pleas and begs to people so low and cruel.

They stopped responding after a time, with the weakened movements of my limbs proving to be of little interest. Mrs Curry dropped me first, hitting my head on the boards with a hard thump. Solomon followed, dropping my legs and taking a few steps to watch as I cradled my head.

'At least they won't hear her up here,' mused Solomon.

'I know, son,' sighed Mrs Curry casually. 'A bit of respite at last.'

My head pounded, my blood pulsating in my ears in dull rhythms. My vision was blurred, but I crawled to the door in one last reflex of humiliation. They waited for me, standing by the top step, locking the door when they could finally see the whites of my eyes. They stood, watching, smiling at their creation.

Solomon spoke first. 'It's such a shame, eh? Looks like Algernon did you dirty.' He smiled, wiping the blood from his lip.

'All you had to do was stay away. You couldn't even manage that? That's the problem with you landlord types, you've always got to be stickin' your noses in.'

He paused to smile, and for a moment, I thought I saw some glimpse of regret cross his face. With a gurgling pop, the blood ran freely down his chin, a clump of ruby viscera dancing on his lips before falling.

'Thirty pounds was it, Ma?' He spoke loudly, his cuff pressed tightly to his nose.

'Thirty pounds was all it took,' echoed Mrs Curry, standing with her arms crossed against her apron, surveying all in front of her.

'Thirty pounds. Just the promise of a few old crofts. Hell,' she laughed, 'he nearly posted you across the sea himself. Couldn't wait to be rid of you.'

The two laughed, then stood in quiet understanding, observing me through the hatch. As I watched them, the housekeeper moved towards him with tenderness. Solomon smiled weakly as Mrs Curry turned to plant a gentle kiss on his forehead.

'You've done good, lad. Don't be long, she's waiting,' smiled the housekeeper.

Mrs Curry turned and left, not so much as a backwards glance. Solomon stood a while, dabbing his nose, eyes cast downwards.

'You know,' he said, 'I really do think it's a shame.'

I righted myself and rested my back against a beam. There was nothing to be done. I waited for the rest of his speech.

'I think we could have got on. Really made something of it.' He paused, inhaling through clenched teeth. 'But Algernon got there first. It's all a matter of timing with these things.'

He took a step back, motioning to leave, before twisting back to face me through the hatch.

'I think Elsie's quite taken with me,' he smiled, his eyes studying mine. 'A year or two, nice spring wedding... we're as good as betrothed! I would invite you but' — he paused — 'that'll be a bit awkward, with you being dead an' all.'

I said nothing, but studied his bloodied face, the shadows closing in from the corners.

He laughed to himself and cheered, 'Don't worry, Miss, I'll come and visit you!' before descending the stairs, his footsteps heavy and certain. I couldn't hear them beyond that. I don't know where they went.

To be truthful, I cried for a while, but then I waited. Father was an impatient man, but I am not. I have all the time in the world. Algernon will come. As will Solomon. Both will come to me, wanting to watch, wanting to boast. The children told me they would, as did the house. We agree on a lot of things. They tell me such fascinating stories and teach me such wonderful tricks. They know so much about life, and death, and Duncain. And when my dear husband comes, I'll be waiting.

Acknowledgements

There are several people I would like to thank for their insight and support during the creation of *Begotten*. Thanks to Kay, whose unwavering belief in both me and Duncain has kept my head above water many times. Also, thanks to Paul whose constant willingness to drop everything and read, despite not quite 'getting it', has meant so much to me. Thank you to Helen whose humour and kindness has been a tonic, to Ginny and Vaffs for their company, and to Pat and Eric for being ever-present sources of inspiration.

Huge thanks to Dr Scott Brewster, without whom Duncain would not exist, and Karin Besant, the best cheerleader and meddling aunt. Thanks to Guy Mankowski and John Robb for their insight and words of support, and thanks to Sophie Cleverly for her time, help, and friendship.

Ian, thank you for your warmth and for reminding me to 'just get on with it' and not look left and right.

ROUNDFIRE
BOOKS

FICTION

Put simply, we publish great stories. Whether it's literary or popular, a gentle tale or a pulsating thriller, the connecting theme in all Roundfire fiction titles is that once you pick them up you won't want to put them down.
If you have enjoyed this book, why not tell other readers by posting a review on your preferred book site.

Recent bestsellers from Roundfire are:

The Bookseller's Sonnets
Andi Rosenthal

The Bookseller's Sonnets intertwines three love stories
with a tale of religious identity and mystery spanning
five hundred years and three countries.
Paperback: 978-1-84694-342-3 ebook: 978-184694-626-4

Birds of the Nile
An Egyptian Adventure
N.E. David

Ex-diplomat Michael Blake wanted a quiet birding trip
up the Nile – he wasn't expecting a revolution.
Paperback: 978-1-78279-158-4 ebook: 978-1-78279-157-7

Blood Profit$
The Lithium Conspiracy
J. Victor Tomaszek, James N. Patrick, Sr.

The blood of the many for the profits of the few... *Blood Profit$*
will take you into the cigar-smoke-filled room where American
policy and laws are really made.
Paperback: 978-1-78279-483-7 ebook: 978-1-78279-277-2

The Burden
A Family Saga
N.E. David

Frank will do anything to keep his mother and father
apart. But he's carrying baggage – and it might
just weigh him down ...
Paperback: 978-1-78279-936-8 ebook: 978-1-78279-937-5

The Cause
Roderick Vincent
The second American Revolution will be a
fire lit from an internal spark.
Paperback: 978-1-78279-763-0 ebook: 978-1-78279-762-3

Don't Drink and Fly
The Story of Bernice O'Hanlon: Part One
Cathie Devitt
Bernice is a witch living in Glasgow. She loses her way
in her life and wanders off the beaten track looking for the
garden of enlightenment.
Paperback: 978-1-78279-016-7 ebook: 978-1-78279-015-0

Gag
Melissa Unger
One rainy afternoon in a Brooklyn diner, Peter Howland
punctures an egg with his fork. Repulsed, Peter pushes
the plate away and never eats again.
Paperback: 978-1-78279-564-3 ebook: 978-1-78279-563-6

The Master Yeshua
The Undiscovered Gospel of Joseph
Joyce Luck
Jesus is not who you think he is. The year is 75 CE. Joseph
ben Jude is frail and ailing, but he has a prophecy to fulfil ...
Paperback: 978-1-78279-974-0 ebook: 978-1-78279-975-7

On the Far Side, There's a Boy
Paula Coston
Martine Haslett, a thirty-something 1980s woman, plays hard
on the fringes of the London drag club scene until one night
which prompts her to sign up to a charity. She writes to a
young Sri Lankan boy, with consequences far and long.
Paperback: 978-1-78279-574-2 ebook: 978-1-78279-573-5

Tuareg
Alberto Vazquez-Figueroa
With over 5 million copies sold worldwide, *Tuareg* is a classic
adventure story from best-selling author Alberto Vazquez-
Figueroa, about honour, revenge and a clash of cultures.
Paperback: 978-1-84694-192-4

Readers of ebooks can buy or view any of these bestsellers by
clicking on the live link in the title. Most titles are published
in paperback and as an ebook. Paperbacks are available in
traditional bookshops. Both print and ebook formats are
available online.

Find more titles and sign up to our readers' newsletter at
www.collectiveinkbooks.com/fiction

Printed and bound by CPI Group (UK) Ltd, Croydon, CR0 4YY

24/04/2025

01852443-0001